SIXTH SENSE
A Reverse Harem Tale

Lovin' the Coven
Book 6

Jacquelyn Faye

∞ Untold Press ∞

SIXTH SENSE
A Reverse Harem Tale

Lovin' the Coven, book 6

ISBN: 978-1-945893-16-2

First Publication, June 2020

Published by Untold Press LLC
114 NE Estia Lane
Port St Lucie, FL 34983

www.untoldpress.com

PRODUCED IN THE UNITED STATES OF AMERICA

10 9 8 7 6 5 4 3 2 1

Dedication

This book is Dedicated to my fingers. The poor little bastards. They work perilously, sometimes faster than my brain, but after the day is done, they are the reason this book was finally finished. Magical little fuckers that they are. Wink wink.

CHAPTER 1

I refused to take my eyes off his in the rearview mirror. Dating him had been one of the highlights of moving north with my best friend and starting a completely new life in Cedar Falls. I'd ended up with the chief and a hunky fireman and it had all started with a broken coven. Chief could be a huge pain in the ass, we bumped heads constantly, but at the end of the day...I loved him.

Sitting there in the back of his police car, hands cuffed behind me, after he arrested me at my *other* boyfriend's house...I started to doubt that warm and fuzzy corner of my heart I had reserved for his pompous, righteous, self-centered, egotistical ass. We'd driven three blocks, and he had yet to acknowledge my presence or meet my smoldering gaze.

He picked up the dash mic for his police radio and keyed it up. "Charlie-one-nine in transit with prisoner."

"Copy, Charlie-one-nine," came the response, and the radio clicked dead with a loud hiss of static.

"Dot," he finally let my name slide from his lips.

I leaned forward, putting my face almost against the relatively clean looking plexiglass. "Don't. Don't you fucking dare utter a Lady damned word to me right now. I can't guarantee your safety." I sat back and stared out the window.

"Do you think I *wanted* to arrest you? Do you think this is fun for me?"

I smirked and looked back up at the mirror, not saying a word.

"The DA was given the pictures by a concerned citizen. *He* motioned for the arrest warrant. *He* convinced the judge that you were a menace. *Not* me. The Mayor and I argued on your behalf for an hour, saying that it was crazy that you could possibly have *lightning* flying from your hands. I'm *sorry*!"

"You could have warned me."

"What?"

"Why the fuck didn't you just call me. Why the fuck didn't you let me know that there was a warrant out for my arrest. I would have showed up at the station with my lawyer. You didn't have to come arrest me."

"Yes, I did."

"Why?"

"Because I love you." He kept looking at me, worry etched clearly on his face and pleading in his eyes. Pleading for me to understand why he had done what he did.

He could go fuck himself with his police issued nightstick. "Funny way of showing it."

"They used the word witch, Dot. You know how stupid humans can get when they start throwing that word around. I came and got you before somebody else did."

I huffed. "Who used the word witch? People don't believe in witches anymore."

"Cedar Falls. Sure, nobody talks about it, but everybody remembers the demons in town square."

"So, a group of concerned citizens showed up with pitchforks and torches? Bullshit."

"No. Just one."

"Who?"

"I'm not at liberty…"

"Fuck off."

"I could lose my job, Dot."

Reality can be a funny thing. Events around you can be so set in stone as you plod through life day to day. Sometimes, you can even take things for granted. Like the sunshine in the sky, a steady supply of water, the air around you. Even the people you love. You depend on them. They're part of your life and you assume they will always be there. You assume they'll *always* feel the same about you and prioritize you in their life as you have with them in yours. The funny thing about reality is it isn't always real, and that it can be *completely* shattered by the simplest of things. Like a thoughtless sentence from the man you love.

I stared at him in the rearview mirror, mouth open in a silent cry of shock as tears flowed freely from my eyes. He had arrested me for wanton destruction while he sat there guilty of murder, and they'd never find the weapon he used to stab me in the heart.

"Silly me for thinking I was more important to you than your job," I said icily, not daring to let the tears, hurt, or anguish into my voice.

"Dot...I..."

"Save it, Bill. We're done here."

"We will get you through this! I promise."

"Don't want, need, or expect your help. I can handle this just fine without you. You drew the line, and I'm turning around and walking away from it. You know damn fucking well I did what I did to save everybody in that restaurant. Sure, it was my fault they were attacked in the first place, but I damn well made sure there were no innocent casualties. So, you can drop the fucking boy scout routine."

"What would you have me do?"

"I already told you what you *should* have done. You chose who you are over what you are. Tell you what. While I'm sitting in your little jail cell, why don't you ask your *coven* if you did the right thing."

9

"That's not fair, Dot, and you know it."

"And sitting in the back of your car in handcuffs is?" Leaning forward to spit on his little plastic window, I almost screamed as a buzzing sensation filled me. For a moment, I thought an insect had flown into my hair by my ear, but then I knew it was coming from inside me, *much* lower than my ear.

No. Fuck no. Oh, hell fucking no. Jason. I'm going to kill you, so help me lady, shut the fucking butt plug off now. Please. No. Oh, wow. Why now? Oh. Ooooooh.

I scrunched my eyes and lowered my face, pressing my chin against my chest and not daring to breathe. The buzzing increased in intensity and then began pulsating in waves of delicious agony. It might have been in my ass, but it felt like it was hardwired to my lungs. My breathing matched its pace as it came in frantic gasps.

I threw myself back in the seat and my head flipped up against the top of the headrest. Staring at the roof, little stars floated across my vision. I may, or may not, have even mewled.

"You okay?"

Apparently, I mewled. Ignoring him, I focused on not paying attention to the three-inch-long piece of surgical steel making my ass feel like the inside of a sub-woofer.

There is no vibrator. I'm only imagining it. I must not fear. Fear is the mind killer. I will face my fear. I will permit it to pass over me and through me.

It stopped. I gasped a sigh of relief and lifted my head, trying to control my breathing as I opened and closed my eyes repeatedly.

Maybe we got out of range.

I could almost picture Jason sitting in the middle of his trailer, thumb on the control, cackling maniacally as he slammed it to warp factor ten.

"Fuuuuuck," I screamed as my ass lifted off the seat, and my hips started bucking in the middle of the police car.

"Dot? What's wrong? Dot! Did you get bit by a werewolf? What the fuck is going on?"

My speech capability was reduced to incoherent, sobbing chipmunk mating calls. Falling over on my side, my head pressed against the seat as my ass was assaulted by an industrial boring rig. The orgasm hit and I rolled over on my back, almost breaking my wrist in the handcuffs as I started convulsing while speaking Klingon.

Fear is the mind–fuck that feels good. Oh, my lady.

"Dot?"

"Call Jason…" I had managed to squeak out between contractions. "Stop."

"Jason? What does he have to do with this?"

"Please," I sobbed, turned my head and started crying in pleasure.

The sound of a dialing phone filled the Jeep as Chief called him via the handsfree Bluetooth. He picked up on the third ring and my fourth orgasm.

"Hey, Bill. What's up?"

"What is going on right now?"

"Nothing. Sitting at home having a beer."

"What does that have to do with Dot?"

"Dot?" I could hear the panic in his voice.

"Yeah… She's rolling around in the back of my police vehicle like she's having some sort of seizure. Did you give her something? You're not doing drugs again, are you?"

"What? Nooo. Hold on a second, I'm getting another call."

The line never clicked, so I knew he was lying. Bless his fucking face. You could hear his finger tapping the screen as he desperately tried to switch apps. I could *almost* hear his finger squeaking as it slid across the screen and the vibrations inside me slowed to a stop.

"Thank fuck."

"What?" Chief turned his head and looked at me through the divider.

"Fucking drive. Take me to the station. Book me. Whatever. But get me out of these damn handcuffs and let me go to the fucking bathroom."

∞ ∞ ∞

"How are you holding up?"

"Peachy," I lied to Sherry through the gray iron bars separating us. Chief had booked me into the local jail, saving me from the indignity of being thrown into the local population of the county lockup. For which I would be eternally grateful. Orange might be the new black, but with my hair, I would have totally looked like a carrot.

"Well, it's almost morning. Judge Blankenship owes me a favor or two. As soon as he's up, I'll see about speeding things along to get your bail set and get you out of here."

"Thanks, Sherry. For everything."

"I'm just sorry I couldn't get the arrest warrant nipped in the bud. The district attorney was pretty adamant about filing charges."

"That doesn't make any sense. How the hell could he think I could destroy a restaurant by hurling lightning at it. Does he believe in witches?"

Her face narrowed. "My thoughts exactly. It almost seemed…personal. Every argument I had against it, he dismissed and decided to plod forward. This case is going to get thrown out the minute the presiding judge looks at the evidence. How he got one to sign off on the arrest warrant is beyond me."

"Chief said that a concerned citizen showed him the picture. Maybe they know each other?"

"District Attorney Materos doesn't have friends. Any."

"Materos?" I gulped.

"Yes? Do you know him?"

"No. While he may not have any friends...he might have a brother...."

"Dr. Materos. The one who got Jimmy kicked off the fire department..." She nodded in understanding. "He's making this personal. He may have screwed you in the process, but he might have just helped Jimmy's case if I can prove that he's doing this out of spite."

"You can be sure of that. It seems to be his motivating drive for everything. I bet his power ties are even angry."

"Everything makes a little more sense now. You'll be okay for a little while? I need to make some calls. Promise I'll have you out of here as soon as possible."

"Thanks, Sherry. I'll be fine."

"Call me if you need anything."

"A cake with a file in it?"

"Seriously doubt you'd need one if you *really* wanted to get out of here." She cocked an eyebrow and gave me a look.

I grinned and smiled.

Without another word, she headed toward the door separating the holding cells from the rest of the station. That walk had been the longest of my life. Not that I'd never been arrested before, but it was the first time it had been my boyfriend who had done it. I snarled in the direction of the door.

Are you all right? Dar's voice intruded on my rage, gingerly. Almost as if he knew I'd be pissed.

Been better.

You need help escaping?

No. Riding this one out. If I escape, I'll become a wanted criminal.

You already are. I want you. Shea wants you. Yuki looks like she's about to disembowel Chief. Jimmy is staging a coup. Jason is crying. Dennis is organizing a strike at the fire department. Things are getting ugly.

Tell everybody to calm down. The charges should get dropped and Sherry is hounding the judge. Everything will be okay. Eventually. Especially once I got my magical paws on the Materos brothers. Or my mother did...

I sighed, wishing I could communicate with everybody telepathically. Chief had taken my phone, wallet, keys, and everything else I had on me and put it in a box behind the counter. Everything but the butt plug. That went into the trash in the bathroom. While the pleasure had been exquisite...the humiliation attached to it rendered it useless to me. Maybe I'd pick up another one in a few dozen decades. In a different color, shape, and size. Maybe even manufacturer. I *never* wanted to be reminded of that night again as long as I lived.

Tell Josie to call my mother. Tell her that I'm not ignoring her and not to do anything stupid.

She does not know.

Welcome to Cedar Falls. It should only be a matter of moments before Marge tells her.

She's calling now.

Thanks, Dar. Tell everyone else I said thank you, too.

Yes, Master.

I leaned back against the gray painted concrete wall, looked up at the ceiling, and sighed heavily. Perfectly content sitting there, my reverie was broken by the click of a lock and the clang of metal as the door opened to the holding zone.

"Hey, Dot."

"Officer Brown. How nice to see you again." I was lying and he knew it. His braying laughter echoed off the concrete walls.

"Sorry. I didn't come here to tease you or anything. Chief sent me to see if you needed a bathroom break. Sorry our tiny cells don't have toilets."

"Actually, yes. I do. Tell him I said fuck off and die. But thank *you*."

14

He reached out and shoved a key in the lock, turning it and pulling the door open. I got up off my comfy slab of concrete and stretched, ignoring the chill in my butt. Thankfully, I had enough padding it hadn't seeped into my bones. "Don't suppose you have a cushion you can lend me?"

"I'll see what I can do. Want some coffee?"

"You can do this?" I practically grabbed his shirt.

"I can. I has the power."

"I'll love you forever."

He gave a short bark of laughter and motioned me toward the single bathroom in the holding area. "Shouldn't be too much longer, Dot. Sherry looked pissed. Not to mention, you have the mayor as your lawyer."

"Yeah, I know." I slipped into the bathroom and closed the door behind me.

"I was there in the square, fighting alongside you guys. You might be different, but you're all good people. Mostly. The Jimmy dude kind of gives me the creeps."

Laughing wasn't conducive to peeing, but I managed. "He's harmless. As long as you're not dating him."

"I think I'll be safe," he said with a chuckle barely audible through the door.

"I don't know. He's pretty cute." I washed my hands and opened the door. "Ready to be locked back up."

"Come on. Let's get you some coffee first. I'm sure if you were going to escape you would have been long gone by now."

"Yeah. Running from the law isn't exactly a good idea when you're trying to maintain a good guy image."

He nodded and headed toward the exit. I followed him out of the holding area and into the tiny kitchen. "How you like yours?"

"Black."

He cocked an eyebrow. "You *are* a hardened criminal."

"Just love the taste of coffee."

He handed me a Styrofoam cup and filled up his own mug, adding cream and sugar to his. I was just taking a sip when *he* walked in.

"Marcus, what is she doing out of her cell?"

"Just getting some coffee, Chief," he answered without looking at him.

Chief sighed and looked at me. "Doing okay?"

"Fuck off," I said and turned around, heading back to my cell.

Unfortunately, it was him who followed me back instead of Marcus. I liked Marcus. He didn't arrest me.

Ignoring Chief Runs-with-stick-in-ass, I pulled the door closed behind me and sat back down on the cement block bench, sipping my coffee and looking *everywhere* but into the cornflower blue eyes staring intently at me.

"Dot," he said through the bars, but I stopped him with an outstretched hand and a pointed finger.

"No. I don't wanna hear it."

"I know. I'm not going to try and explain myself to you. Maybe when you're less pissed off at me, I'll try. I was just letting you know that I contacted the coven, warning them to stay low and that the DA is poking around."

That got my attention. "He is?"

"Yes. He's been poking around case files."

"Is there anything incriminating in them for the rest of the coven?"

He sighed and leaned against the bars. "Between the murders, demons, abductions, and everything else... Yes. Unfortunately."

I sighed and leaned my head back, returning my eyes to the ceiling. It was almost comforting staring at the slightly darker spot on the white paint... "You son of a bitch."

"What?"

"You spelled the Lady damned ceiling with a tranquility spell."

He chuckled and sipped his coffee. "Maybe."

"Did you do that to keep me calm?"

"No! That was one of the first things I did when I joined the force. If you look around, there's one in every cell."

"That's kind of brilliant."

"I have my moments."

"Not very often."

"No."

"Do you regret arresting me?" I turned my head to look at him, wanting to *see* his answer more than I wanted to hear it.

"No. I did what I thought I had to do. I *do* regret not warning you first. That was kind of fucked up on my part. I'm sorry."

"Yeah. Well. You're still a dick."

"I know." He turned around and walked out of the holding area, pulling the door closed behind him with a loud *clang*.

"At least you know. Knowing is half the battle," I whispered with a little smile. He pissed me off, but that was part of his charm.

CHAPTER 2

"So, how does it feel to be free?" Jason snickered under his breath as we walked next door to the bookstore.

"Laugh it up. Next time, *you're* getting the remote-control butt plug. No lube for you."

He winced and unlocked the solid wood door, pulled it open, and let me inside. "Yeah. Sorry about that…"

"I know. But not as sorry as you're *going* to be." I chuckled evilly.

"Dot?" Josie squeaked and ran out from the café, Candace right behind her. I braced for the impact and they didn't disappoint, Josie hit high and Candace low around my waist. A small *oomph* escaped my lips, but I smiled and hugged them both back.

"Yep. Didja miss me?"

Josie lifted her head and narrowed her eyes at me. "If it was one night in jail, I would have said no. But I hardly see you anymore."

Candace nodded in agreement against my stomach.

"Yeah. Well, I'm not going anywhere. For a while."

"Good. Come on, Candy. We're opening in twenty minutes."

I looked over at Jason. "We're ready?"

"As we'll ever be. I was going to postpone until you could be here, but when Chief called me a bit ago that your bail had been set, I figured what better way to keep your mind off being locked up." He winked to let me know he was teasing as he re-locked the front door.

"Well, I'll stay until you open, but I *need* to go home and have a shower."

"Want me to call someone to pick you up?"

"No," I answered without thinking. Only Shea and Dar knew about my shadow walking ability, and I kind of wanted to keep it that way. The rest knew about my dad, and that I wasn't just a witch. They didn't need to see just how different I had become. Thankfully *none* of them knew about growing fangs and vamping out on Ellis, the gorgeous dark elf whose mother had kidnapped Jaeren in an attempt to get me to marry her son. That would have been awkward. More awkward. "I'll have Yuki bring my car," I lied.

"She can drive?"

"I think so."

"You don't want me to call Jimmy?"

"No. I will. He can let everybody know I'm out of the hoosegow."

The knock on the front door almost startled me. Sherry was peering through the glass, cupping her hand over her eyes to cut out some of the bright background light. She waved when she saw me.

I walked over and twisted the deadbolt, gently pushing the door open. "Hello, Mayor."

"Glad to see you're out and about." She stepped inside, and I relocked the door.

"Thank you, for getting the judge to set bail so quick."

She narrowed her eyes at me. "That wasn't me? I couldn't get ahold of him."

"Then how am I out already? It isn't even nine."

"Maybe you just got lucky," she said and reached over and patted my arm.

I might have bought it, but Jason was looking even more guilty than when he decided to play DJ with the butt plug controls. "Spill it."

"I don't know anything."

"Uh huh. Your face is saying different. Talk."

"I can't."

"Want the butt plug inserted horizontally?"

"It was Chief." He didn't hesitate to answer. "He went to the judge's house and had him set bail and sign the papers. He told me not to tell you."

I was almost disappointed. My mother was in town. My grandmother lived in town. I'd have expected him to tell me one of them bedded the judge to get me out of jail. Chief doing it didn't make any damn sense. He'd arrested me in the first place. "Why?"

"You'll have to ask him. I know he felt horrible for what he did, maybe he wanted you free, but by the book."

"That sounds a little more like the boy scout." I turned toward the front door, half tempted to march my ass back to the station and demand an answer. But then I'd have to see him again. Maybe it was better to let things be.

Sherry cleared her throat. "Anyway, the DA absolutely refuses to drop the case, which is weird. Even he has to know there is absolutely no *way* he's going to win this. He's just wasting taxpayer dollars."

His motivation clicked in my head. "Not if putting me behind bars isn't what he's after."

"What would that be?"

"Exposure. He's going to glorify this case to let the entire town know that I'm a witch. Scratch that. I'll be lucky if it's just me he's after. He'll probably drag Jimmy into this, too," I said with a little frown. *Come after me, I'll let you live. Go after my coven and they won't find your body.*

"What are you going to do?"

"You're my lawyer. I'll leave that up to you. As long as I lay low, and everybody else does, too… He won't have a shred of evidence other than the lightning flying out of my hands. Maybe I should sue the power company. It was their electricity that hit me. Luckily, I wasn't hurt," I told her with a wink.

"That's kind of scary fucking brilliant…"

"I have my moments."

"More often than you think. If you're suing the power company for faulty wiring, or a blown transformer…" She practically squealed and hugged me and ran for the door. At least she remembered to unlock it before running outside.

"Anything I can do?" Jason tilted his head and smiled at me.

"Yes. Get this damn store open. Josie!" I waited for them to come out of the café again.

"What?"

"I'm going home to shower. I'll be back later. Just wanted to say good luck."

She jogged back over and gave me another hug. "Thank you. For everything."

"What are sisters for?" I'd said it jokingly to her a million times growing up. This time, I meant it. Even if she didn't know the truth behind my words.

"You're not going to stay for the opening?"

"No. I changed my mind. I *really* need a shower. And a nap. And some coffee and food. I'll be back later to check on you all." I looked at her, Candace, and Jason. I hoped the three of them could handle everything, but I wasn't exactly expecting a mad rush of people on the very first day. Not wanting to take a chance, I gave Jason a *look*. "If it gets too busy and you can't handle it, call me. I'll be here in five."

"You're worrying too much. Go and get cleaned up, then come hang out."

22

"I will. And thank *you* for everything you've done. And bailing me out."

"It was uh…the least I could do." He blushed again.

"All right, kids. I'm heading home. You got this!" I leaned over and gave Jason a not so chaste kiss on his lips. "Love you," I whispered.

"Love you, too."

"I don't get one of those?" Josie was teasing. Josie was always teasing about an inappropriate relationship with me. She'd done it since we were kids. It is the main reason I was never surprised when she came out as bisexual. Knowing she was my *actual*, blood-related sister, the thought turned my stomach in about thirty-seven knots. She must have noticed my reaction. "Damn. I know I'm ugly but that's just plain rude."

"No! And shut up, ho. You know you're hot. I uh…just got out of jail. Things were pretty rough on the other side. Big girls named Bertha who told me I had a pretty mouth…"

"Oh, Lady. I'm sorry, Dot!"

She bought it. "It's okay… I'll be all right. I'll be back in a little bit."

"Okay. Sorry. No more lesbian jokes, I promise!"

"Thanks, Jose. Have fun! Candace, if she starts skimming money out of the register, you smack her, okay?"

"I will, Lady." She grinned at me, and I ruffled her hair.

I turned and waved at everyone over my shoulder as I slipped out the still unlocked front door and into the bright sunlight. *Dar? Yuki?*

Yes, Master? Dar was the first responder.

Anybody home that can come pick me up? I'm outside the bookstore.

Glad to see you are finally free. I shall call off the rescue operation.

23

What rescue operation?

The one I'd planned on executing sometime early next week. When we ran out of foodstuffs in your humble abode.

You're a shit.

I'm not the one who got arrested.

Is there someone there who can drive a car and pick me up?

Yuki is already on her way.

Yuki, pick me up at the diner. I'm grabbing a coffee.

Yes, Master. Her voice sounded strange. Almost like she was concentrating *really hard* and too busy to talk.

I let it go and headed for the diner, ducking under the window of the police station, and peering through the front window of the diner, just to make sure there were no Chiefs in there ordering burgers. Luckily, he was nowhere in sight. Ignoring the chill of the handle, I yanked open the door and slipped inside, inhaling deeply of the smell of burgers and freedom. One night in a jail cell and I was already appreciating the simple things in life. Burgers, bacon, and grease. That's what life boiled down to.

"Dot!"

Marge's voice stopped space and time. Every head in the diner turned and focused on me. "Hey, Marge."

"Cop a squat. I'll bring you some coffee."

"Thanks," I mumbled and slid into my booth, putting my back to the rest of the diner and watching the front for signs of my car or Yuki.

Marge delivered the promised coffee quicker than I expected, sliding into the booth across from me. "You hungry? Poor child."

"You know?"

She put her head on her hand, leaning her elbow against the table, nodding emphatically. "Herb was taking out the trash last night, saw Chief bringing you in the back in cuffs. That rat-bastard. Told him he better not show his face in here again until you were home free. Guess I should have the kid deliver a burger. Does he deserve one?"

"No. Yes. Wait, put hot sauce and jalapenos on it. He'll eat it if he's hungry enough." *May your ass be as sore as mine, fuck nut.*

"Evil. I like it. I'll have Herb soak the burger in Texas Pete."

I chuckled. "Thanks, Marge." I was grateful for more than the payback. She, in a totally uncharacteristic Marge moment, was actually whispering.

"Saw your mother this morning…"

Shit. "Did you tell her anything…"

"Sorry, kiddo. I did. Figured she was on the need to know list. My bad. She said for you to call her the moment I saw you."

"Not your fault, sweetie. I will. After I get home and have a shower after I finish this coffee."

"You gonna eat?"

"No time. Yuki's picking me up any moment."

"Gotcha. Be right back, I'll make you a coffee to go. Hold tight." She slid out of the booth and patted me on the head before practically jogging across the restaurant. "Herb, emergency rations."

"Comin up!"

Two minutes later, she dropped off a plastic bag with a takeout container in it, and a foam cup filled with coffee and the promise of a better day. "Here you go, Dot."

I grabbed my bank card out of my wallet, but she shook her head, putting her hand over mine.

"Herb says come by later and drop off the check for the house, if you have time to make it to the bank today. You won't be able to move anybody in right away, but he can give you the key. House next door to you is yours at the end of the month."

"Perfect. Thanks, and tell him I said thanks, too."

"Will do."

25

"Wait. What day is it?"

"The twentieth, why?"

"Just making sure I didn't miss the great turkey cookoff. Don't forget, you're having Christmas dinner at my place."

"You sure you're still up for everything?"

"Wouldn't miss it for the world."

"All right, but don't be afraid to back out of cooking dinner with us. I know you have a ton of shit goin' on."

I downed the last of my coffee in my mug. "I meant what I said. Looking forward to it," I answered with a grin, just as my vampire chauffer pulled my car in front of the diner door. "Ride's here. Thanks, Marge," I said, got up, and gave her a quick hug before heading out the door.

"You take care of you, too!"

"I will," I managed to shout just before the door closed between us.

"Hey, Boss," Yuki said as I opened the passenger door.

"Thanks for picking me up."

"Prison bus doesn't go by the house?"

"*Et tu,* Yuké?" I gave her an exasperated look. It was bad enough I'd gotten arrested. If they kept teasing me about it, I was going to snap.

"Dar gave ya shit, too?" She grinned at me before looking over her shoulder and pulling away from the curb. I wasn't completely sure *why* she looked before she leaped, a big pickup locked up its brakes and the guy laid on the horn.

"Thank you," Yuki called out the window and gave him a little wave. Then she almost sideswiped the car parked in front of us.

"You…um…have driven before, right?"

"Sure. Lots of times."

"Thank the Lady."

"The whole steering wheel thing is a little weird, though."

"What?"

"I mean, the little joy sticks on the Xbox are waaay easier. I'm just sayin'."

"You better not be fucking just saying. Are you kidding me right now?"

"A little."

"Yuki, you suck."

"Blah blah blah," she answered it a Transylvanian accent and bared a fang at me.

A mental image of me standing over Ellis flashed through my mind. I could taste the sweetness of his blood and feel the tenderness of his flesh against my lips. Swallowing guiltily, I focused on the road ahead of us.

"You okay?"

"Yes?" I turned my head and cocked an eyebrow at her.

"You went totally broody."

"Broody?"

"Yes. Your face darkened and you were staring out the window like a brooding vampire."

"Huh?"

"Never mind. Maybe I miss hanging out with other vampires."

"You do?"

"Sure. My dad's a dick, but I love George like a cousin. Which works out good. Cuz he is. And don't get me wrong, I love you guys and my new family, but I feel like the oddball out. No late-night snacks to share with your buds, you know?"

"Have you talked to them at all?" It was her turn to get broody, which told me she had. "I'm sorry, Yuki."

"Don't be. It is what it is. I'm sure if dear old Dad hadn't commanded it, George would have at least checked on me."

"At least he isn't forbidding you from visiting the blood bank."

"Money is money. Doesn't matter if it comes from his excommunicated daughter or not." She swallowed guiltily.

"At least he's practical in some things."

The whine of a diesel engine sounded like a 747 taking off as the truck Yuki had cutoff gunned its engine and passed us on Main Street, horn blaring again. The passenger rolled down his window and launched a half-filled foam dip cup across our windshield. I gagged as the tobacco infused spit splashed across my mostly clean car.

"That's fucking disgusting." I stared in disbelief.

Yuki had hit the windshield wipers just in time to see the truck skid to a stop in front of us. Her arm shot out with inhuman speed as she stomped on the brake and held me against the seat simultaneously. We fishtailed to a stop with just inches to spare.

"Nice reflexes."

"Thanks." She undid her seatbelt, opened the door, and stomped out.

"Yuki!"

She ignored me as she stomped the entire way to the driver's side of the truck. I winced as the total hillbilly stepped out and towered over Yuki with a smirk on his face, a cowboy hat on his head, and enough muscles to probably fold her in half and tuck her in his back pocket. If she weren't a vampire. I practically kicked my door open to stop him from getting hurt.

I had just gotten out of the car in time to see him take a swipe at her. With a resigned sigh, I leaned over the door to watch the show. Whatever he got, he deserved it after that.

He'd only meant to grab her, but his hand never got close. She reached out and wrapped her hand around his wrist, yanking him toward her as she sidestepped while keeping one leg firmly planted against the asphalt. I doubted a moving car could have uprooted that foot, so his shin didn't stand a chance. As soon as he tripped, she used his momentum to flip him with the hand around his wrist.

28

She looked like a tiny little judo master throwing a mannequin, but the move saved him from plowing a ditch through the asphalt with his face.

Then the other one got out of the truck.

My hands pushed back against the car, ready to intercept him and protect her, but then reality kicked in. Yuki didn't even remotely *need* my help. Nor did she probably want it. And I was in enough trouble with the police.

Skoal-boy was shorter than Flippy McRoadkill, but stockier. He looked like a hairy tank in sleeveless plaid. "Make sure he cleans the windshield, Yuki," I called softly.

She grinned at me and turned to the rapidly approaching source of amusement, still holding on to his disbelieving friend's wrist. He wasn't unconscious, his ass having taken the brunt of the landing, but judging from the way he was holding his ass off the pavement, he would be sporting a sore tailbone for a few years. Those damn things never healed.

"You heard the lady, go clean the windshield."

"Fuck off, you little twat!" He went to shove Yuki away from Flippy and got a hand to the throat. It was kind of mesmerizing watching his face register the shock of not being able to breathe and the ineffectiveness of his fists against Yuki's face and arms. It took all of thirty seconds for him to start tapping out frantically.

"Don't kill him."

"You're getting soft, Master."

"No. There are witnesses," I answered, playing along with her big-bad mini bodyguard routine.

With a sigh, she let him go. "I said go clean the windshield. Now." He wasn't going to be able to for a few minutes at least. He was too busy trying to suck in air through his rapidly bruising neck.

The sound of a police siren behind us stopped the fun. Slowly, I turned, hoping against hope that it wasn't Chief who had stopped behind us. Hope betrayed me, and I winced as he slowly got out of his car and slid his sunglasses up onto his head. "Fancy meeting you here."

"Gonna arrest me again?"

"Depends."

"On?"

"What did you do this time."

CHAPTER 3

"Dot?"

"Yes, Chief?"

"Please. For the love of the lady, stay out of *trouble*." He shut my car door.

I started the engine, happy to be back in the driver's seat. Yuki had seemed a little put out that I refused to let her drive. Ever again. "Tell trouble to quit throwing shit at my window."

"Thankfully there were witnesses. I've warned Jackson and Davis about their tempers. They're lucky they didn't cause an accident." He leaned down enough to look at Yuki in the passenger seat. "Next time you might want to show a little restraint. The whole town thinks you're some kind of ninja now," he said with a chuckle.

"Luckily, I didn't bite his face off. I kind of wanted to."

"Well, with as many people who recorded the whole incident with their phones, I'll call that a good thing."

He slapped the car door and motioned for us to get going. We'd blocked traffic long enough. The rednecks were in the back of the cop car for assault and we had to give our statement. Thankfully, I had the takeout container of breakfast food Herb had thrown together. I sat in the car eating while Chief did his thing. I still wanted a shower, but my stomach wasn't trying to gnaw its way out of my abdomen in search of food.

I gave him a little wave as we drove away, the pickup truck finally having been removed by a hunky looking tow truck driver. Sparing Chief one last glance, I smiled at his image in the rearview mirror standing in the middle of the road, hands on his hips, watching me drive away and shaking his head.

"That was fun. I miss the good old days when I could have bled a mortal in the middle of the street, and nobody would have batted an eyelash."

"I'm going to agree with you on that one."

"You would have bled him?" She was joking, but the mark hit a little too close to home.

"No, but I'd have set him on fire if he tried to hurt me. But then again, I wouldn't have cut off the big diesel Ford with my tiny assed car."

"He was in my blind spot."

I spared her a glance. "You're a vampire. You could have heard that truck coming at you from three counties over."

She sighed and sank into her seat a little. "Okay. I suck at driving. I've done it probably a dozen times. I don't even have my license. Luckily, your boyfriend didn't ask me for one."

I patted her on the head. "We'll practice. I'll teach you if you want to learn."

She perked up at that and turned on the radio. Full blast. Blaring K-pop in my Kia, ironically.

"What station is this?" I stared at the radio.

"WUKI. Yuki radio, all day and all night!" She wiggled her phone in front of her.

"You hooked up your phone. To *my* Bluetooth."

"Yep."

I let out a sigh, followed quickly by a little smile to let her know I was kidding. We bopped along with the music all the way to the house.

The last thing I was expecting was a moving van in front of the neighbor's house. The pastor, his wife, and a crew of five guys were steadily loading boxes into the back. I waved at him and gave him a tiny smile out of pure spite for his wife.

Evil. Thy name is Dot. He was going to be sleeping on the couch for a while, but I didn't care. If they had been less nasty and talked to me like a human being, I would have been more than happy to be the friendly neighbor. Instead, his bitch wife had to tell everybody about her slutty neighbor. Good riddance, and thanks for the house. Which reminded me that I needed to go to the bank after my shower and nap.

Dar opened the door as soon as we got out of the car. He was in his elf guise, for which I was grateful. The neighbors didn't need to see a blue demon leaning against the door, shirtless and looking hot as hell. The elf body was bad enough. Out of curiosity, I turned back toward the neighbors. Mrs. Pastor had just handed off a box to the mover in the back of the truck and was staring intently at my Dar. The perv.

Chuckling, I walked up to him and locked my lips to his, much to his surprise. He got over it quickly and wrapped his arms around me, pulling me in tighter. I gasped as his hands slid down over my ass and lifted me into the kiss. "I assume this show was for your nosy neighbor," he whispered as he pulled away.

"No. Don't know what you're talking about. I *wanted* to kiss you."

"Yes, Master," he whispered and licked my ear, pulling away and letting me in through the door.

The kiss had gotten me a little excited. The sultry way he whispered the word master made my knees a little weak. I ran my hand across his chest as I walked past him.

"Welcome home, Lady," Shea said with a smile and a little bow.

"You are free!" Jaeren added from the living room, standing up from the couch. "I am glad."

"Thanks, Jaeren," I said, stifling a small laugh. He was cute when he wanted to be. "If anybody needs me, I will be in the shower and then I'm going to sleep for a little bit."

Heading into the bedroom, I stripped on the way to the bathroom, turned the water on in the shower to the molten lava setting, and brushed my teeth while I waited for the pipes to drag the water up from the seventh level of Hell. Nothing makes you feel dirtier than spending the night in jail.

Sliding open the glass door, I stepped in and winced as the scalding water hit my leg. I skirted around the spray, edging my way in slowly as I got used to being boiled alive. By the time I finally made it all the way under, I already felt cleaner. Steam cleaned.

I was shampooing my hair when I heard the door slide open. Unable to see, I tilted my head a little, trying to hear who had joined me, but the sound of the water drowned out any telltale sounds. "Yuki?"

They didn't say a word, merely grabbed my hands, pulling them away from my hair. Their fingers took the place of mine and started massaging the shampoo into my hair, dancing across my scalp and sending shivers down my back.

"Dar?"

Still no response. I started to turn, but the hands stopped me as they gripped my shoulders. They were definitely not Yuki's, and whoever it was wanted to remain a mystery. At least for now. It was either Dar or Shea, it had to be. Jaeren didn't have it in him to climb into the shower with me unasked, and probably didn't have the desire to, either. Unless Jimmy stopped by, it *had* to be one of the other two.

The hands worked the lather through my hair, brushing the back of my neck with the back of their fingers. I felt myself sigh in contentment. "Keep your eyes closed," a voice whispered in my ear, soft enough that it didn't give away who they were. Finally, they turned me around, easing me back gently into the spray and tilting my head back.

If I were being honest, I kind of wanted to look. But I didn't. Not knowing who was washing my hair was ten-thousand times more exciting than knowing. Instead, I focused on the feel of the gentle fingers sliding through my hair as they rinsed away the suds and how exposed I was to whoever was standing in front of me.

When they finished, they pulled me slowly forward and turned me back around. I heard them rummage through the bottles of shampoos and soaps I kept on the rack beside me. They found whatever they were looking for and I heard it squirt out of the bottle. When they replaced it, the hands rubbed conditioner in my hair, I could tell by the scent. "Thank you," I said softly, a smile spreading across my face. One of the hands caressed my neck, acknowledging my thanks.

Again, they pulled me out of the water, rinsing me again.

"Can I open my eyes now?"

Instead of answering, they leaned forward and gently kissed my closed lids, moving from one to another without saying a word. I took it as a no, sighing outwardly, but nearly screaming in excitement internally.

I listened to their movements and breathing the best I could as they rummaged some more. When I felt the wet, soapy bath scrunchie slide across my chest gently, a little moan *did* escape my lips.

Steady hands lifted my arms and washed away my troubles and cares, caressed my breasts, and lightly ran their thumbs over my nipples. My hand snaked down over my stomach, gathered some suds, and rubbed the flesh of my lips between my thighs.

35

Whoever it was with me grabbed my wrist, stopping me from pleasuring myself, and I almost whimpered in frustration. Until his fingers found me. "Yesss," I hissed as my hips bucked against his hand. He cupped me, letting his middle finger slide through me as the rest of his fingers rubbed against my lips. When his finger curled and slid inside me, I moaned in ecstasy as my hand reached out and grabbed his already hard cock.

"Dot," his voice came out as a breathless whisper, tinged with heat.

My eyes flew open.

"Dennis?" I backed away from his hand in shock.

He sort of embarrassedly smiled at me. "Yeah."

"Hey, bud. What are you uh…doin' in here?" One arm crossed my breasts and the other covered my almost aching crotch. I didn't want to stop almost as much as I wanted an explanation.

His eyes opened wide in shock and then narrowed in what looked suspiciously like suspicion. "You… Let me guess. You didn't want me to join you… Fuck me." He sighed and covered his eyes with his hands, a blush spreading across his cheeks that had absolutely nothing to do with the temperature of the water.

"Jimmy," I said to him, simply. It wasn't a name, it was an explanation.

He nodded, not daring to look at me.

"He's out in the living room, isn't he?"

He nodded again.

I wanted to walk out there, stark naked and stark raving mad. But I could kill him later. Right then, there was something I wanted to do more. I wrapped my arms around Dennis and pressed my head against his chest. "I'm sorry your best friend is an asshole."

He laughed. "I'm sorry your boyfriend is an asshole, too." He awkwardly patted my back with the hand that wasn't still covering his eyes.

I kissed the chest that was tantalizingly close to my lips.

"Well, I'll let you finish your shower. I'm gonna go," he said and let go of his face long enough to gently grip my shoulders, steadying me as he took a step back.

"Don't."

"Don't what?"

I took a deep breath, steadying my nerves. "Go. Don't go. Stay." I scrunched my eyes, clearly not knowing what I was doing.

To his credit, he didn't immediately agree and jump right back in. Instead, he stared at me incredulously.

I pressed myself against him, tilted my head up and gently kissed his chin. His mouth quickly found mine. There was more pent up frustration in that kiss than I thought possible, but it wasn't forced or awkward, fumbling or over eager. It was potential, a crouched lion ready to spring. I grinned against his mouth as the tip of his cock bobbed in front of him, slapping me lightly in the stomach.

"Somebody's happy," I whispered.

"That makes both of us." He smiled back at me.

"Let's get you clean, get out of here, and go punish Jimmy."

"Good plan." He chuckled evilly.

I carefully worked my way around him, difficult in the shower with his broad shoulders, and what made it harder was tearing my eyes away from the look he was giving me. This, what was happening between us, was a long time coming.

Taking the scrunchie from him, it was my turn to run it over the smooth skin of his chest. My guys varied in amounts of body hair. Dar and Shea were completely hairless, and Jason wasn't far behind with just a hint of stubble across his face. Even his leg hair was sparse, getting denser the closer it got to his pubic hair. Jimmy and

37

Chief had the most, and Chief took the crown by a long shot. Dennis was smack in the middle. Hair and arms, a thick patch around his beautiful cock, and a patch in the middle of his chest that fanned out over his pectoral muscles. A happy medium. I'd always found him handsome, seeing him naked was better than I'd imagined. And I had. A lot.

He tilted his head back into the spray, running his hands over his short hair and rubbing his face as I washed his body. The water cascaded down his chest and over his stomach, instantly washing away the suds. Taking a hold of his cock, I pulled him forward a little, soaping him up and letting my hand glide over his hot flesh.

"Keep that up and you're going to make a mess." His voice sounded stained. He wasn't kidding.

I pushed him gently back under the water, dropping the scrunchie and using my hand to get the suds off him again. Then I lowered myself to my knees, putting him at eye level. "We can't have any messes in the shower…"

I licked the tip of him. He was already leaking precum in all his excitement. We were definitely going to fuck, but I wanted it to last. Our first time should be something we would both remember with a smile for a very long time. So, I pulled him into my mouth and ran my tongue against the underside of his sensitive tip.

"Dot!"

I pulled him out and looked up at him. "Go ahead," I answered simply, meaning it. I wanted him to explode, letting that pent-up frustration out before I *really* got what I'd always wanted from him. My pussy was practically throbbing in anticipation and I hadn't even cum yet. I needed to, almost as bad as he did.

As I sucked him back into my mouth, I reached beneath me and slipped two fingers inside me. He was blocking the spray of water with his broad back, but my pussy was practically dripping on its own. Pulling my fingers out, I mashed my clit between them as I covered them in my slickness. Groaning against him, I started sucking in earnest.

Of all of them, he had the most ridges and veins. Even more than Dar. I very much looked forward to feeling him inside me. Immensely. I practically whimpered as I felt him throb against the roof of my mouth. He was closer than I'd imagined.

"Dot, I'm going to come..."

"Mmmhmm," I mumbled around him. That was more than he could handle.

He groaned as he unloaded. I doubled my assault against my hard clit, wanting to come almost as bad as I'd wanted to make him. The first splash completely coated my tongue, giving it that numbing feeling and onslaught of saltiness. The second puffed out my cheeks a little. By the time the third made it a little uncomfortable, I came.

Opening my mouth in a silent scream, I pulled him from my mouth and panted through the orgasm, not caring that he was still coming and feeling the fourth and fifth spurts splash across my lips and chin.

"Fuck," he managed to stammer as I still worked him with my hand.

"You said it." I looked up at him and grinned as I washed his come from my skin and onto the shower floor.

"I thought you didn't want to make a mess," he said with a chuckle.

"I thought you were going to come like a normal human. Been a while, huh?"

He gave me a sad nod, reaching down and offering me a hand up. "Are you okay?"

"Why wouldn't I be?" I got to my feet.

"Well, we were kind of forced into this... Just wanted to make sure you were okay with it."

I leaned in close and looked him right in the eye. "First thing you should always remember about me. I will do absolutely *nothing* that I don't want to. Ever. Got it, Mister? This wasn't pity, this wasn't an accident, I've *wanted* to do this for a very long time."

"Okay," he said with a chuckle, putting his hands up in the air for emphasis.

"Our timing just sucked in the beginning. Then you met Alista. I'm sorry things didn't work out with her, but I'm also *not* sorry. Does that make sense?"

"Not only do I understand, I agree."

"You're happy you broke up with her?"

"No. I'm happy that you like me."

I couldn't help it and leaned in for that kiss.

He chuckled, used his hand to wipe off my chin, and met my lips with his. He reached down and lifted my leg, intent on taking me in the shower, but I pulled away and shook my head. "No. I want our first time to be in a damn bed. Please."

He smiled and nodded. "I'd like that, too. Sorry, you're just a little hard to resist."

I reached down and took his cock in my hand. "You're a lot hard to resist." I wiggled my eyebrows. "Let me rinse off. Towels are in the cupboard by the shower."

"Yes, ma'am." He kissed me one more time, traded places with me, and opened the door. "You fucker!"

Dennis's shout and Jimmy's laughter told me all I needed to know. Grinning, I slid under the water and rinsed away the evidence while I plotted my revenge.

CHAPTER 4

Jimmy flopped back on the bed, grinning at me as I straddled his waist. His cock poked at the entrance to my pussy and I pushed back against him, letting the tip sink inside me before stopping.

"Oh, you feel sooo good, Jimmy."

"So do you," he answered as his eyes widened. His hips began to push forward, but I matched his movements, keeping him just inside me.

I put my hands on his chest to steady myself and looked deeply into his eyes as I felt Dennis settle on the bed beside us. Sliding my hands over his shoulders and down his arms, I grabbed his wrists and gently guided his arms up against the head of the bed, leaning down and brushing his lips with mine. "I want you," I whispered.

"You have me. All of me. It's yours."

"To have and to hold?"

He nodded.

"Forever and ever?"

He nodded again.

"To do with as I please."

"Yes," he said solemnly.

My tongue darted out and licked his lips as I drank in his desire, his want, and his need. But mostly his love. "*Ceangal agus tost,*" I said as I sat up, grinning at him.

The wood of the headboard warped as tendrils grew from the surface, binding his hands against it. His legs began kicking behind me as they bound his feet. His mouth opened but no words, or sound, escaped him.

"That was my binding and silence canting. Behave, or I'll try out my immobility spell." I glared at him for emphasis. "You were a *very* naughty monkey, Jimmy. So, I'm going to punish you. Would you like that?"

He nodded, his eyes taking on a gleam I hadn't quite expected.

"Good. Now you get to lie there and enjoy the show." I pushed back against him, fully impaling myself on his throbbing cock. Bound and unable to move, completely at my mercy, he was more turned on than I'd ever seen him, harder than I'd ever felt him.

I put one leg down on the floor beside us and lifted myself off him, but reached down and stroked him a couple of times, smearing my wetness all over him. His hips bucked in pleasure.

Then I focused on Dennis. Sweet Dennis who was grinning at me in appreciation and stroking his own cock while he watched the show. "Shall we?"

"Please," he practically begged.

I motioned for him to get up and meet me at the end of the bed. He met me there with open arms and I fell into them, kissing him like I'd always wanted to. His hands traced lazy circles down my back until they made their way over my ass. He lifted me up further into that kiss, practically devouring me. Moaning against him, I returned the favor, pulling him into me and twisting, rubbing his cock between our stomachs.

"You drive me insane," he said with a throaty chuckle as he pulled away.

"Just you wait. I really do drive people insane." I kissed the tip of his nose.

"I thought we were going to do this on the bed?"

"Oh. We are. I was just giving Jimmy the best seat in the house. Remember when he made me fuck him on the couch right in front of you?"

He blushed, clearly remembering. It was the first time I'd seen his cock. He'd masturbated and came right in front of me while I rode his best friend. My pussy practically drooled at the memory. Okay, it did drool. I felt my wetness dripping slowly down my leg. Even bound and gagged, he was still able to make me insane with desire.

Sitting down on the end of the bed, I grabbed Dennis's hands and pulled him with me as I scooted back between Jimmy's legs. I leaned back against him, his hard cock sliding against my neck as my head rested on his stomach.

Dennis leaned over me and kissed me again as his hand found my pussy, fingers parting my flesh and sinking inside me. He was ignoring his best friend's dick only inches from us as his tongue found mine.

"You're so wet," he said as he pulled away.

"You're so hard," I answered, glancing down at him, wanting nothing more than for him to sink into me.

He didn't though, he curled his fingers inside me, letting the tips brush against the flesh just behind my mound before he began to finger fuck me in earnest.

"Dennisssssss," I hissed his name as pleasure kicked the shit out of me. My eyes crossed, and then rolled up as I closed them. The rest of his fingers were banging against me, only adding to the frenzy that had enveloped me. He put his other hand on the flesh of my stomach, just above my pubic hair, and applied a little pressure as his other hand became a blur of motion.

What flew from my mouth was unintelligible, primal, and I probably looked like a complete spaz. The orgasm that hit me was almost immediate, and when he leaned down and kissed my pussy, I exploded. My eyes opened and I yelled his name as the room darkened, either from the

43

shadows reacting from my orgasm or just my vision failing me. I was betting on the latter as stars also filled my vision.

"Stop. No more," I whimpered as he slowed his assault. "Holy fuck. Woah. Wow. Yeah um…where'd you learn that one?" I blinked slowly, trying to bring his face back into focus.

"Internet," he said with a grin, wiping moisture that had escaped from my lady bits off his forearm.

"Gotta love the fucking internet. Wow."

He gave my clit a gentle kiss and scooted forward on his knees, bringing the tip of his cock to my entrance. "Need a minute?"

"I want to say yes, but not as much as I want you inside me. Go slow, please."

He reached down and grabbed his shaft, bringing the tip of his cock to my clit and rubbing it slowly with that soft patch of skin just under the head.

"Oooh," I cooed.

He looked at the cock beside me and smiled, glancing at me and looking back at it, commanding me without words.

"You want me to suck Jimmy while you fuck me?"

He nodded shyly.

"Do you think he deserves it?"

A smile and a shake of his head.

"But you want to watch me do it."

"Yes."

He was beyond fucking cute. And now he was mine. Jimmy was being pleasured and punished by being left out of our fun. Life was good.

I turned my head and kissed the side of Jimmy's cock. It was moving on its own as it bobbed beside me. He was flexing his muscles, trying to give himself a modicum of pleasure. I captured the head of it with my mouth, shifting my back and pulling him in a bit more. He couldn't even groan, but I felt him throb hotly in my mouth.

Dennis stopped rubbing my clit with his dick and sank the head inside me. I groaned around a mouthful of cock. The deeper he went, the deeper I took Jimmy into my mouth. He was still feeding himself inside me long after Jimmy had touched the back of my mouth. Any farther and things would have gotten ugly.

When Dennis pulled back, I did the same, matching him stroke for stroke. I moaned in pleasure, Dennis feeling better inside me than I had ever imagined.

"You are so fucking beautiful. And hot. Sexy. Kinky. Would it be too soon to tell you you're everything I ever imagined I wanted?"

Letting Jimmy go, I looked up at the gorgeous man leaning over me, my legs over his thighs as he drove himself inside me. "You should have told me sooner." I gave him a small smile, embarrassed a thousand times more by his words than the situation.

"I should have told you that night in the bar. When we were playing pool. Jimmy is way better at me than flirting."

I reached up and rubbed his chest. "But you're much better at being sweet."

He smiled at me, earnestly, without reservation, and my heart turned into a puddle of goo as my smile matched his. Then his took an evil uptake as he drove his cock into me, grinding himself against me.

"Yes, Dennis! Fuck me."

And he did, driving himself in and out of me almost at the same pace he had almost wrecked my sanity with his fingers.

"Fuck fuck fuck."

Jimmy's cock slapped against my cheek as I turned my head in agony and ecstasy. I wanted him, needed him, back in my mouth while Dennis drove me insane.

"*Pléisiúr,*" I mumbled around Jimmy's cock.

I'd gotten wrapped up in the moment and didn't think about what I was doing. My spell shot into Jimmy *and* Dennis.

"Dooooottttttttttt," Dennis groaned as he practically tried to crawl inside me, his cock diving in as far as it could go as he convulsed against me.

Jimmy erupted into the back of my throat. I almost gagged and quickly freed him from my mouth, trying to guide him away with my face. Unfortunately, he kept spewing all over my mouth and neck, some spurts landing on my breasts and lower. Dennis' was flowing out of me and quickly running down the crack of my ass, pooling beneath me.

I'd wanted Dennis's and my first time to be something special. It was, and then some. It turned into a bukkake threesome with me covered in silvery strands of hot wetness. I should have been disgusted. My error in magical judgement should have been very apparent. But...I loved every second of it. Jimmy splashing all over me, Dennis unloading inside me, feeling him twitching and spasming as his face contorted in primal pleasure...

I was lucky I survived. Orgasm after orgasm raced through me, tearing up the track. My back arched and my head pivoted against Jimmy as I tried to roll away and curl up in fetal position. Dennis collapsed on top of me, not caring in the slightest that Jimmy's cock jabbed him in the face and then the room went dark as the shadows pulled from the walls, encircling us and wrapping the entire bed in a cocoon of silky blackness that glittered in my vampiric vision.

With a defeated sigh, I let go of all the magic of the pleasure and binding spells that were still going. Jimmy gave one grunt of pleasure, sat up, and fell back on the bed. "Woah."

"Woah is right," I managed to answer back.

"Can we do that again?"

One thing was for damn certain, I needed a bigger shower. The three of us had barely fit and I got to the point where I couldn't take it anymore. We were literally just showering, but the closeness was overwhelming. I soaped up, rinsed off, and got the hell out of there, letting the two of them finish on their own. I didn't even stick around and watch to see if anything happened. I was sore, tired, and in desperate need of a nap.

Call me weird, call me insane, but I wanted a cup of coffee first. Sex like that deserved coffee. And cheesecake, but I doubted my ability to stay up long enough to bake one. Even if I had the ingredients in my fridge. Which I didn't. I desperately needed to go to the store.

Slipping on a pair of leggings and a T-shirt, I padded quietly into the kitchen. Shea wasn't around, so I assumed he had gone back to his apartment. I reminded myself to call him later, spend some more time with him. I hadn't *planned* on the impromptu threesome, things like that just seemed to happen around me lately. I grinned in satisfaction.

"Lady! Are you rested?" Jaeren sprang from the couch and met me in the kitchen.

I chuckled in response. "No. Just got out of the shower."

"Again?"

"Er…yeah. Where's Dar and Yuki?"

"Yuki's face went white and she started to tremble. She left so she would not be embarrassed by your amorous festivities."

"Amorous festivities. That's a very succinct way to put it."

"Thank you. Can I get anything for you?"

"Nope. Thanks J-run. Just makin' a coffee."

"J-run?"

"Nickname. Don't like it?"

"I do. Thank you." He bowed.

Since I'd rescued him from the clutches of the tyrannical dark elf who turned out to be not so tyrannical...he'd been very accommodating and meek. I guess gratitude went a long way with the fae. "Oh, I got you something!"

I grabbed a mug and shoved it into the maker, popping a pod in and setting it to brew before heading over to the fridge. I'd set aside his surprise until we rescued him from Faerie. In all the recent commotion, I'd forgotten to give them to him. Reaching up on my tippy-toes, I barely got the cabinet above the fridge open, not wanting to hunt for the step stool.

"They're in there if you want to grab them." I pointed.

I moved back to my coffee but watched him out of the corner of my eye with a little smile on my face. *This should make his millennium...*

He moved closer and easily reached over the fridge, grabbing the green and yellow box out of the cupboard. He seemed disappointingly uninterested until he saw the picture of the crayon on the front. I almost reached over to steady him as his hand started shaking. He grabbed the other side of the box, cradling it between his hands and staring at it.

"You bought me more color sticks?"

"I did."

"There are many," he said softly, his voice quivering almost imperceptibly. Almost.

"Sixty-four of them."

"In all different shades?"

"Every color of the rainbow and then some."

"Why?"

"Why what?"

"Why would you do something so extraordinarily nice for me? I have brought naught but trouble for you. I have not even been that nice to you. I even tried to kill you. Twice."

I sighed, ignored my sputtering coffee, and turned to him. "Because. Just because. You're my friend now. Friends do nice things for each other when they can."

"But I have not for you."

"Are you more inclined to now?"

He looked up at me, eyes glittering with moisture. He nodded solemnly.

"That makes me happy. But that's not why I did it. I did it for a million reasons, but that look on your face, happiness, that's the main reason. I wanted *you* to be happy."

Without warning, he set the box on the counter and threw his arms around me in a hug, openly weeping. Not very masculine, and not befitting of an elven king, but the entire thing made my eyes more than a little wet, too. "You have my thanks, my lady."

I scrunched him back, returning his hug. "There's more in the cupboard you know. Go look."

He gasped and pulled away from me, almost not believing me. I nodded and pointed over the fridge. "You might not be able to see them, but they're up there."

He reached over and put his hand down, feeling around. He grabbed all four of them between his fingers and pulled out the coloring books I had bought with the crayons.

He was fully trembling as he brought them out and ran his fingers over the covers. "What is this?"

"They're books. They have pictures in them. More like the outlines of pictures. You use the coloring sticks to fill them in, bringing them to life. In any color you want."

"I may choose?"

I nodded.

"The unicorn on the front, I could make it blue if I wished?"

I nodded again.

He hugged them to his chest, flashed me the most grateful look I'd ever seen, a smile more brilliant than the sun, grabbed the box and practically ran to the dining room table.

"If any of the crayons get dull, there's a sharpener built into the box!"

"Truly?"

"Truly," I answered with a little laugh, joining him at the table.

He fumbled getting the box open but managed to do it without ripping it. He gasped when he saw all sixty-four crayons neatly packed inside. "Glorious!"

He set the box behind the book and opened it to the first page. He touched his index finger to his lips as his eyes scanned the colors, and the moment he found the exact shade he wanted, he smiled and pulled it from the box.

He was a hummer. As the tip of the crayon almost magically filled in the open area he was shading, he started humming softly to himself. He was like a little kid and my heart may have skipped a beat or two just watching him. He blushed when he saw me.

"Don't mind me. Enjoy yourself."

"Oh, I shall. Thank you again, Lady."

"You're welcome."

Yuki came through the front door. She still looked flustered, but not angry. She blushed furiously. "All done?"

"Yes. Sorry."

"What the hell were you doing in there?"

I cocked an eyebrow at her. "Do you really want to know?"

She turned a little green, shaking her head. "No. Not even a little."

"Is it that bad? You can still feel everything?"

"It's worse."

"Because there were three of us?"

"No. This isn't the first time. And the other time, Dar was with you and the intensity didn't change, even though he's your familiar. Something is different. Your...power is growing or our link is getting stronger."

My father's power. Shit. "Huh. That's weird. Maybe it's the new cell tower they built up the road. It could be amplifying our signal." I was so full of shit it scared me.

Dar came out of Yuki's room looking way too happy. There was no doubt what he'd been doing. He blushed, too.

Yuki refused to look at him and cocked an eyebrow at me. "Cell tower? You're joking."

"Kind of, yeah." I sighed. "It's probably the whole 'my dad is a god' thing. But I don't wanna think about it."

"I don't blame you. Just wanted to let you know."

"Thanks, Yuke," I said and patted her spikey little head.

She frowned at me. "Whatcha doin, J-man?" She looked at him coloring.

"Painting with colored wax. Would you care to join me? I have multiple canvas books."

"Sure! Gimme one."

He slid one from the bottom of the pile across the table to Yuki and then put the box of crayons in front of me so they could both reach them.

"Want to trade seats?" I pointed at my chair.

"If you want."

"Don't wanna get in the middle of your color war. This could get ugly."

I got up and let her slide over, taking her chair just as Dar stepped up behind me and put his hands on my shoulders. "I see you gave him his present."

"Yep. He was a good boy," I answered with a grin.

51

"There! I have finished my first work!" He slid the book over to me and I couldn't help but gasp. Not only had he finished it in a few moments…it was perfect. It didn't even look like it had been colored with crayon either. It was almost as if the crayon had melted and spread across the page, collecting in spots that should have been shaded and spreading thinner where the light would have been reflected. I almost waited for the butterfly on the blue unicorn's head to start flapping its wings and the entire image stood off the page.

"Woah."

"Do you like it?"

"Jaeren, it's amazing."

Even Yuki whistled.

"Do you wish to have it?" He asked softly.

"Can I?"

"I would be honored, Lady."

"Then let me show you our gallery. It's where you put all works of art done in crayon."

"You have such a place?"

"Every house does."

"Truly?"

"Truly," I answered and carefully pulled the page out of the coloring book, careful not to put any rips in it. I don't think his heart could have taken it. When it was finally free, I stood and took it into the kitchen while he followed behind me.

"It goes in the most used room of the house? Other than your bedroom, I mean."

I hoped to the Lady he didn't mean it like I thought he meant it, but knowing Jaeren, he probably did and didn't think anything wrong with it. With a sigh, I grabbed the tape dispenser out of the junk drawer, plastered the page against the fridge, and taped the four corners to the black stainless-steel.

"A place of honor," he whispered next to me.

52

"Befitting such a treasure," I answered.

"Lookin' good, buddy," Jimmy said behind us. I hadn't even heard him come out of the bedroom.

"Thank you, James. It is my first work."

"Did you sign it?"

He turned to look at Jimmy. A horrible feeling settled itself in my stomach. I turned and cocked an eyebrow at him, but he refused to look at me.

"Was I supposed to?" Jaeren asked shyly.

"Hell yeah. All arteests sign their work." He grabbed a pen off the counter. "Go ahead."

"But I only know elvish. Nobody will know my name," Jaeren said worriedly.

"Tell you what. You sign it in elvish, and I'll write it in English under that. Sound like a good plan?"

"No, James. That sounds like an amazing plan. I thank you."

"You're welcome, buddy."

Jaeren positively beamed. He took the pen and began scrawling something across the bottom corner of the page. I looked over at Jimmy and he was practically salivating. This wasn't going to end well.

Jaeren turned and offered the pen to Jimmy, who took it without question and hastily scrawled something beneath it. I was afraid to look.

"There you go! You're all set. Now, you're officially an artist of the mortal realm!" He tossed the pen on the counter and slapped Jaeren on the shoulder, heading toward the living room.

"Thank you, Sir James," Jaren said with a respectful bow, rising to stare appreciatively at his picture, signature, and the translation I knew was nowhere near what it should read. I sighed as Jaeren followed Jimmy, breaking off to color some more.

With vast amounts of trepidation, I leaned in to read just exactly what Sir James had written, stifling a giggle when I did.

JERUN. AGE: 6

He should have written it in crayon.

CHAPTER 5

Waking up with something slithering up your leg is not a pleasant way to actually wake up. I screamed and sat up, blinking in the darkness. Brushing off my leg, something squawked and landed on the bedspread beside me.

My vampiric eyes adjusted, brightening the room with silvery hues. Fidget, the tiny shadow creature that had adopted me as its mother, was looking up at me from the bed. I could feel the sadness radiating from him.

"Fidget? You okay, buddy?"

He chirped and hopped closer. I held out my hand and he melted, sliding across my comforter and into the palm of my hand, re-solidifying, and blinking at me with tiny glowing red eyes.

"What's the matter?" I looked out the window, it was dark, but not night yet. A storm had rolled over Cedar Falls. I grabbed my phone off the nightstand. I'd only intended to take a quick nap and head back down to the bookstore. My nap had lasted five hours. I stared at the shadow in my hand. "Thank you for waking me up. I'm starving. Should we go get some dinner?"

He chirped again.

"Next time, don't slither up my leg. Smack me in the face or something."

Another chirp. I vaguely wished he could talk. I should have been lucky he could make any noises at all. He was a shadow. He was a cute little shit though. I ran my finger over the top of his head and blinked in confusion. He had more of a realistic feel than he ever had before. When he first appeared to me, my finger would have passed right through him. Now, it brushed against him with the feeling of soft fur with the sponginess of marshmallow beneath it.

"Look at you! Who's a big boy?"

He chirped again and I set him down on the bed.

"I'm going to get dressed. Then we can hit the diner and stop by the bookstore."

Chirp chirp.

"Should we invite Shea? You like Shea, don't you?"

Chirp chirp.

I grabbed my phone and fired off a quick text to him, asking if he wanted to go to dinner. I was just setting my phone back down on the nightstand when he emerged from the shadows in the corner of my room.

"That was fast. Hungry?"

"Greetings, my Lady."

"Hey, Shea." I opened my arms for a hug. He took the offer and wrapped himself around me, cloak and all. "You're kind of overdressed for the diner."

He sighed as he pulled away, dropping the cloak off his shoulders and catching it with his arm as it fell. "Old habits die hard, I am afraid."

"We should go shopping sometime. I'll buy you a nice modern trench coat or something. Maybe a nice hoodie."

"Hoodie? Like those that you wear?"

I nodded, having a flash of brilliance. He was hot in his leather pants. That I could work with, but I promised myself to at least get him some jeans for a more casual look, but in the meantime, I had several hoodies he could make do with. Then he wouldn't stand out so much. Hell, if I put him in a *dress* he would stand out less than wearing his damn cloak. He looked like an escapee from middle earth. In Asheville, people dressing outside the norm

56

was…normal. In Cedar Falls, it practically screamed, "I'm not human." Which is what we were trying to avoid.

I grabbed the biggest, blackest hoodie in my closet and tossed it to him. It was a pullover instead of a zippered one, but beggars couldn't be choosers, and I was begging him internally to wear it. Thankfully, he did without batting an eyelash. "Wow. You look…"

"Weird?"

I busted out laughing. "Try the opposite of weird. You look…human. Hot, young, but human."

"My thanks," he said with a little bow.

I looked down. I was wearing sweats and a light gray sweatshirt. Hardly dinner worthy. I stripped and went back into my closet, grabbing a fluffy sweater that would go nicely with my skull leggings.

Coming out of the closet holding the sweater, I busted Shea staring at me intently. "Something on me?" He wasn't one to stare at my bare flesh for no reason.

He blinked and looked up at me. "You are crawling with shadows."

"What?" I looked down frantically. It was still dark enough in my room that they didn't stand out right away and I hadn't seen them when I pulled my sweats off. Sure enough, little waving lines of shadow stuff were weaving across the skin of my legs, arms, and chest. "What are they doing?"

He stepped closer and reached out to run his finger across them. Wherever he tried to touch, they moved away from him like a living anemone. It was creepy and weird, and I was trying very, very hard not to freak the fuck out. They were literally coming out of my skin.

Shea reached over and turned on the bedroom light.

They disappeared almost instantly, creeping back inside me.

"What the fuck is it?"

"I do not know," he answered honestly, staring at the wobbling pillow and creeping slowly toward the bed.

"That's just Fidget."

"He's moving the pillow on his own. In the mortal realm?"

"Yeah. I'm not turning into a shadow, right?"

"It is said the lord of shadows gave birth to all the shadows of the world. Maybe…"

"I'm pregnant?"

He chuckled. "Nay, but maybe…"

"Which is it, Shea? Yes or no?"

"Not in the conventional sense. You are not giving birth to shadows…"

"Shea?"

"Yes?"

"This feels really unnatural."

"You have the blood of a god running through your veins. Be thankful you are not having offspring pour from your head like some of the myths and legends."

I felt like I was going to throw up. Sitting down on the end of my bed, I stared at my arm. "Turn the light off."

He reached over and flipped the switch. The room plummeted into darkness and the tendrils of shadow reappeared. I wanted to cry.

"Get them off me," I practically pleaded with Shea.

"Can you feel them?"

I wanted to say yes, but I couldn't. Even if I imagine what they felt like. "No. I can't," I said and ran my finger across them. They didn't shy away from my touch like they had with him. They seemed to reach for my finger. One of them wrapped a tendril around my finger and I pulled it away from my arm, the edge of the tendril rounding off and blinking at me with a solitary red eye in the center of it.

"They're baby fidgets." I looked over at the bed. "What did you do?"

It blinked in surprise, seemed to get agitated, and chirped once.

Shea let out a few notes of his magical laughter. "I do not think he is the culprit. You are."

"Pardon?"

"Mother of shadows," he said with a shrug. "Try to tell it what to do?"

I looked at the lengthening shadow wrapped around my finger. "Begone," I said with a bit of authority.

It screeched as it dissipated into nothingness. Fidget squawked and Shea hissed.

"Where did it go?"

Shea's look told me all I needed to know. I'd killed it. I stared at him blankly and felt like a complete and utter shit. "I didn't want to kill it! I just wanted it to get off me."

"Be very careful, Lady. Your will can alter reality, especially for the creatures beneath you. Words have power, especially your words. Focus your intent like you would with a spell before you utter a word."

"Think before I speak?"

Shea nodded.

"Fuck me. I've never been an expert at that."

Shea gulped. "You just did it again."

I realized what I'd said the moment I'd said it. At least he didn't jump my bones. That would have been my luck lately. "Let's go eat. Thinking hurts my head right now."

He opened his mouth to make a joke, but I squashed that with a perfectly timed look and outstretched finger. His mouth closed almost comically.

I needed to take my mind off the shadows hanging around me. Fidget was one thing. A hundred tiny shadow puppets were another. Seriously creeped out didn't begin to describe how I felt at that moment.

"Let's get out of here. Some place bright. And teal."

"Yes, Lady."

We're going to dinner. You guys wanna go? I sent the thought to Yuki and Dar.

Steak? Dar asked hopefully.

Only if you want eggs with it. We're going to the diner and the bookstore.

That is acceptable.

I'll watch you eat. Can we swing by the blood bank?

Of course.

∞ ∞ ∞

Shea looked uncomfortable in the vehicle sitting next to me as we parked in front of the diner. He never looked comfortable in a vehicle, which made sense since he shadow-walked wherever he went. I should have let Yuki drive. His expression would have been much more gratifying.

I put it in park and shut the engine off. "Everybody hungry?"

"Starving," Yuki replied, which made me more than a little nervous.

"Don't eat anybody."

"No promises," she said huffily, as we all got out. Hopefully Marge still had a supply of blood in the kitchen.

Dar pulled the door open, Shea entered, and I followed Yuki inside. As usual, the place was mostly empty, but we were a little late to have hit the dinner rush. What surprised me most was the booth of five younger vampires huddled in the corner, looking *everywhere* but in our direction. I felt Yuki tense beside me.

"Friends of yours?"

She shook her head. "Nope. They're noobs. At least to the area," she whispered back futilely. They were vampires. They could probably hear the mice fucking in the walls.

60

"Hey, Sweetie," Marge said as she headed toward the booth on the other side of the entrance.

"Hey, Marge." I slid into my usual booth and scooted in toward the window. Yuki immediately slid in next to me, we were facing the vampires, and I was sure she wanted to keep her eyes on them.

Shea sat across from me and Dar settled in next to him, giving him a small smile as he sat. It might have just been my imagination, but he seemed to be sitting a little closer to him than one would have expected, not that I minded. They could hold hands while eating dinner and I wouldn't have minded. I might have drooled a little bit, but that was just me.

"What can I get you all to drink?"

"I'll have a coke," I answered first.

"Water."

"Water."

"Usual, hon?" Marge winked at Yuki.

"Yes, please."

Leave it to Marge. I swear the woman was really a genie who granted wishes. She always had what everybody wanted. Even when it was whiskey.

"Is it truly okay if I get these steak and eggs?" Dar looked over the menu at me.

"Yep. Knock yourself out. The steak is usually pretty thin, so don't expect medium raw."

"Anything is fine as long as it is meat."

Shea uncharacteristically snickered next to him. Dar's elvish cheeks got a little pink. Something was definitely going on between the two of them. *Maybe they fooled around when I was in prison...* The thought sent a shiver down my spine and tickled me in my lady bits.

"You okay?"

I looked over at Yuki and nodded. Her eyes kept flicking between me and the table of vampires. "How about you?"

Just nervous. Getting some bad vibes from them. Nothing to worry about. They feel young, she answered non-verbally.

Keep an eye on them. We can leave if we need to.

No. They can leave.

Yuki…

Leave the vampire stuff to me, Master. They are bottom feeders on the power pole. If we run, it will open us up for an attack later. There are rules to this sort of thing.

Oh. Okay. Let me know if I need to help.

Dar and I can handle them.

She must have been broadcasting to him, too. He suddenly tore his eyes from Shea, looked across the table, and nodded at the two of us.

Just don't wreck the diner. Marge would forgive us for a lot of things, but never that, I sent to the both of them but didn't get a response.

"Here ya go, folks," Marge said and slid Yuki's mug of blood in front of her. She dropped off the waters and coke and I took a sip while she pulled out her order pad. "Whatcha want to eat?"

"Burger," I answered. She knew how I liked it.

She looked at Shea. "Chicken Caesar salad, please?"

"You got it, sweetie. What about you, hon?" She looked at Dar.

"Steak and eggs?"

"How do you want your steak?"

"As rare as possible."

"And your eggs?"

"Without the shell?"

"Herb's a klutz, sweetie, but he won't get none in your eggs. How you want them cooked?"

He gave me a panicked look, not knowing how to answer.

"Scrambled," I told her for him. It was the safest way.

"Scrambled?" Dar answered again, very unconfident.

"You've never had eggs before, have you." Marge didn't make it a question.

"No," he said and shook his head.

"You'll like them." She patted his shoulder and headed for the kitchen.

"I know they are the unfertilized young of chickens, why did she ask how I wanted them cooked?"

"You can have them fried to where they yolk is runny, or they can flip them over and cook it until it's hard. You can boil them with or without the shells to varying degrees of doneness, too."

"What is scrambled, I'm sorry to ask. I have heard the word, but I do not understand how it applies to eggs?"

"They break the eggs and mix the whites and yolks together. They come out fluffy and have a different taste than just cooking the egg whole. Try them with some ketchup."

"I shall." He nodded, completely mesmerized by the whole conversation.

My bladder decided I needed to pee. "Let me out, Yuki?"

"Why?"

"I have to pee."

She glanced nervously at the table of vampires and gave me a worried look. "I'll be fine. You can come save me if they get bitey."

"Maybe I should go with you."

No. I can take care of myself, and you going with me might taunt them into doing something stupid.

But…

No buts. Let me out.

Yes, Master.

She wordlessly slid out of the booth and gave me enough room to get out. Barely. Patting her head, I walked across the black and white checkered floor toward the hallway leading to the restrooms. Their booth was right

63

outside the hallway and I focused on the bathroom door at the end of the hallway instead of sparing a glance in their direction.

The closer I got, the tenser the situation became. I could almost feel them coiling in anticipation. The very air around them began to vibrate with their intent and...fear.

I blinked in surprise, still not letting myself look in their direction. They didn't want to start anything. They were afraid of me. I could literally feel and smell their fear. With every step it got stronger and stronger. It was almost delicious. It was baking apple pie and wounded human delicious, if those two smells could drift together and create one incredible, irresistible smell. My mouth started watering and I almost cut my tongue on one of my fangs as I tried to wet my parched lips.

Fangs? I turned my head to look away from them as I passed by. I didn't want to hurt them, I wanted to bleed them, and that thought scared me. *Fuck. Fuck. Fuck.*

Are you okay? Yuki's thought interrupted my chant.

Yep. Peachy fucking keen.

Why did you stop walking?

I hadn't even realized I had. I was standing next to their table, staring at myself in the glass and watching their reflections in the dark glass. *Yuki. Come here.*

Did they do something to you? By the time she finished the thought, she was by my side. The vamps had slid as far away from me into the booth as they could. The two on the outside were practically sitting in the laps of the other three.

Tell them I won't hurt them.

What?

Do it.

Her hands went around my arm, putting herself between me and them. "She...uh. She wants me to tell you she won't hurt you."

"What is she?" One of the braver ones asked.

64

"A witch. I am her familiar."

"You're Princess Yukina!"

Fuck, Yuki's thought drifted into my head, helping to clear it a little. Or maybe it was their awe for Yuki. Their fear had ebbed, helping a little with my control. "Yes. Sorry to disturb you," she said with a little bow and pushed me toward the bathroom.

"That means she is the head of the local coven. The one Lord Abernathy told us never to…cross?"

More like never to feed from, I thought to myself, keeping Yuki out of my conversation.

"Yep. That's her. Excuse us."

"But she felt like another vampire lord, not a witch."

Yuki stopped and turned around. She gave me another gentle nudge toward the bathroom with her outstretched hand and I heard her walk away, sitting down with the vampires. *Go pee. I'll handle this.*

What are you going to do?

Tell them how very wrong they are. Try to convince them that it must have been me they felt. If they blab to my father about this…

Gotcha. Sorry, Yuki.

You can tell me what happened when you get out. Stay away from them if you can.

I will.

The connection between us went quiet, she was doing her damnedest to keep me out of it. Instead of trying to eavesdrop, I headed for the bathroom and realized I didn't have to pee at all.

"What the fuck?" I stared at myself in the bathroom mirror and got the shock of my life. My face had gone pale and my green eyes were now an ice blue, staring back at me and burning with inner fire. My lips were the only thing with color, nearly beet red and struggling to cover the fangs behind them. Fangs I didn't want and didn't want to see. It would make them too real. I was losing control over everything I'd become. Shaking uncontrollably, I wrapped my arms around myself and stood there in the bathroom, afraid to even move.

There was a soft knock at the door. *You okay?*

No.

Let me in?

No.

Unfortunately, I never locked the door, and Yuki discovered that fact. She twisted the handle and walked right in, locking the door behind her and stopping short when I looked up at her.

"You're…"

"A vampire."

"Holy fuck. How the hell did that happen?'

"My father's power obviously. I can't control it."

She made a shushing noise and switched to mind-speech. *That's what happened? You vamped out when you were next to them?*

I nodded. *I smelled their fear. Looked away and lost control.*

You're hungry! You're part vampire and haven't ever tasted blood.

I stared at her, guiltily.

You've fed before?

Once.

When?

Remember the dark elf? Elleslyn?

Her mouth dropped open. *Why didn't you say anything?*

I almost stomped my foot in frustration. Hating what I was becoming, talking about it only made it worse. Even to my best friends. *I couldn't. I'm losing me, Yuki, and I'm afraid.*

She took the step between us and held me in her arms, pulling my head into her shoulder and patting the back of my head. She'd done it to comfort me, but she put my mouth in the crook of her neck. I tensed in her arms. She smelled like fresh snow and cotton candy. Until she felt me tense and then her scent took on something more flavorful. Food. "Dot?"

I pulled away from her before I did something epically stupid. Like eating her. Backing away, I pressed myself against the far wall.

Did you almost feed on me?

I'm sorry. You smell...

I stink?

No. You smell delicious.

You can't feed from vampires. Our blood is poisonous to each other.

Bullshit. You smell like food.

That's not right, either. We do not smell...appealing to each other. My parents can barely stand to be in the same room. It's why they've been married so long. It's why you always see vampire consorts walking with their fingers entwined and arms up, keeping each other at arm's length.

Well, you smell pretty fucking good to me. So did the booth full of vamp kids out there...

She narrowed her eyes at me and then looked down at her hand. Pricking her finger against her fang, she held out the shiny droplet to me. *Taste it. You'll see.*

She didn't have to ask me twice. I practically pounced on her hand, grabbing her wrist and bringing the drop of nectar to my tongue. I moaned as soon as it touched. Trying to use her finger like a straw, I sucked on the end of it, getting as much out of it as I could before the wound closed. *Delicious...*

I can't be. This isn't right? She pulled her hand away from me slowly, not wanting to offend me, but the fear pouring off her only made the hunger unbearable.

Yuki?

Yes?

Run. Get away from me. Now.

I can't. You're not going to get the hunger under control until you feed.

But if you don't leave, I'm going to feed on you! Bloody red tears began to pour from my eyes as I fought the monster inside me. I knew they were red because I watched them drop to the floor, staining the white linoleum tile pink by my feet.

Then feed. The fear stopped pouring from her like roast beef. She stepped forward and offered me her neck.

Oh, my sweet Yuki. The thought was my own, I didn't share it with her as the tears fell even harder and I buried my mouth in the crook of her neck.

I'd only fed the once, and it was almost explosively pleasurable. Yuki had to have known how it was going to affect her and me, yet she didn't care. She was asexual, had no interest in it whatsoever, yet my trysts battered her sensibilities almost every day. Now she was going beyond that and letting me feed from her. The tears that had been falling for me, fell for her instead.

"I'm sorry," I whispered as I bit down.

The pleasure washed over the both of us as she melted against me. She whimpered as the blood welled into my mouth. I drank it in as fast as I could, trying to ignore the pleasure touching places it had no business touching. I fed for mere moments before the hunger was sated, but it felt like a lifetime. Finally, I pushed her away. "Sorry. Sorry. Sorry," I whispered over and over, unable to look her in the face.

"Shush. It's okay. It's over."

I nodded and turned to the sink, trying hard to get past what I had just done to one of the sweetest people I knew. Turning on the water, I wiped my face with the cold water, washing away my blood-stained mouth and cheeks. I went to grab some paper towels and snarled at the hand dryer mounted on the wall. "Fuck it." I turned the jet up and hit the button, letting the warm blast of air blow away my shame.

"Come on. Your food is going to get cold."

"Okay."

CHAPTER 6

"**W**hy didn't you call me? How the hell do I ring this up?" I paused and forgot to welcome the next customer. "Hi. Welcome to First Moon Books. Will that be all for you today?"

Jason laughed at me from the next register. The line had been twenty people deep when we walked in. He pointed at the other register and unlocked it for me. As soon as I got behind it, half the people shifted to in front of me and I started to panic.

"Deep breaths, Dot. Just scan the books with the reader. You'll be fine."

I shot him a glare and scanned the gray-haired lady's book. "Do you have any books on local history?"

"Jay?"

"Not specifically on Cedar falls, but for Syracuse and the surrounding areas, yes." He pointed to the back wall. "See the historical non-fiction section? Just to the left there's a small section marked local. It's only one shelf, but it's there."

"Thank you, young man!"

"My pleasure."

"Can I set this aside and go look?"

"Uh, sure. I think. I'm sure. Go ahead." I gave her a nod, not tearing my eyes from the touchscreen, trying to figure out how to cancel the sale. Jason reached over and hit the big red cancel button. It was official, I sucked as a cashier.

"Do you wish me to take over for you, Lady?" Shea tugged on my sleeve and pointed at the register.

"You know how?"

"I think I can figure it out. I was the town librarian for sixty years. We used a similar cataloging system."

"You're hired. I didn't know it was going to be this busy. On the first night. Ever. Holy crap." I cleared the register and let Shea in to take my place.

He took the next person in line and actually had them out of the store before Jason. Watching him work was almost mesmerizing as his fingers danced over the buttons. In my defense, watching Shea do *anything* was kind of mesmerizing. Standing behind the registers, I had the best seat in the house. Between Shea in his leather pants and Jason in his jeans, I didn't know which ass to look at. My head kept shifting between the two of them. A fact that didn't go unnoticed by women in line closest to the registers. Half looked jealous, and the other half looked even more jealous.

"I'm going to check on Josie."

They both waved over their shoulders without stopping. I still couldn't believe that we were that busy. I figured Jason would be behind the counter reading a newspaper or something for most of the day. Guilt reared its ugly little head. I should have had him hire someone, just in case. It wasn't as if I couldn't afford it and it was always better to be safe than sorry.

As I wove through the throngs of people, I came up with a plan. Offer Shea a position. He had expressed interest in working at the store, and obviously had the skillset. Hell, maybe even Jimmy would want a job. I didn't know how long his settlement from the fire department would last, and he wouldn't take charity to help with paying the bills. It might give him a way to make some money in the meantime.

Then there was Dwight. He'd been stuck in that hellish factory for long enough. Maybe Jason could teach him how to do the ordering for the store. I could make him the stock manager or something.

By the time I walked through the entrance of the café, I'd already formulated a plan to take care of everybody that I could. It was a good thing I thought quickly, because the café was packed. A haggard looking Josie and Candace were struggling to deal with a line comparable to the one inside the book section of the store, but with only one register. Yuki had hopped back behind the counter and was helping to make coffees. The bakery case was completely empty and looked like it had been for a while.

"Holy shit. Are you guys okay?"

"No," Josie answered and gave me the 'kill me now' look that I'd seen a thousand times before. Just never that bad.

"Has it been like this all day?"

"Since Jason opened the doors this morning. Like right after you left."

"Why didn't you call me?"

She blushed as she handed two teens their cappuccinos. "We didn't want to bother you."

"I'ma smack you."

"Good. It might wake me up."

"Well, I can't run registers for shit. Want me to make coffee and you and Candace can alternate breaks?"

"No. It's died down a lot and it's almost closing time."

"Wait. It was worse than this?"

She motioned to the line of people. "This is nothing. You should have seen it at lunch."

"Holy crap."

"Yep."

73

"All right. Holler if you need me. I'm going to check on Dar."

Josie spared me a brief nod. Candace turned around and waved at me almost cheerfully. Almost.

Maybe Dwight knew how to make coffee. Unless Yuki wanted a job... The three of them seemed to be comfortable around each other in the small enclosed space. If Yuki didn't want the job, maybe hiring some local teens might be a good alternative.

Shaking my head and getting lost in thought, I headed back out into the bookstore proper. Dar was there, stocking up another display of books on the endcap. "I can't believe this place."

Dar looked around the store and nodded. "It is much busier than I anticipated."

"That's the understatement of the world."

"Makes you wonder why."

"Pardon?"

He rubbed his chin. "Given the state of this town and the hardships it has faced, for this many people to be spending hard won money on books and coffee is..."

"Unbelievable."

"Yet here we are." He chuckled and went back to stocking books.

"Need a hand?"

He shook his head. "I didn't know what else to do. I found a box of this particular book, so I decided to fill up the display. I wouldn't know what else to have you do."

"I feel your pain. I own the place and can't even run the register." That made me feel even more guilty. The bookstore was more Jason than me, and it had always been my dream. Maybe it was time I got to know the reality of it. It had always been my dream to own a small bookstore in a small town, but lately, I'd been dumping *everything* on Jason. Who knew small town living would be so rough? "I'll be around. Going to figure out where everything is.

Ignorance is bliss, but not when you're trying to run a business."

"Very wise."

"Sometimes." I gave him a quick kiss and walked away.

Learning the layout of the store was *numero uno* on my list of priorities. The quickest way to ruin a bookstore's reputation was by having unknowledgeable employees. And owners. Sending someone to the erotica section when they were looking for needlepoint techniques might be beneficial to that person in the long run, but they might be a little upset at the beginning.

I made it as far as the self-help section when I felt him. A vampire had entered the store, my store, and was watching me. Not wanting to turn around and make eye contact, I kept weaving through the shelves. They were tall enough to block most of my view, but not all of it. When I rounded the endcap, I took a chance and lifted myself up on my toes.

Amir was staring back at me. The vampire who had come to me for help. The one who had joined Lord Abernathy's clan of vampires. Him, I trusted. For the most part.

I gave him a little wave and he nodded back, looking toward the back of the store and then returning his gaze to me. Turning around, I made my way toward the stock room to see exactly what he wanted.

He made it there first, leaning against the frame of the double doors. "Greetings, Lady."

"Hey, Amir. What brings you to the bookstore?"

"It is you I sought out."

"Everything okay?"

His weary sigh set me on edge. It was usually the precursor to bad news. "No."

"What's the matter?"

"Is there somewhere more private we may speak?"

I leaned against the metal bar and opened the stock room door, the one he wasn't leaning against. "Step into my office." Technically, my office was beside the checkout area, but he didn't need to know that.

He looked toward the front of the store, and satisfied we weren't being watched, ducked into the storeroom. His cautiousness made me paranoid. I'd felt him walk into the store, and I was hopeful I would have felt any other vampires beside Yuki inside. We were relatively safe, I hoped.

"What's wrong?" I figured it was better to get straight to the point as soon as the heavy metal door closed behind us.

"When I came to you and asked you for help, you did so without question. That is a debt I could never repay in a thousand years." He paused to give me a little bow of appreciation. "It is with a heavy heart that I tell you that you are in danger."

"From?"

"Things have transpired in the local clan, and Lord Abernathy has been informed. He plans on visiting us early next week."

"Why?"

"You were in an altercation in the middle of Main Street earlier today?"

"Yeeesss?" How he knew that was beyond me, but I wasn't going to lie to him.

"Many people recorded the incident on their smart phones," he said by way of explanation, and obviously intended me to infer what was wrong from that statement.

"And?"

"Princess Yuki was in the footage shown on the local news station.

"Yeah, but she didn't use her vampire powers. People probably just thought she was some sort of martial arts badass."

He sighed again. "Yes. She was quite impressive without seeming supernatural. However, that was not the issue."

"What was, Amir. Just tell me."

"She was standing in the middle of the street. In broad daylight…"

Oh, fuck me. I'd been so worried about her showing the world she was a vampire, I'd forgotten not to show the vampire world she could walk in the daylight. "Shit."

"Yes. Lord Abernathy was *more* than interested in that fact. So was young George. He was rather put out." Amir nodded.

"As are you?"

He shrugged. "While it would be wonderful to be able to walk freely beneath the sun again, I am sure it comes with a hefty price tag."

"Yeah. I can be pretty annoying."

"So, it is true."

"What?"

"That you are the reason she can," he answered with another sigh. He was sighing quite a lot. I also had *that* effect on people.

"Between you and me…"

He stopped me with a motion of his hand. "No. I have taken a vampire as my lord. If asked, I would be unable to keep any of this conversation from him. It is better that I do not know."

"Fair enough. But it's not really a secret. She's my familiar. Lord Abernathy knows this, and that is the only reason why she can walk in the sunlight. You should have seen her face when she figured it out."

Amir just nodded.

"So that's the reason he is coming here? I could have saved him a trip if he had just called."

"If that were the only reason why, I'm sure he would have."

Uh oh. "What's the other reason?"

"Some of our youngest clan ran into you earlier in the restaurant they like to frequent." He pointed in the direction of the diner.

"Oh. Those kids. Yeah, they're really sweet."

"You frightened them beyond belief."

"Me?"

"They came right home to report that they had encountered a vampire lord in town, in the company of Princess Yukina."

This just keeps getting better and better. "Look at me. Do I look like a vampire to you?"

"Truthfully, no."

"See?"

"But you feel like one. I have stood before Lord Abernathy as I pledged myself to his clan for all eternity."

"Yeah, he's kind of scary."

"I am more afraid of what you could do to me right now in this moment than during my entire stay at his abode. I can feel the power pouring off you."

"I'm not a vampire, Amir!"

"No. You are something very, very different, but you feel like kin." He bowed his head again.

He wasn't lying either. I could smell his fear, almost taste it. I begged my fangs not to make an appearance. That would have been the fuse in the powder keg. The detonator in the C4. Either way, shit would blow sky high. That wasn't exactly something he would be able to keep from Lord Abernathy.

I needed to get away. "Well, I appreciate the worry, but I'm sure Lord Abernathy will see that I am no match for his awesome greatness."

"I hope that you are correct. My loyalty to you forced me to warn you of the storm that is coming. It might be prudent not to be here if at all possible."

"No matter where I went, he would find me if his interest is that piqued. It's not like I can abandon everything I have tried to build here, either."

"I know. But you know I had to try."

"Thanks, Amir." I reached out and patted him on the shoulder. That had been my intent. As soon as my palm touched him, fire flared between us. Not actual flames, but a searing heat passed from me to him and he gasped at the onslaught of the power, dropping to his knees on the concrete in front of me.

One thing was for certain. I was a fucking moron.

"What just happened?" I tried to play stupid.

He rose in front of me, eyes filled with fear as he took a step back away from me. "What are you?"

"Just the same old Dot," I tried to lie. He caught it and narrowed his eyes at me.

"You are unsure, yourself."

"Yes."

He started shaking his head and the fear he had felt before was suddenly wafting off him like the smell of roasting turkey. My mouth involuntarily started watering. "Amir. You need to go." I covered my mouth with my hands and tried to concentrate on anything and everything around me that wasn't him. The smell of the bare concrete floor, the musty delicious smell of the boxes of books on the shelves around us. The sound of the fluorescent lighting high above us. Anything to get my mind off the delicious aroma of him.

The door behind us burst open and Yuki shot into the room, putting herself between us and snarling at Amir. He held up his hands in surrender. "I mean her no harm, Princess."

She stopped snarling and turned around to face me. She knew exactly what was going on as soon as she saw my hand covering my mouth. "Fuck."

I nodded.

79

"You just ate!" She stared at me incredulously.

"It's not my fault!"

She cocked an eyebrow. "Come on, Amir. I'll buy you a coffee."

Without another word to me, she turned around, grabbed his arm, and led him out of the stockroom to safety. It was totally unfair, I wanted a coffee, too.

∞ ∞ ∞

"I am to get you out of here and back home?" Shea gave me an inquisitive look.

"Yes. Please."

"What about your car?"

Yuki, bring my car home.

Yes, Master. Just please go.

I am.

Do you wish me to accompany you? Dar's inquisitive voice broke into our conversation.

Stay with Yuki. Keep an eye on Amir. Things got weird.

Yes, Master.

I nodded at Shea that I was ready. He grabbed my hand and pulled us into the shadows. Sure, I could have done it myself, but the way things were going for me lately, I might have shadow walked myself into a black hole or something. The dark side of the moon was also a distinct possibility.

Everything turned to black and white around us and I felt a sudden, unexplainable sense of belonging. Gazing out of the shadows at the mortal realm around us was a voyeuristic wet dream. Literally. It was amazing the things people did in the safety of their own bedrooms when they thought nobody could possibly see them. The sheer number of residents in Cedar Falls into bondage surprised me.

A gasp escaped my lips, a gasp that normally would have been muted in the Realm of Shadows. Sights and sounds felt almost normal. But what shocked me and caused me to gasp was the fact that I could see every shadow as we passed by it. One step had always felt like leaping across town whenever I tagged along with Shea. This time, every shadow settled in my vision and the world outside became frighteningly clear. We weren't walking, still in mid-step, but I saw and heard *everything* as we whisked by with frightening clarity. I tugged on Shea's arm to stop our momentum.

We settled in the shadows of a streetlight halfway home.

"What is it?"

"I can see everything."

He looked around. "Yes?"

I shook my head, unsure as to how to make my point. "Every shadow we passed, from the bookstore to here, I saw. Saw what was on the other side. Thirteen people were having sex between here and there, four of those involved one of them being tied to the bed. It was like time stopped."

He stared at me like I had lost my fucking mind. Maybe I had. "That's not possible. I was focused on our destination and was taking us directly there. This wasn't a journey. It was stepping into the other room."

"I'm telling you. Should we go back, and I'll show you?"

He stared into my eyes. "No. I believe you. Let us get you home. It is never wise to dwell in the Realm of Shadow."

I looked around, not even needing to close my eyes to feel them all around us. It started as a humming in my chest, quickly progressing to a song in my head. There were no words, just a chaotic hum as swarms of them began to converge on us. It was a song of greeting.

"They're singing."

"What?" Shea started tugging on my hand.

"The shadows. They're singing. Don't tell me you can't hear it because I can feel it in my chest." The closer they came, the louder it got, sounding almost like humpback whales.

One second, Shea was holding my hand and the next, he was yanking me through a shadow into the mortal realm. "Lady!"

"What?"

"Did you not hear me screaming at you?"

I blinked at him in confusion. "No?"

"Shadows cannot make noise. I don't know what you thought you were listening to, but it couldn't have been good."

"Uh, I beg to differ. Shadows make noises. Fidget cheeps and chirps."

It was his turn to blink at me. Only it wasn't in surprise. It was more like I had lost my mind. Maybe I had.

"Fidget," I called softly.

He slithered out of the sleeve of my jacket and coalesced in the palm of my hand, giving a little chirp of greeting.

"See?"

"Dot…"

"I told you he made noise."

"Lady. It didn't make a sound."

"He's chirping right now. And he just squawked. You're going to sit there and tell me you don't hear a Lady damned thing?"

"Not a sound."

"I'm losing my ever-loving effin' mind."

His face got a little too serious. "No. Maybe you can hear what I cannot." He might have just been trying to comfort me, but he sounded a little put out. Almost jealous.

He'd been a shadow walker his entire life, and then there was me. The freak.

"I want to go home."

"Tis a nice night for a walk."

"That's the best idea I've heard in a week."

CHAPTER 7

Sleep not only eluded me, it packed its shit, took the kids, and moved across town to live with its mother. I'd been lying under the covers staring at the plaster designs in the ceiling for the better part of three hours and I hadn't even yawned.

"I give up." I threw the cover off me, slipped on my T-shirt from the floor, and headed into the kitchen. The rest of the house was silently sleeping the night away. Josie and Candace were tucked away in their room. Yuki was in her room. Jaeren had gone back to Faerie to deal with his kingly duties. And Dar was sleeping on the couch. I leaned over the edge to check on him and frowned when he wasn't there.

Dar?

Lady? Wherever he was, he was sleeping. I could hear it in his voice.

Where are you?

Is everything okay? The sleep left his mental voice and was replaced with fear that I was in danger.

I'm fine! Just couldn't sleep. You weren't on the couch.

Oh. I am at Shea's.

Oooh? You are?

Yes. He has a spare room. We were discussing how to keep you safe.

Are you lying?

There was a brief moment of silence. *And we watched a movie.*

I laughed out loud so he couldn't hear me. *You guys Netflix and chillin'?*

Yes. We watched a movie on Netflix. What do you mean by chillin'?

Are you guys getting busy? Touching each other inappropriately?

Maybe.

I knew it!

Lady, I am sorry. I will come home right now.

Don't you dare.

You're that mad? He almost sobbed across our link.

It was time to quit teasing him. *Absolutely. Not. You guys have fun!*

We already did. We were sleeping.

Ooops. Dar, seriously though. I meant what I said. We're all in this relationship together. I have absolutely no problem with you guys taking care of each other, either. I was just kind of sad I didn't get to watch, but I didn't want to tell him that.

I know you said it, but when you called...I felt guilty?

Don't. I'm serious. This makes me happy.

Me, too. I felt his little grin.

Goodnight, sweetie.

Master?

Yes?

Are you lonely? I could come home...

Nope. I just can't sleep.

Okay. Call me if you need me.

Always. Love you, Darling.

Love you, too, my master. And Happy Yule.

Happy Yule. I smiled. It was Yule, the first day of winter. The coven had wanted to celebrate, but with everything going on, I'd postponed until Christmas since we'd be helping at the diner anyway. An after party would be easier. I promised myself that next year would be different. And hopefully, things would be a little quieter.

When I severed the link, I realized I had made a cup of coffee without paying attention. Caffeine for the win. Taking a deep breath of my favorite smell in the universe, I took that quintessential first sip and rolled my head around on my neck, trying to relax.

While most people would argue until they were blue in the face that I shouldn't be drinking coffee if I was having trouble sleeping, I begged to differ. Coffee relaxed me and I was one of those caffeine mutants who could literally drink a pot of coffee and go straight to bed. I'd probably have to get up thirty times to pee, but I could sleep just fine.

I grabbed my phone off the charger and parked my ass on one of the kitchen stools. That and the coffee staved off my boredom for all of five minutes. *Why can't I sleep?*

The door to one of the bedrooms opened, scared me a fraction of a tiny bit, but then I grinned in anticipation of some company. Unfortunately, it was just Candace wandering into the bathroom. Frowning, I let her do what she had got up to do. When she came back out, she saw me sitting in the kitchen, waving at her like a moron.

"Lady?" She shuffled toward me.

"In the flesh."

"Why are you up?"

"Couldn't sleep."

"Should you be drinking coffee?"

Not wanting to share my thoughts on the matter, I shrugged. "Figured it wouldn't do any harm."

Without a shred of modesty, she came around the counter completely naked and hugged me. "I would stay up with you, but I can barely keep my eyes open. Today was…"

"Unbelievable. Go get some sleep, sweetie. I'll be fine."

"Are you going in with us tomorrow?"

I nodded. It was the least I could do, and I had plans on finding them some help if day two was as busy as the first day. Jason had been adamant about not hiring help, but it was my money. It's not like he could fire me. "You betcha."

"Try to get some sleep."

"I don't think that's going to happen. Maybe I'll go get something to eat and meet you guys at the store."

She narrowed her eyes. "You will take someone with you?"

I booped her nose. "I'm a big girl and everybody is asleep. I'll be fine."

"I will go with you."

"No. Your cute little butt is going to bed." I turned her around and gave her a little shove. She looked at me over her shoulder and stuck her tongue out in a very uncharacteristic display of bravery. I was proud of her and gave her a quick smile before polishing off my coffee.

∞ ∞ ∞

The Cedar Falls Diner was my second home. Like all diners, it was open twenty-four hours a day. I knew it, I'd seen the sign on the door a hundred times, but actually pulling the door open at almost four o'clock in the morning was kind of weird. I didn't know why, but I expected Marge and Herb to be working. I knew it wasn't possible for them to be there all day, every day, but it just didn't seem like the same diner without them. There were two people in the kitchen and a much, much younger version of Marge. She even had the same style hair.

"Howdy. Sit wherever you want, sweets."

She even sounded like Marge. I'd have accused her of being her daughter, but I knew for a fact Marge and Herb had never had kids. It was like an episode of the twilight zone. "Thanks," I managed to stammer and slid into my booth.

There were only two couples sitting in the back of the diner, and one guy eating at the counter. To be honest, it was more than I was expecting so late in the evening. Or early in the morning, but at least there weren't any vampires. I'd checked before I walked in, feeling around for them with whatever it was that let me sense them. Vampire sense.

Marge Jr ambled up to my table. She had to be related to my favorite waitress, somehow. They were too much alike. "What can I get for you, sweets?"

"Coffee. And pie."

"That's a funny breakfast."

"Too early for eggs." I shuddered at the thought. I loved eggs, but sometimes, they didn't love me. Four in the morning was one of those times. Even the thought made my stomach turn a little.

"What kind of pie?"

"Hot. With ice cream. Any of the rhubarb left?"

She gave me a curious smile. "You must be someone special to get some of Uncle Herb's rhubarb pie."

"Uncle?"

"Yep. My mom is Marge's sister."

"Huh. I never would have guessed it." I grinned to let her know I was joking.

"Funny. I have fresh apple, or you can have blueberry, cherry, or pecan."

"Oooh. Fresh apple, please."

"Get that right out for you..." She was trying to be polite and ask me my name subtly. Maybe she wasn't related to Marge.

"Dot."

She looked up at the advertisement for the Dotwich in the window and looked back at me. I nodded and shrugged.

"Ha! Need to get your autograph before you leave," she said with a wink and flipped her order pad closed one-handed. "I'm Tabitha. Pleased to meet you!"

I reached out my hand to shake hers and she didn't disappoint, her handshake more like Herb's than Marge's. She gave me one more grin before grabbing the pot and a mug. She practically beamed at me as she filled it and dropped it off to me, walking and pouring in a flurry of movement without spilling a drop.

"Thanks," I said gratefully and took that first tentative, temperature gauging sip.

"My pleasure," she answered and took off toward the kitchen.

The door chimed behind me and a moment later a hand touched my shoulder. I looked up over my shoulder at a very concerned looking Chief. I wanted to smile at him, I really did. Unfortunately, I also wanted to stab him in the face with a spoon. I ended up frowning at him.

"Happy, Yule. You okay?"

"Peachy. Happy Yule."

"What are you doing up already?"

"You know us convicts. Scoping out the area for some armed robberies. Maybe a few kidnappings. Are sacrifices illegal? I could do some of those, too."

"Think that falls under murder."

"Sweet. That's at least life in prison, right?"

"Depends on the circumstances surrounding the murder."

"Good to know."

"Seriously, why are you up?"

"Trouble sleeping. Too many crimes to plot, not enough time in the day. Pie sounded like a better choice than drinking."

He nodded, almost as if he understood.

"Not that I care, but what are you doing up already?" I narrowed my eyes.

He motioned to the seat across from me. I pointed at the stools in front of the counter, but he ignored me and sat down in my booth, anyway. "I don't sleep much."

"Whoa. Hold the phone. You're up at this un-Lady hour on purpose?" The shock made me forget the seating arrangements.

"Don't get me wrong, I'd rather be snoring on the couch or curled up in bed. As I said, I don't sleep much. It's not a lifestyle I would have chosen."

The look on his face said it all. "You have nightmares," I said without thinking. He sighed internally. I saw the subtle jerk of his shoulders.

"Night terrors, actually." A small blush spread across his cheeks. Manly Chief was embarrassed by it. It made him ten-thousand times cuter, but I *almost* felt bad for him.

"That sucks. Sorry," I said begrudgingly.

"Well, you do invade my dreams quite often. But you're not to blame for the night terrors. In fact, they've been somewhat better since you came to town. Even more so since Becca's killer was laid to rest. Thank you."

It was my turn to blush, just as Tabitha brought my coffee and pie. "Hey, Gorgeous. Usual?"

"Please."

She nodded and left us sitting there. "Gorgeous?" I kind of wanted to gag.

He shrugged. "Nickname."

"Because you're curious?"

"From high school."

"Bi-curious."

"Nope."

"I'll just ask Mini Marge."

He lost it and started laughing in the middle of the diner. Everyone turned around, and I fought the urge to cover my face. Maybe I should have insisted he didn't sit with me. "I am sooo calling her that. For the rest of her

91

life." He unrolled his silverware and used his napkin to wipe his eyes.

"You're just trying to change the subject. I made you laugh, now you tell me why they called you Gorgeous in high school." His lips mashed together, and darkness pushed away the smile.

"Can I tell you something?"

I nodded. "Always. As long as I'm not in handcuffs when you're trying to have said conversation."

"Fair enough. I *really* try not to talk about Becca around you. If you ask me something and I'm avoiding answering, it's because of that."

"Because it's painful for you to talk about, or you're trying to spare my feelings?"

"The feelings part. My pain is my own to deal with."

"Then you have nothing to worry about. I know how much you loved her. It doesn't bother me when you talk about her." I was lying through my fucking teeth, but whatever.

Without missing a beat, he answered. "Becca called me Gorgeous in high school. I was on the football team. They heard her, and it became my nickname. Tabitha," he paused to point in her direction, "married the kicker."

"I take it he didn't go pro."

"He's cooking in the kitchen. Blew out his knee senior year."

"Ouch."

"Yeah."

"What position did you play?"

"Promise not to laugh?"

"No."

"Quarterback."

"That's the guy who throws the ball, right?"

"Yes."

"Did you blow out your arm? Because, I have a feeling you're going to be strengthening your arm muscle a lot over the foreseeable future."

"Never said I was any good at it." He was getting pretty good at avoiding my jabs. Maybe I needed to resort to punching.

"So, I'm dating the captain of the football team?"

"Are you?" Tabitha chose *that* exact moment to bring our food. She placed the dish of warm pie and melting ice cream in front of me before setting a mug of coffee and a pile of strawberry pancakes in front of Chief. She even drew a smiley face on top of it with whip cream.

"Need anything else?" Mini Marge put her hands on her hips as she waited for our answer.

"I'll have some more coffee when you have a chance," I told her and then nodded at Chief's food. "Bring my friend a shot of insulin, too."

She cackled and headed for the coffee pot.

"Says the girl eating pie for breakfast."

"It's too early for breakfast. This is a late-night dessert."

"Ahhh. I stand corrected as that vastly changes the amount of sugar and calories in it."

Tabitha reappeared and filled up my mug. "Thanks, Tabitha."

"Tabby," Chief said.

"Don't you get her started, too. I swear I will smack you with a spatula. I like *her*."

"Stop calling me Gorgeous, and I'll stop trying to get everybody to call you Tabby." He smiled at her over his coffee.

"But Tabby's cute. Gorgeous makes you sound..." I didn't know how it made him sound. Certainly un-chiefly.

"Gay?" He sighed.

I frowned at him. "Nothing wrong with that. I was going to say pompous. Maybe I should start calling you Gorgeous. It fits."

He chuckled. "I know there's nothing wrong with being gay. For some reason when I hear the word gorgeous, I think of Boy George."

"Okaaay." I took a bite of pie and gasped. If it were possible to live off pie, I would. *Fresh* pie was everything.

"That good?"

"Better."

The fucker had the balls to reach over and scoop out a bite with his fork. I didn't know whether to scream or whack him in the knuckle with my spoon. All I could do was stare. "That is good. Marco makes a killer pie."

I shook my head to rid it of the murderous urges. "I only know Herb, Marge, and Miguel."

"Night crew. Are we still helping for Christmas? You'll meet everybody then. Unless you want to go back into the kitchen and meet them now."

"Yes, we're still helping. And no. I'll just enjoy my pie." *And fantasize about a thousand ways to hurt you.*

"You never answered my question."

"I know."

"So, we're not dating anymore?"

I sighed and set my spoon down, crossing my arms impetuously. "You arrested me."

He took a bite of pancake and stared at me while he chewed. At least he ate with his mouth closed. He swallowed and nodded. "I did."

"You're not even sorry, dickhole."

Washing down the pancake with his coffee, he set the mug down and folded his hands on the table in front of his breakfast. "I'm sorry I had to. I'm sorry I didn't call you first. Being a cop is what I am used to. Having a girlfriend isn't. Would I go back and do things differently? Absolutely."

"You really still want to date me?"

"And you think I ask stupid questions."

"Is that a yes?"

"That is a resounding thousand-times yes."

"You gonna bust me ever again?"

"Not without calling you first."

"Can I get that in writing?"

"No, but I swear it upon my soul."

"Deal."

He reached out his hand to shake mine. I took it, strawberry and whip cream sticky as it was.

"Still love me?" I had to ask. If he could say it…I could forgive him. Eventually.

"I do. Indubitably."

I smiled and started back on my pie.

"Well?" He was waiting for me to say it back.

"Well what?"

He made an impatient motion with his hand.

"Pie."

"Pie?"

"I love pie."

He narrowed his eyes.

"And you." It wasn't a lie. As crazy as he drove me, I loved him. It was as simple as that. If he ever fucking arrested me again, I would continue to love him long after he was dead.

The smile I had killed earlier found its way back on his lips. He picked up his fork and cut a slice of pancake, nodding as if everything had worked itself out. That's when he was the cutest. When he thought I wasn't watching him, and he was having happy little moments to himself.

We ate in companionable silence. I finished my pie well before him and just sat there, drinking my coffee and staring out the window.

"You okay?"

Turning my head, I nodded and for the first time in a while, I meant it. Sitting there in the diner, munching pie with him well before the sun was up was almost therapeutic. "Yep."

"Penny for your thoughts."

"Just kind of happy."

"Because we made up?"

"Don't get ahead of yourself. We're dating and I love you. But I'm still going to make your life hell until I feel as though you've redeemed yourself."

"I wouldn't expect anything less."

"This is just a snack. You'll have to wine me and dine me if you expect panty privileges."

"Well, that's not a big deal."

"It's not?"

"Nope. I don't wear panties."

"I meant *my* panties."

"I don't wear your panties, either. They wouldn't fit." He grinned at his own joke. I may have, too. Just a little bit.

"Well, you might have to break your own rules. I might want to see you in panties before I let you remove mine."

He lifted the corner of his mouth. "You would like that, wouldn't you."

"Humiliating you? A little. If you're a good boy, I'll put you in handcuffs and stuff you into the back of my car."

He chortled. "I meant seeing me in panties."

I cocked an eyebrow and stuck out my lips while I thought about it. I answered him with a nod. "Yep. I kinda would."

"Why?"

"Because I think you'd be gorgeous in them."

CHAPTER 8

The handcuffs were chaffing my wrists, but as Chief slid my leggings down and off, the sensation in my wrists was the last thing on my mind. Especially when his lips found mine, his tongue parting them and slipping inside me. I hissed as pleasure coursed through me.

"Fuck that feels good."

He pulled away. "All that teasing about panties, and you weren't even wearing any."

"Eat me, pig."

"Oh, I will…"

My back arched against the cold surface of Chief's desk as he dove back in, sucking my clit into his mouth as he lifted my legs over his shoulders and wrapped his arms around my thighs, using his fingers to pry me open while he feasted.

Bringing my cuffed wrists down, I hooked them over his head and pulled him in harder. I wanted to come, and then I wanted him to fuck me on his desk until I blacked out in pleasure. I didn't want it, I needed it. I needed him.

And at least he had kept his promise. As soon as we entered the police station and walked past the desk sergeant, my phone started ringing. I'd pulled it out of my purse and looked down at it. CHIEF DINGALING was plastered across the screen. Without looking back, I answered it.

"Hey, Dot...I'm going to arrest you now," he whispered into the phone. He gave me enough time to put my phone in my jacket pocket before he took it off, and my sweater, and then pushed me up against the wall, hands over my head. I almost came when he whispered, "Spread em."

I like a man who kept his promises. Especially when he spread me out over his desk and was lightly grazing my clit while his tongue was undulating inside me.

"Oh fuck, Bill. Right there. Don't stop."

His tongue sped up and he rubbed my clit a little harder, just enough to throw me over the edge of the Cliffs of Insanity. I tried so hard not to scream and failed miserably. High pitched wheezes escaped from my lips in time with the throbbing contractions tightening my canal around his tongue.

"Stop, please," I begged.

Sighing as he pulled his tongue free, I gasped as he attacked my clit with his lips, sucking me back into his mouth and flicking me with the tip of his tongue as he hummed. *Another* orgasm ripped through me like lightning. My contractions turned into convulsions as my back lifted off the desk and I curled from the ecstasy. Relief finally came as I collapsed back against the desk when he finally let me go.

"You're evil." I brought my cuffed wrists up to my face and covered my eyes, still spasming with after quakes, my clit still angry at the beating it had taken.

He must have unzipped himself while he was performing his oral acrobatics. When he stood up, his tip nudged my entrance, throbbing against me. "Muahahahaha," he said with an evil laugh and skewered me with the first three of his many inches.

"Oh, you fucker!"

"Why, yes. Yes I am."

"Slowly."

He pulled me closer to him, stepping back with me to not fully impale me as he leaned over me and found my upper lips with his. After the onslaught he'd given me, his kisses were positively gentle. His lips lightly grazed mine as his tongue gently prodded me into opening my mouth and moaning against him.

"I do love you. It kind of scares me how much," he said softly after he broke the kiss, I would have kept going for the rest of forever. He had his faults, but not in the bedroom. Or the office.

I lifted my wrists off my eyes, careful not to hit him in the face, and stared into his cool blue eyes. "I bet you say that to all the girls you handcuff on your desk."

"Nope. You're the first one I've said it to." He nodded emphatically.

I growled. "And how many women have been handcuffed on your desk?"

"Including you?"

"Yes."

"One." He smiled at me.

"Good answer."

"Only answer."

"Smart man."

"The others said no to the handcuffs."

"You fucker!" I hooked my legs around him and pulled him closer, fully driving him inside me. I squealed through the kabobbing and threw my arms over his head, pulling him back down to my lip level. "You're my prisoner now."

"I admit my guilt and am ready to serve my sentence right here."

"The length of your punishment?"

"Definitely life."

It wasn't until the first tear slid down over my temple that I realized just how sweet he could be. When he wanted to. My lips smashed against his and there was no gentle prodding with my tongue as I invaded his mouth. His

99

kisses were strawberry flavored from the pancakes and… I tried not to think of the other flavor coating his lips.

When he came up for air, I had to stifle a laugh. "Why?"

"Why what?"

"Why is it always *strawberries* with you."

He grinned at me, knowing *exactly* what I was referring to. "That was the hottest night, ever."

"I don't know…this one is pretty close. I like being impaled on your cock on your desk in handcuffs. I'm writing this one down."

"We'll have to make a list."

"Of?"

"Favorite places to fuck. And favorite flavors. And positions."

"Chief Dingaling, in the office, with the baseball bat." I pulled him in closer with my legs, driving that last inch inside me and then letting him go, giving myself a reprieve.

"What about flavors?"

"Always strawberry…" I kissed him again.

"And Dot…"

"Shut up. I'm trying not to think about it."

He chuckled. "Don't like the taste of you? I do."

"I don't mind it…it's just. I'd rather not think about it."

"I think it's hot. I make you come with my lips and then you kiss me. It makes me even harder," he answered and pushed forward with his hips.

"Fuuuck," I groaned. "Turnaround is fair play, Chief. Remember that."

"You're gonna fuck me on my desk?"

"No. I'm going to make you come with my lips and then kiss *you*."

"Ew."

"See?"

"Okay. Your logic has prevailed. You win. No more kisses for you."

"I didn't say that…"

He lifted himself off me, stopping to lift my handcuffed hands off his neck, and let his hands settle on my hips. "You shouldn't be saying anything. You should be moaning." He pulled himself halfway out and thrust back in. My eyes crossed as his face blurred.

"Keep doing that and I'll be unable to talk."

"That's the plan." *He* groaned as he started slowly picking up the pace after every third or fourth stroke. He wasn't wrong, I was totally incapable of making coherent sounds, let alone rational thoughts. He felt incredible, like he was splitting me like firewood, but what was really sending me to the celestial planes was the feel of his balls as they slapped against my ass. It was then that I felt truly *full*.

"Going…to…come," I managed to spout between thrusts.

"Oh, I am, too. Do you want me to fill you?"

I mewled, the thought of it nearly triggering the orgasm welling from deep inside me. His thrusts picked up and he started grunting as he drove every inch inside me, holding himself in for a moment and then pulling back. It was only three or four of those incredibly long strokes that caused my brain to explode in a shower of sparks. At least that's what it looked like from behind my closed eyes.

"*Fuuuck*," I shouted as he jammed himself in, his cock throbbing as he emptied himself completely inside me. My orgasm matched his as I whimpered in time with his twitching, throbbing cock.

"Holy shit," he panted as he collapsed against me, head against mine.

We were both out of breath, sweaty, and exhausted. It was perfect, and I was totally happy I'd been unable to fall asleep. "You can say that again," I panted against him, my lips against his neck. He smelled incredibly sweet, unlike his usual aftershave enhanced aroma. "Okay. The cuffs were fun, but you're lying on my arms. I can't feel my fingers."

"Oh. Sorry," he said and lifted himself off me, still inside me. I wiggled my fingers, trying to get the circulation flowing through the starved digits.

"That's okay." I looked down at where we were still joined. "That's gonna make a mess," I said thoughtfully, not looking forward to him pulling out.

He held up a finger, gave me a smile, and opened the desk drawer by my ass, pulling out a neatly folded towel.

"You are such a boy scout."

"What? I keep towels in my desk. It gets hot in the summer."

"Uh huh."

"You try chasing criminals in July."

"Uh huh."

He narrowed his eyes. "I do *not* masturbate in my office. If that's what you're insinuating."

"Why not?"

"Why not what?"

"Rub one out in your office every once in a while. I'm going to."

"You're going to finger yourself in your office?"

"Yep." I grinned at him. "Once I get the security cameras installed so I can see hunky police chiefs wandering around in my bookstore. I'll let you know when they're in. You can 'catch' me doing naughty things to myself in my office."

He was staring at me incredulously. *But* he liked the thought. Mr. Twitchy was throbbing inside me again.

"Maybe I'll let you cuff me in *my* office and have your way with me on *my* desk. I should stock up on towels."

He lightly smacked me in the face with the towel in his hand. "You're insane."

"Sometimes. But you like the insanity."

"I do." He leaned over and kissed me before he pulled out of me and gently wiped me with the towel. I'd never felt more vulnerable, or loved, in my life.

∞ ∞ ∞

You suck. Yuki's sleepy voice caught me off guard.

Actually, I didn't. My lips remained virginal this morning.

Ewww. Way TMI. I swear she gagged over the mind speech.

Sorry. I was making a joke.

It's bad enough being woken up with your...you know. Know how frustrating it is to wake up being pelted with all sorts of warm and squishies, and then try and fall back asleep?

Why yes, Yuki. Yes, I do.

Ew. You're not normal.

I smirked, leaning against the door to the bookstore. The sun was just barely over the horizon, but technically we didn't open for another three hours. I could have magicked the lock, but Main Street was getting a little busy. I didn't want someone to see me and call the police on me for breaking and entering. I'd already been fucked by them once, and I wasn't referring to my early morning tryst.

Is Josephina up yet?

No. But Candace is. I can hear her in the shower. Want me to wake up Josie?

Not if you want to live. Let Candace do it. I'm sure she has creative ways...

You're trying to make me barf blood, aren't you?

Maybe.

You're evil.

But you love me.

103

I do, she answered without hesitation. *What do you need the Josiemonster for?*

I need her key to the bookstore. Jason has mine and I never had another one made. There are too many damn people around to magick the lock open.

Dot...it's seven o'clock in the morning. Why are you at the bookstore?

Nothing else to do...

There was an awkward pause in the conversation. I thought she might have shut me off and gone back to sleep. *Hang on.*

Not like I have a choice...

Seriously, how busy can Main Street be? It's too damn early.

For a vampire.

Har har.

I could have found a shadow somewhere deserted and tried my hand at shadow walking into the store, but I wasn't comfortable with that option at all. Too much weird shit happened any time I used powers related to my father's three spheres. So far, I'd only had to deal with vampire and shadow stuff. I shuddered to think what would happen if I did something stupid and took a trip to Gehenna.

I got em, Yuki's thought interrupted my musings. *Want me to bring them to you?*

Can you get here without making the 5 o'clock news?

Can a vampire shit in the Transylvanian woods?

Wait. Vampires shit?

No. It's a figure of speech.

I should have known. *How long until you get here?*

"Now."

I screamed and spun around, nearly lashing out with a bit of fire in spite of the ton of people I was *trying* not to do magic in front of. During our conversation, I'd been slowly wandering around in circles and she emerged from the parking lot behind me. "You little shit."

She grinned and held out a key. She was still wearing her pajamas. "I'm going back to bed, unless you need something else?"

"No. Thank you. You do that," I answered grumpily.

She just laughed and turned around, heading back the way she'd come. "That was payback for this morning," she called from out of sight.

"Just wait 'til later!" I wasn't sure if she heard me or not, but it didn't matter. Even if I ended up alone in my bed, I was going to abuse the hell out of myself, just to get her back. My leggings weren't exactly dry and she didn't help the situation any. I'd nearly pissed myself. In fact, I was dancing from foot to foot, fumbling with the key to the front door. Finally getting inside, I ran toward the bathroom after twisting the lock shut, not bothering to flip the store lights on.

Bookstores, by nature, are quiet. Bookstores that aren't open and you're the only person in there are eerily quiet. Bookstores with all the afore mentioned and not a single light on are fucking creepy. Even when you can see in the dark. I stopped halfway to the stall and turned around, walked back, and flipped the switch.

"That's better," I mumbled to myself and peed as quickly as I could.

The sinks were standard white ceramic, but Jason had spared a little extra expense with the fixtures. They were almost nicer than the ones I had in my house. I turned the one for the hot water, dispensed a little soap, and ran them under the tap. The hot water heater was on the other side of the store and my hands were frozen before the hot water finally kicked in. Shaking my head, I looked up at myself in the mirror.

There was no stopping the scream as it tore from my throat like the wail of a banshee. Every hair on my arms stood on end as adrenaline coursed through my veins. Standing behind me were three people in various stages of decay, all of them burned. One of them had suffered burns so bad, his facial features were *beyond* recognition. He looked like a walking piece of burned meat. All of their arms were outstretched, nearly brushing my back.

I spun and did let forth a blaze of fire as my hand whipped around, ready to defend myself...and met empty air. The air around me had dropped in temperature enough for my breath to be seen. With every ragged breath, a jet of steam escaped.

"What the ever-loving fuck?" My voice echoed in the now empty bathroom.

My butt dropped to the counter behind me, right into a puddle of water I had splashed on the counter. I didn't care. Getting my breathing under control was my main priority. Passing out on the bathroom floor from hyperventilating was not how I wanted to be found when Jason finally opened the store.

"I'm losing my mind," I mumbled and turned back around.

They were still there.

I screamed, closed my eyes, and ran for the bathroom door. When I was past where they were standing, only then did I pry my eyes open just in time to grab the handle, fling the door open, and escape into the relative safety of the bookstore. My bookstore. My *haunted* bookstore.

I didn't stop until I hit the front door, fumbled again with the lock, and spilled out onto the sidewalk in front of a couple out for a morning stroll.

"Miss Blackwell?"

"Oh. Hey, Abe." It was the elderly man who owned Abe's Fine Furniture.

He reached down and offered me a helping hand up. "Are you all right?"

In the head? No. "Yeah," I answered, dusting off my leggings. "Tripped on the way out. That threshold is a little high. Gonna have to have the contractor take a look at it before I have a lawsuit on my hands." I concentrated on getting my breathing under control. Enough to talk to my business neighbors, at least.

"Definitely. That was quite the spill."

"I've had worse. I'm such a klutz." I looked at the woman standing next to Abe. "Hi. I'm Dorothea Blackwell. Dot."

"This is my wife Virginia," he answered with a smile.

"Hello, Dorothea. Pleasure to meet you."

She was so cute, I wanted to pinch her cheeks. "What are you doing out? Don't tell me you open up this early?"

"Oh, heavens no," Abe answered, shaking his head. "Today is the Christmas parade. We haven't missed a single one since 1967. They're not much, but they're festive."

"Oh. That explains all the people."

"Yes. It's quite popular. They are just securing their vantage points," Virginia said with a smile.

"Front row seats."

They both nodded.

"I'll have to check it out. What time does it start?"

"Eleven."

"You guys are going to sit out in this cold for three hours?"

They each held up a matching thermos and Abe turned, showing off the folding chairs in a sling on his back. "Hot cocoa and chairs," he said with a wheeze of ancient laughter. "Part of the tradition."

"Well, don't you freeze! And enjoy yourself."

"Are you opening this early?"

"No. I just stopped in to check on a few things. My manager will be here in an hour, but we don't open until ten."

"You were booming yesterday!" Abe sounded impressed.

"I couldn't believe it. Going to have to hire a few more people if it keeps up."

"I wish you all the luck," he said with a nod of his head.

"Thanks, Abe. Oh! That reminds me. I bought another house. I'll come see you for furniture in a few days."

"Thank you!" He patted me on my shoulder and Virginia gave me a little wave as they ambled away. They were adorable, and I found myself sighing wistfully as they headed closer to the center of town.

I had a little vision of me at their stage of age, being followed by the guys, and I laughed to myself in the middle of the sidewalk. Then the reality of the ghosts in my store snapped me out of my musings. "Mother."

I needed to talk to my mother. She or Nanna would know how to get rid of them, hopefully without blowing up my brand-new bookstore.

"What's the matter? You look like you saw a ghost."

I gave a little yelp at Chief standing there giving me a concerned look. "You scared me!"

"Sorry. Thought you knew I was there. I was waiting for you to finish talking to the Andersons."

"Abe and his wife?"

He nodded.

"Didn't know their last name."

"Ahhh."

He took a step closer. "What happened?"

"Saw three ghosts, actually. I need to call my mother. And maybe my grandmother."

"You think they're playing a prank on you? With actual ghosts?" He stared at me like I'd lost my mind.

"No! But they might know how to get rid of them."

"Priest?"

"Nope."

"Why the bookstore?"

I stopped before I hit the call button and looked at him thoughtfully. "I don't know. They were burned horribly. They looked like firemen. Just a little over cooked. Did anybody die in the fire?"

He shook his head. "No."

"Are you sure?"

He nodded. "No. It wasn't that bad of a fire. Are you sure…you saw what you think you saw?"

"If I had seen them once, I may seriously be doubting my sanity. I saw them in the mirror, turned around and they were gone. But when I finally calmed down and looked back in the mirror, they were still there. Not moving except to reach for me."

"That's some seriously creepy shit."

"You're telling me."

"Mind if I take a look?"

"Knock yourself out. Women's bathroom," I answered, with no intention of going back in there. Not without backup that included more than handcuffs and handguns. I had my own arsenal. I'd never met another witch that compared to Mother and Nana. Witches grew in power as they aged, and my family had an abundance of magic to begin with. Add centuries to that power and they could easily wipe a town off the face of the map. Much to the chagrin of Ashville, Virginia. It had taken the brunt of their petty arguments for those centuries. Luckily, my family also excelled at restoration magic.

As soon as he left, I dialed my mother.

"Oh, you finally recalled I am in town after you begged me to stay?"

"Sorry. Having a bad week."

"How bad could it possibly be, Daughter?"

"Uh…got arrested, in trouble with the locals, and now I am vampire enemy number one. To top all *that* off, I just had a run in with a trio of ghosts in my store."

"Where are you now?" She'd gone from cranky to worried faster than Josie went down on a box of donuts.

"Standing outside the bookstore."

"I shall be there shortly."

I could feel the storm approaching. "Thank you, Mother. I'll buy you breakfast. Meet me at the diner."

"Very well."

"Should I call Nana, too?"

There was a pause on the other end of the line. At least she was thinking about it before telling me to go fuck myself with a broken bottle. "As *loathe* as I am to admit it. She is closer in age to most of the spirits roaming the mortal realm than I. Call her. Have her join us."

I looked up to the sky in search of the meteor that was about to strike the earth, ending all life as we knew it. But there was only blue sky. She had agreed. Something bad was going to happen, I just knew it. "Okay," I answered meekly.

"Only *you* could find yourself in enough trouble for me to willingly spend time with my mother."

"Boy, if I had a dime for every time I said that," I said jokingly.

The line clicked dead.

Hopefully I wouldn't. With a silent prayer to the Lady that my mother left my voodoo doll at home, I stuffed my phone in my pocket and waited for Chief. Outside. Away from the ghosts.

When he finally came out, he frowned and shook his head. "Nothing in there."

"Great, I'm crazy or I'm the only one who can see them."

"Maybe a bit of both?"

"You're hilarious. Now you get to have second breakfasts."

"Uh...why?"

"Because I'm meeting my mother and grandmother at the diner. We may need your handcuffs and taser."

CHAPTER 9

"And you are sure that no one perished in the fire?" My mother set her tea mug down on the table and stared at me intently. Nana was, too. How the hell they thought I would know was beyond me. I looked at Chief for verification, even though he had been adamant of the fact.

"Yes. I'm positive. It was only twentyish years ago, and I'm certain."

"Then they couldn't have been ghosts," my mother said surely.

"What if it wasn't from the firehouse fire? What was the building *before* that?" Leave it to Nana to bring logic to the table.

"It's always been a firehouse, since the founding of the town in the late 1800's."

"That building isn't two hundred years old," I said, getting a bad feeling. "I saw it stripped down to bare walls. There's no way it's more than fifty. What happened to the original building?"

He opened his mouth, but nothing came out while he thought about it. Finally, his face darkened. "Honestly, I don't know. I can tell you about the history of the police station, but not the firehouse. Maybe ask Jimmy or Dennis?"

I nodded. That wasn't a bad idea. Maybe they shared spooky firehouse stories around the kitchen table over firehouse chili. Grabbing my phone, I shot off a quick text to see if Jimmy was up yet.

Yes? Everything okay?

I smiled at my screen. *Yes. Was there ever a fire at the old firehouse before it burned the last time?*

What? One more time in English.

The fire at the firehouse twenty years ago...was there another fire before that one?

I think so. Half the town burned down in 1929. During prohibition.

Wow. Did anybody die in the fire?

A lot of people died in the fire.

Wow. That sucks.

I'll ask the chief about the firehouse. Just out of curiosity...why?

I'll tell you tonight.

Okay, baby. Love you.

Love you, too, my Jimmy.

Everybody was staring at me and the goofy ass smile on my face. Setting my phone down, I cleared my throat. "Apparently, half the town burned down in 1929. Jimmy is going to ask the chief about the firehouse."

My mother's face darkened considerably. Which, for her, was quite a feat.

"What?"

"If that many people died in the fire, why are there only ghosts at your bookstore?"

"Just lucky, I guess."

She didn't look convinced. Instead, she raised her eyebrows and stared into her cup of tea as she took a sip of it.

"What?" I wanted to know what she was thinking. It was the whole point of inviting her to breakfast.

"Seems a little *too* coincidental, if you ask me."

"When my granddaughter is involved, there are very little coincidences."

My mother looked at her mother and nodded solemnly.

"What? You think I'm responsible for the three burnt stooges in my bathroom?"

Nana shrugged. My mother nodded.

"How the hell is it my fault?"

Calmly, my mother set her tea on the table. "Perhaps you should ask your fellow shopkeepers if they have had any recent run-ins with the undead?" She made a sweeping gesture down both sides of the street with her hands.

"Maybe they can't see them?"

"Maybe. Or maybe it is your power that has given them form. Think about it, Daughter. Think about who your father was."

"Is."

"Was. His mantle has fallen squarely upon your shoulders." I opened my mouth to protest, but she held up her hand and continued. "Yes, yes. I know of your grand designs on mounting a rescue, but in the meantime, you have dominion over the night, the shadows, and most importantly, the dead… Perhaps they are *seeking* you out for release."

"Ew."

"From earthly constraints," she added with a sigh and shook her head again, rubbing the bridge of her nose. I was giving her a migraine.

"That's just fucking dandy," I said and slumped forward, burying my face in my hands and leaning on the table. Chief patted my shoulder in an awkward attempt at comforting me.

"I should just move to Antarctica. Bet there's no ghosts, vampires, demons, or shadows there."

"You would be surprised." Nana scoffed.

"So, tell me about your vampire problem. Do I need to get involved?"

I'd momentarily forgotten about my *other* dilemma. "Had a run in with a few of the locals. Yuki made some new potholes in Main Street with their faces. In broad daylight. She made the news and the vampire clan saw it and told her father. He is most curious and probably on his way here."

My mother's face twisted in evil glee. "Then it is most fortuitous that I stayed at your request!" She loved butting heads with people. And not just people. Especially Lord Abernathy.

"Yeah. Have at it. I don't have time for that bullshit right now."

"So glad I could be of service," she said drolly.

"Not what I meant, but I'm glad you are here. He freaks me out."

"He is powerful. But not *all* powerful. Do not forget that."

"I won't. So back to the ghosts. How do I get rid of them?"

"That is not a question I can answer." She shrugged her shoulders and I looked at Nana.

"There are spells. But I am unsure if that would be a plausible solution if there are going to be more than your trio. I shall pore over the family records and see what I can find."

"Thank you, Nana."

"My pleasure, Grandchild."

"Great. Well, I need to get to the parade. It should be starting soon. Are you ladies going to watch?" Chief asked lightheartedly, knowing full well that the last place on earth my mother and grandmother would be was at a Christmas parade.

"Humans celebrating Christmas by driving slow moving vehicles covered in flowers while freezing my *tuchus* off?" My mother looked at him as if he had gone insane.

"There's a hot chocolate stand."

"I shall accompany you, then." Mother stood and exited the booth. At first, I thought she was joking, but she was staring at Chief impatiently.

"I'll...uh...see you later," I told him and gave him a quick kiss. Just in case something happened to him. "I love you."

"Should I be afraid?"

"Just don't let her sense any fear and you should be fine."

"Anything else I should know?"

"Her vision is based on movement. Like a T-rex. If she smells blood or fear, just freeze. She won't be able to see you."

"Very funny, Daughter."

"I know. Don't hurt him. Or sleep with him." I narrowed my eyes at her to let her know I wasn't fucking kidding.

"I never dip my toes in another witch's pond, dear."

"It's not your toes I'm worried about, Mother."

She cackled and wrapped herself around Chief's arm as he stood up, letting him lead the way.

"Should I trust her?"

"About as far as you can throw her with T-rex arms," Nana supplied unhelpfully. "But you should trust in your man. This might be a good test for him."

"If he can stand the mother, he can stand me?"

"More like, if he can stand your mother, he has the patience of a fucking saint and you could probably lock him in a small room with a rabid velociraptor without fear."

"Look at you go with the dinosaur references."

"Well, your mother brings them to mind."

I cocked an eyebrow at her.

"Please, Child. We are witches. We only *act* our age and I caught her laying eggs and hunting in packs just the other day."

"You should really save these for when she's around."

"Definitely not. I *abhor* having to explain my jokes.

∞ ∞ ∞

The subtle smell of shampoo and aftershave wafted off Jason as he pushed the bathroom door open and flipped on the light switch. The fluorescents flickered twice overhead and filled the room with brilliant white light.

"There's nothing there."

"That's just what they want you to think. Go stand at the sink and look behind you in the mirror."

He glanced at me over his shoulder and sighed. "Okaaay."

I watched him take every step. When I'd told him about the ghosts, he very subtly let me know he thought I was hallucinating from sleep deprivation. Telling him I was checking out the store because I hadn't gotten a lick of sleep and then saw ghosts in the bathroom wasn't the brightest thing I'd ever done. I didn't blame him for thinking I had imagined the whole damn thing.

As soon as he was in front of the sink, he turned and gave me one last look before facing the the mirror. From the doorway I watched his face contort in fear as he turned to me, opened his mouth to scream, and started laughing. "There's nothing there, Lady."

"You're a shit." I shot him the dirtiest look I could manage and stomped into the bathroom. Raising my hand to poke him in the ribs, I froze. They were there, in the mirror, still unmoving. The stench of charred flesh filled my nose. I nearly gagged as I watched them out of the corner of my eye, refusing to turn toward the mirror or in their direction. Still unmoving, Jason gave me a concerned look.

"Are you okay? You're white as a—"

118

"Don't you dare finish that fucking sentence." My breath came in ragged gasps, condensation puffing out of my mouth with every breath as the temperature in the room plummeted. Jason at least noticed that and rubbed his arms as he looked up at the vents.

"What the hell? I left the heat on. Feels like the AC just kicked in."

"They're here. That's why it's cold."

He turned back toward the mirror. "Dot, there's nothing there."

"You can't see them?"

"No. Not at all."

"Well, I can. I'm leaving." Closing my eyes, I turned around and walked out of the room, not wanting to take the chance of being able to see them without the mirror. I was done dealing with it.

"Woah," Jason said as I was going through the door.

"What?" I asked over my shoulder.

"As soon as you left, it got warm again."

"Seriously?"

"Yes. Come back in for a moment. I want to see if it gets cold again."

"No." I let the door close and headed for my office. There were no mirrors in there.

I shouldn't have left him in there alone. He couldn't even see them, so I thought he would have been completely safe. The store had been open all day yesterday and we didn't have one damn complaint about ghosts in the bathroom. When I'd made it halfway across the store, he let out a heart-rendering scream. I spun and ran back when the realization he was probably pranking me again kind of pissed me off.

Grabbing the door, I flung it open and shouted, "Jason!"

My heart stopped. He was lying on the ground gripping ghostly hands wrapped around his neck and fighting to breathe.

"Get the fuck away from him!" Anger coursed through me with adrenaline as I strode into the room and swung a fist at the burned, ghastly image floating over his prone form. I slowed my swing, expecting it to pass through the specter, but it connected. It felt like punching a wet newspaper. The ghost screeched and flew away, hitting the wall and disappearing through it, discoloring the paint where it hit.

Jason started choking, trying to get air into his lungs.

"Are you okay?"

He nodded, wheezing. "Cold."

I reached down and grabbed his arms, pulling him to his feet and dragging him out of the bathroom. When he was safely outside, I stormed back into the bathroom and looked back into the mirror. The other two were still milling about, arms outstretched and searching for something.

"Get out!" I held up my hands as the shadows in the room coalesced, slid along the floor, and burst from the ground around me. The non-visible ghosts became quite visible after that. Fidget slithered up my forearm when he reached my hand, stretched and screeched like a bird of prey. Surging out of my palm, wings sprouted from his massive form as he lashed out with clawed appendages.

Moaning in fear and pain as he slashed at them, they lifted from the floor and raced after the third one that had vanished through the wall. Pulling Fidget back, I walked to the spot and slapped my other hand against the frosty concrete wall, slamming up a ward.

Whenever I'd cast wards in the past, I could feel the magic as it seeped into the perimeter and formed a thin barrier that could be passed through or flared, depending on the person's intent. What poured from my hand didn't

120

seep softly into the walls, it became an instant part of the walls and foundation, slamming up with an audible clap of thunder, causing the walls to shimmer in the light in opalescent beauty. I had to blink a few times as my eyes refused to focus on the tan hued paint Jason had picked for the bathrooms.

"What the fuck?"

I dropped to my knees, my hand sliding down the wall as I fell, and pressed my head to my arm. Refusing to cry, I breathed in and out, trying not to focus on what was happening to me. Things were getting out of control. *I* was getting out of control.

The hand on my shoulder broke me out of my spiral of self-pity. "Are you okay?"

Jason's voice sounded a little raspier than usual, but thank the Lady, he was okay. "Peachy."

"I'm sorry. Sorry I didn't believe you."

I reached up and patted his hand on my shoulder. "It's okay. I still don't believe it, either."

"That was pretty fucking scary. I'm not going to lie."

"Tell me about it."

Fidget slithered off my hand, or at least part of him did, and touched Jason's hand just below his wrist. He jerked back and Fidget squawked in protest.

"What the hell is that?"

"Fidget. He's my shadow buddy."

"Like a pet?"

"More like a guard dog."

"He bites?"

"I don't know. But he claws and chokes things when I'm in danger."

"Woah."

"Yeah."

"Thank you, Lady."

"For?"

"Saving me."

121

I got up and wrapped my arms around him, pulling him closer and putting my head against his chest. "I'm just sorry I couldn't turn those bastards into ghost dust."

"I'm alive. More than I was expecting, to be honest."

"He had just started choking you…"

"But that's just it. He was draining me as he did it. I could feel it. Then you came charging in and punched him in the face… Not too many people can actually say they punched a ghost in the face."

"I could see him."

"Uh, yeah."

"But I couldn't before. Only in the mirror."

"Okay?"

"I think you're right. He was draining you to become…real? Corporeal?"

"What about the other two?"

"The shadows made them visible."

"This little guy?" He reached out and nudged Fidget.

"No. The shadows in the room."

"They're alive, too?" He was starting to panic, eyes darting around the room.

"I don't think so. I think shadows come from another realm and into ours through them."

"Oh. That's much better." His eyebrows practically disappeared into his hairline.

"Don't think about it. Just trust me."

He sighed heavily and nodded. "Always."

That earned him a smile and a kiss.

"So, what the hell was that noise?"

I pointed at the wall. "That's an outside wall. When they were knocked out of the store, I slapped up a ward that will keep them out of here for the rest of forever."

"To roam around town? Eating people?" He gave me a look.

"I'll deal with that when, and if, it happens. I think they were bound here. Long story. I have my mother and

122

grandmother looking for a way to banish them completely. Until that time…at least we hopefully won't have any more incidents in the store."

Jason nodded, but didn't look to happy with the situation in general. He was young. He still needed to learn the age-old adage of picking your battles wisely. Fighting an unknown enemy never ended well.

"Come on, I'll buy you a cup of coffee and we can get the store open."

"You got it, Boss."

I left him to get everything running and I headed into the café. Josie and Candace were busy stocking everything. You could see the worry etched on both their faces. I frowned a little, unsure what they were worried about.

"Mornin', beautiful ladies." I said in the deepest, huskiest voice I could manage in an effort to cheer them up.

"What was that noise?" Josie scrunched her face after she asked.

"Just figured some wards would help protect the place until we get the alarm going. Might have overdone it a bit," I lied, trying to not make them worry more.

Josie nodded, but Candace narrowed her eyes at me in suspicion. "Gotcha. You can help us clean the storeroom later. Your overzealous wards knocked half the stock off the shelves."

"I didn't break anything did I?"

Candace shook her head before Josie could answer.

"How come you two look so happy?"

"You saw this place yesterday. While I appreciate the business, that was almost too much. We didn't get a break."

"You need to hire a few people."

"I had a couple of girls ask for applications, but I haven't had a chance to look at them yet."

"Want some help for today?"

Josie shot me a nervous glance. "Yuki?"

"Yep. Dar, too, if you need him. I was planning on Shea helping at the bookstore. Maybe Jimmy, too. Until I can find full timers."

"As much as I *don't* want the tick around my fiancé," she said and paused when Candace smacked her in the tummy for the tick comment, "we could really use the help." She rubbed her stomach and grinned at her fiancée.

"I'll see what she says."

"Thanks, Dot. Coffee?"

"Two. Please. Bless your face."

Josie stopped stocking and walked over to the espresso machine. She loaded it and set it to brew, already looking like an expert barista. But then again, she probably made ten-thousand cups yesterday. She'd better have gotten the movements down pat. The only problem was I didn't want espresso... "Uh, reg coffee is fine, Josie. Don't have to get fancy with me."

"Candace told me you were up all night. We call this one The Columbian Car Bomb." She slapped two paper cups down on the counter, poured coffee from the pot into it, leaving a little bit of room. When the espresso machine finished sputtering, she took the two shot glasses of espresso, dumped them into the coffee and pushed a couple of lids down on the cups. Once she popped the cups into the recycled cardboard sleeves, she handed them over the counter to me.

"How much I owe you?"

"Don't make me kick your ass in the middle of the Café."

"Fair enough," I answered with a grin, taking a sip and bracing myself.

Surprisingly, the espresso didn't alter the flavor of the coffee much, just gave it a darker roast flavor that was actually quite good. I didn't even know what kind of beans they were using for the regular coffee, not that it mattered to me. Coffee was life. There was no such thing as a bad cup of coffee. Unless it was iced. Shudder.

"Good?'

"Really good. Thanks. I'll let you know about Yuki."

They went back to work without another word, but Candace did spare me another worried glance and a little wave. She knew something was up, but she didn't press for details. It was one of the reasons she was my favorite.

Yuki? I whispered her voice mentally in case she was sleeping.

Yes, Master?

You up?

Yes... I could hear the fear in her voice.

Wanna make some money?

Who do you want me to kill?

Laughing to myself, I wandered through the store, avoiding the throng of customers rapidly filling the aisles. He still looked a little shaken as I handed him his cup of coffee. "Thanks."

"No problem," I said to him and then replied to Yuki. *Nobody, yet. Want to work in the coffee shop today? There's a paycheck in it for you.*

Is Josie going to keep giving me dirty looks all day?

Probably. But you have my permission to bite her if she gives you too much of a hard time.

Ew. Can I smack her in the head instead?

Don't hurt your hand.

On my way.

Is Dar home yet?

No. I see you know.

About him and Shea? Yep. Gave them my blessing.

Want me to call him?

I will. I need to talk to Shea, too.

Just gonna hire the whole damn family, huh?

If they want. See you shortly.

I'm almost there…

One problem down, one to go. Without looking back at Jason, I pulled my phone out of its secret hiding place in the waistband of my leggings. It's where I usually stashed it when I wasn't carrying my small purse. I found Shea in my contacts and sent him a text instead of calling. Just in case he was still sleeping. I could have just contacted Dar directly, but I wanted to hear from Shea first.

Hey, sexy. You up?

It took him a few minutes to answer. Hopefully, I didn't interrupt anything. I smiled at my phone when I felt it vibrate in my hand, my imagination had been running wild. *Yes, Lady. Is everything okay?*

Yep. Just wanted to know if you want a job.

At the bookstore?

Yep.

I was hoping you would ask. When do you need me?

Always and forever. My grin got a little bigger. I loved being sappy with him. All of them. It gave me the happies.

I meant for work… As for the other, forever is too short of a time. Need me until the end of always and I will be happy.

It took me a moment to answer. The happies had turned into full-blown holy shits. *As soon as you can get here. It looks like it's going to be another busy day.* Happy tears were wetting my cheeks.

I shall be there soon.

I was half tempted to have him ask Dar if he would help in the coffee shop, but that would have been a little impersonal.

Dar?

I shall accompany him, Master.

I laughed as I sat down at my desk. Things were finally coming together. Especially with the spectral eviction. With one last text to Dwight, asking him if he'd like a job and get out of the factory, to which he responded extraordinarily positively, I finally had a moment to myself.

CHAPTER 10

"You want cheese on that?"

Dar gave me a thoughtful look before shaking his head. "No, thank you. Just the burger and fries. Do you wish me to accompany you?"

"I'm literally walking a few doors down. I think I can manage. Besides, the way the books are flying off the shelf, Jason needs you more than I need an extra set of hands."

Dar looked around the still full store. There hadn't been a moment's peace since we unlocked the doors. Even with the Christmas parade. I'd expected it to be completely *dead*, but the lure of warm cappuccinos, lattes, cocoas, and coffees were bringing them in, and the warm glow of the store kept them inside. It was almost magical, and if I didn't know my witches better, I might have accused one of them of casting a spell on the store. "I shall do my best to keep up."

"I'm sure your best will be more than enough." I ripped the page off the white pad of paper and stuffed it in my pocket. Dar had been the last order I needed.

Stopping by my office, I tossed the notepad and pen on the wood surface and grabbed my purse out of the drawer. I had to mill my way around the people crowding the store, but finally made it to the door and smiled as I exited into the cold afternoon.

The streets seemed to be mostly empty. My guess was that the parade had finally ended, and people were getting on with their day. Hopefully the diner wouldn't be too crowded to put in a to go lunch order. If it was, I could always grab my car and hit the drive-thru at McD's, but that was a last resort option. I craved their fries every so often, but nothing, and I mean nothing, compared to the diner.

The door chimed and Marge waved from behind the counter while armed with two coffee pots. She was going down the line and topping everybody off. When I didn't plop my ass in a booth (mine was taken by some miscreants) she cocked an eyebrow at me when I walked up to the counter. "Hey, Darlin'."

"Afternoon, Marge."

"To go order?"

I was amazed at how quickly she had put two and two together. She didn't always seem like the brightest bulb on the strand, but she didn't miss much. "Yep."

I pulled out the folded, crumpled piece of paper and held it out to her. She set one of the pots of coffee down on the counter, grabbed a mug, and sloshed some coffee in it for me before taking the paper. "Be ready in a few. Cop a squat."

"Thanks, Marge." I did as she asked and sat down on the teal stool, nodding at the two burly-esque guys on either side of me.

The one on my right nodded back, the other got up and moved a few seats down. I shrugged and nonchalantly sniffed my pit. A move that didn't go unnoticed by the guy who stayed. He chuckled. "No. You don't stink."

"Just checking."

"He just don't like witches."

"Pardon?"

The guy sat down his coffee and reached out with a burly paw and offered it. I raised an eyebrow but took it and shook. "Name's Devin. Pleased to meet you."

"Dot."

"I know. Everybody does. You're the head witch."

"There's no such things as witches..." It hurt me to say it, but the way things were going lately, I figured it was my best option. His chuckle said otherwise.

"Sweetie, I was in the town square that day."

"Oh."

"Thank you."

"You're not freaked out?"

"Sitting next to the Lady who saved the town? Hell, no. Glad I finally got to say thank you."

I blushed and gave him a small nod. "Well, this is a first," I whispered. "Most people are afraid of us."

"Like Benson?" He leaned over and shot the other guy a dirty look.

I didn't even bother turning around. I could feel his eyes on me. "Yeah. Like him."

He nodded for emphasis and leaned in a little closer. "Be careful. Ever since the lightning storm, there's been talk."

"I know." I patted him on the leg. "I got arrested for that."

He sighed heavily. "Heard some rumors about meetings, too. If I hear anything concrete, I'll let Marge know."

"You want the whole town to find out?" I winked to let him know I was kidding and was rewarded with a guffaw.

"You're a good kid. Just be careful. Have a feeling that something wicked is coming this way and we're gonna need you to get through it..."

"Huh?"

He sighed. "Granny had a touch of the shine. I get it sometimes, too. Call it a hunch, call it a feeling. I learned the hard way not to ignore it when it smacks me in the face with a two-by-four."

"Those are wise words. In every case and sense."

He let out a deep belly laugh and nodded, tossed a twenty on the counter and stood up. "If I get hit with another one, I'll let Marge know, too."

"Please. Or you could just stop by the new bookstore. I'll be there most days."

"Will do. Take care, Dot. Nice meeting you."

"Nice meeting you, too," I answered and meant it, shaking his hand one last time. A smile crept up on my lips as I watched him walk away.

"I see you met Devin."

"Yep. Nice guy."

"He should be. He's my brother-in-law."

My gaze tore from his retreating back and shot to Marge. "That's Tabby's Dad?"

She giggled. "I see you met the whole famn damily!" She laughed as she set the three bags of food on the counter in front of me. Then she noticed the vacant seat next to me and scanned the restaurant. When her eyes settled on Benson, she gave him a scowl. He seemed very interested in the contents of the coffee mug in his hands.

"Don't worry about it."

"I'm not. I'm pissed about it. Two different things, Darling."

"It's okay, Marge. Everybody is entitled to their own opinion."

"Not when it's different from mine!"

I laughed and handed her my credit card. She shook her head and held up her hand. "It's on me today."

"Damnit, Marge. Take the money."

"Seriously. I'm pissed off and this will make me feel better."

All I could do was sigh. "Fine." I stuffed my card back in my pocket.

"Don't worry. You'll work it off in three days," she answered with a smile.

"Looking forward to it." I stuck my hands through the handles of the three plastic bags. "Thanks, Marge. Give Herb a hug for me."

"I will later when he doesn't smell like bacon."

"That's the best time to hug him."

"He gets bitchy when I bite him."

That was more information than I needed. Hopefully my appetite returned before I cracked open my lunch.

Heading for the front door, I turned to push it open with my butt and almost fell through when someone opened it behind me. Only a quick shuffle of my feet and the strong hand on my back saved me from ass planting on the concrete outside.

"You okay?"

"Derek?"

"Yes?"

"Oh, hey. Thanks for saving me… Sherry?"

"Hi, Dot."

Derek's face, the face I had kissed a thousand times in my youth before he moved to Ireland with his mother and broke my heart, darkened. "You two know each other?"

I nodded.

"Yes. She's dating my cousin, Jimmy…but something tells me you know this. How do you know Dot?" She shifted her weight to her other foot and her hand slid involuntarily to her hip as she waited for his explanation.

"Well uh…"

"Eloquent, Derek." I turned to the mayor. "We dated a few decades ago…" I didn't know if she knew he was a witch, but she deserved to know. Staring at her, I waited until understanding dawned.

"Oh. Oh! Ohhh…"

"Well, I've got to get back to the store. Have fun, you crazy kids." I started to walk away until her voice stopped me.

"Dot?"

"Yeah?"

She turned to Derek. "Grab us a table. I'll be in in a minute."

"Aye." He smiled at her and tilted his head to me before disappearing through the door to the diner.

As soon as the door closed, she sighed and turned her attention back to me. "I am so sorry!"

"For?" Of all the words to come flying out of her mouth, I wasn't expecting an apology. She confused me.

"For dating your ex! If I had known, I would have steered clear!"

"Sherry. Don't think twice about it. Derek's a good guy and you make a cute couple." Surprisingly enough, I meant it.

Her eyes narrowed for a moment. "You're not interested in him anymore, are you?"

"Oh, hell no. We were kids, for witches, when we dated. He did move to town thinking about rekindling something, but he didn't care for the fact that I was dating multiple people. When he came to terms with it, I realized I had lost all interest in him. He's all yours."

Her eyes opened back up, but she didn't look too happy.

"What?"

"He didn't hurt you, did he?"

"Yes. But by moving to another continent. I was young and stupid. He didn't do anything on purpose. He really is a great guy. I'm just surprised you're okay with him being a witch."

"Well, I hadn't known. But between you and Jimmy...I've found myself getting used to the idea. Hell, I have a feeling that in a few years, the whole town might be forced to get used to the idea."

"Does that bother you?"

Her smile was my answer. "Nope. Kind of looking forward to it."

"If you want to know what it will be like, visit Ashville. Make Derek take you for a getaway."

"I will. Thanks for being honest with me."

"Always. You're my lawyer," I said with a wink and lifted the bags of food at her as sort of a wave and an excuse to get back to the store. "See you later, Sher."

"Have fun!"

"Stop by the store."

"I will."

I was halfway to the bookstore when the first tear fell. Carrying the bags made it difficult to wipe the moisture from my eyes, but I managed with the back of my hand. Before I opened the door, I made sure my face was dry and there was a smile on my face.

∞ ∞ ∞

My well-deserved, long-awaited glass of merlot had just graced the tips of my fingers when the doorbell rang. I looked up pitifully at Yuki. She smiled and headed for the door. After lunch, the remainder of the day had been spent with a very out of shape witch helping Dar to stock shelves after she had given everybody an opportunity to eat their lunch in peace, relieving each one as quickly as possible. While it was a kind gesture on my part, I quickly realized we needed people. I'd called Dwight and offered him a job, to which he immediately agreed to and promised to be there tomorrow at opening. I'd insisted he give the factory two weeks, but he was fed up enough to just walk out.

Things had gotten exponentially worse since Jason had left. I'd asked Jimmy, but he declined with a chuckle.

I'd asked Jimmy why, but he changed the subject.

The man in question followed Yuki back into my living room carrying a wrapped, and slightly shaking box wrapped in festive red wrapping paper.

Dar, who had been lounging on the love seat, immediately perked up and stared at the box. "Is that?"

Jimmy made a shushing motion with his other hand after he shifted the box into the other arm as quickly as he could. "A Yule present for Dot? Why yes, it is."

"Why are you giving it to me now? I thought we were exchanging gifts when everybody was here?"

"Because this one is special."

That statement, alone, was enough to make me worry. "What is it?"

He crossed the distance between us and held out the box proudly. "Happy Yule, Dot."

I gingerly reached out and took the box from him, feeling the contents shifting around inside of its own volition as a soft mew escaped from several holes that had been poked through the paper. Excitement shivered through me as I clutched it to my chest and settled it in my lap. I'd always, *always* wanted a cat. Practically every witch in existence did. We were naturally drawn to the creatures and they made the most wonderful familiars. I could practically see its sleek black fur and yellow eyes as I slowly tore the paper from the box.

The lid wasn't sealed, Jimmy had used the paper to hold it closed. I shot him a questioning glare. "How long has he been in there?"

"Since just after Thanksgiving. I was waiting to give him to you."

"What?"

"I'm kidding. It's alive. I wrapped the box in your front yard before ringing the doorbell."

"Oh." I turned my attention back to the box, grinning like a mad fool as I grabbed the crisscrossed cardboard flaps and pulled them open.

My grin slowly faded from my face...

There was no sleek black fur or yellow eyes. Two dangling tufts of skin hung sadly from its head as it looked up at me disdainfully with bright blue orbs that stuck out from its face like creepy marbles as it let out a nerve-grating meow.

It leapt from the box and hooked dagger-like claws into the knit of my sweater, staring at me with one angry eye. Without a single tuft of fur on its entire body, the effect was rather akin to getting an unsolicited dick pic texted to you from your high school social studies teacher. Sure, you knew he had one, but you never ever wanted to see it. Especially that close.

Meow.

Oh, hell no. You're not a cat, you're a house elf.

"Do you like him?" Jimmy was staring at the both of us.

"Uh...what is it?"

"A Sphinx. A hairless cat?"

"It's not a nut sack with legs?"

Jimmy laughed. "No. They're hypoallergenic, extraordinarily independent, and extremely smart."

"You got me a non-irritant, lone wolf, evil genius cat?"

"Yep."

"That was uh...thoughtful."

"I know right? I call him Mister Wrinkles, but you can change it if you don't like it."

"It's a cat raisin."

"You're going to name it raisin?"

Fuck me, he thinks I likes it. "Uh..." The look of pure joy he was giving me was enough for me to shut my fucking mouth. "Yeah. I thought Raisin would be a cute name."

"It kind of is. *Way* better than Mister Wrinkles!" He reached down and rubbed the cat's foreskin. I tried not to gag as the skin shifted under his fingers. "Isn't he adorable?"

Maybe if I give it a sock, it will run away... "Too much cuteness for one little thing to have."

"You should make it your familiar!"

Then I can change my name to Kim Possible! I even had the naked mole rat. "Oh...I think Yuki and Dar are more than enough! I think they might get upset if I took another. You know how they get."

"I do not mind, Master!" Dar was practically crawling toward us, his eyes fixated on the alien sticking out of my chest.

Shut it. You would be more than offended, I thought at him and gave him a look. He didn't look up, his hand reaching slowly toward the kitten.

No. For such a magnificent creature, I would be more than happy to share familiar responsibilities. He started stroking the skin on its back which caused its eyes to bulge and his face to shift to the top of its head.

You like the kitty?

Yes. He is beautiful.

Will you take care of it and love it?

His eyes finally shifted from the cat to mine. *You do not like it?*

Don't tell Jimmy, but it creeps me the fuck out.

Yuki snorted behind me. She must have been listening in.

We are going to keep it? Dar sounded as happy as I'd ever heard him.

If you like it, we can. Just don't make me touch it. And get it off me.

Thank you, Master!

"You want to hold it?" I asked Dar out loud. He picked up on my subterfuge right away.

138

"May I?"

"Please!" I tried to keep the panic from my voice.

Dar reached down and curled his hand under its belly, using his fingers to pry the kitten's claws from my sweater. I sighed once it was free and off my chest. "Is it okay to give it some milk?" He looked at Jimmy.

"Yes. I have a litter box, litter, and some kitten chow out in the car."

"I'll get it," Yuki said and headed out the front door, still chuckling.

Dar took the kitten toward the kitchen. I picked up my wine and leaned back. Crisis averted.

Jimmy sighed next to me. "You don't like cats do you?"

I took a sip while I mentally debated Jimmy's ability to handle the truth. "I do. But that wasn't a cat."

"What?"

"That was a mutant."

He laughed and leaned back against the couch. "Seriously? I think it's adorable."

"I think you're adorable. Thank you for my Yule present."

"You gonna let Dar keep it?"

"Like I have a choice."

"At least my money didn't go to waste then."

"What? How much was it?"

"You don't want to know."

We were treading into dangerous waters. "Yes. I do. Since Dar is keeping it, I'll give you the money for it. How much was it."

"Nope. My gift, my burden."

I looked over the back of the couch. Dar was pouring a saucer of milk for the mutant kitten. "Dar. Happy Yule. That's from me *and* Jimmy."

"Truly?"

"Truly." I turned back to Jimmy. "Now you *have* to take half of your money back."

He gave me a sad chuckle. "Sorry. I thought you would have liked it."

"I like that you thought of me." I gave him a soft smile and leaned over, kissing him gently. "Besides, I already have what I really want."

"What's that?"

"Your heart. That is more than enough."

"Still getting you something else."

"Fine. Just please, don't go overboard. How much was that cat?"

His cheeks flushed a little red. "It was only two."

"Hundred?"

"Uh...no."

"James Duncan. Are you telling me you spent two-thousand dollars on a lump of scrotum with ears?"

"Yeah. But when you say it that way, it doesn't seem like such a great idea."

I laughed and patted his leg. "That will learn you not to buy me expensive gifts. And I'm naming him Mr. Nutsack."

CHAPTER 11

"You're sure you can handle this?"

Jason nodded at me. "Go."

I cast one last quick glance around the store. Dwight, Dar, Yuki, and Shea were there again helping out. Jason had hired two more people to help with the evening shift. Josie had hired another two to help in the coffee shop. Things were as good as they were going to get, but I still felt like crap leaving them to face the hordes of holiday shoppers. Those people were insane.

I'd spent all of thirty minutes working in the store before almost getting into two fist fights and setting a large woman with a chicken-butt haircut ablaze. She had stomped up to the register demanding to speak to the manager. I one-upped her and introduced myself as the owner. Things went south from there and Jason actually had to step between us just as the words to my spell were tantalizingly wetting my lips.

It was after that altercation that Jason politely suggested I do some retail therapy to blow off some steam. "Okay, but call me if you need me."

"If we are attacked by an army of trolls, your services will be needed. You can't incinerate the customers, Dot.

Even if you own the place," he whispered and pleaded with his eyes.

"She wanted to use a Barnes & Noble gift card. At my store. What was I supposed to do?"

"Offer her a discount on her purchase after politely explaining why we can't accept our competitors' gift cards. She was confused between coupons and them. I gave her a ten percent markdown for her misunderstanding, and she was happy with that."

"I'da been happy if she was charcoal."

"She spent three hundred dollars, just to save enough at our store to match the balance of her gift card. You made out like a bandit. That's what I call a win."

"Reducing your enemies to ash is a win. Giving her a discount is a peace treaty at best and still feels like surrendering to me."

He sighed and rubbed the bridge of his nose. I needed to get out of there before he quit. "Dot…"

"I know. This is why you're the boss, and I just sign the checks." I leaned in and gave him a quick kiss. "You win. You're much better at this than I am. I'm going Yule shopping." I grabbed my purse out of the drawer in my desk and headed for the office door.

"You taking anybody with you?"

"Nope. You need them more than I do."

"But…"

"No buts. I'll be fine. Nice crowded mall."

"We don't have a mall."

"But Amersville does."

"Well, I don't think anybody wants to kill you in the neighboring town, so I'll keep your familiars."

"If they give you shit, tell them if I have a problem, they'll be the first to know. I'm not helpless."

He cocked an eyebrow at me and gave me *the look*.

"At defending myself."

142

"As long as it's not from customers, I'll agree with you."

"Not gonna let that go, are you?"

"Nope. Be safe."

"You, too."

I headed out the door and waved at everybody as I passed them walking toward the front door.

Where are you going? Yuki and Dar's mental voices assaulted me simultaneously.

Shopping.

I'm coming with you, Yuki said with a hint of anger in her voice.

No. Josie needs you.

So do you.

She needs you more.

You are my master, not her. It's my job to protect you. Please?

No.

I thought you were supposed to obey me?

I do. When you're not being stupid.

And just like that, I lost control. Dar's mental snicker was the icing on the cake. *Shut up.*

Yes, Master. I spun around to where he was stocking shelves to find him laughing.

I let out a frustrated snarl, scared four customers perusing the shelves closest to me, and stomped toward the door. Yuki slid up behind me smelling like a cinnamon Vietnamese triple fluff latte with a chocolate drizzle. "You actually serve any coffee today or are you wearing it all?"

"I spilled one. But at least I didn't set anybody on fire." She shot me an evil looking grin.

"This is going to be fun. I'm buying you ten pounds of garlic and a silver crucifix for Christmas."

"Can we stop by the attitude adjustment kiosk? I'll get you a gift certificate."

"Yes. Right after we stop by the joke store. We'll pick you up something nice. And funny."

She cackled next to me. I reached over and patted her spiky little head. She was a pain in the ass, but she was mine and I loved her dearly. "So, where we goin'?"

"The mall."

"Amersville?"

Inspiration struck. "No. We're going to Syracuse."

"Destiny, USA?"

"Yep."

"Can I drive?"

"Oh, hell no. We'll practice around town before we unleash you on the highway."

"Promise?"

"Yep."

She grinned as we walked up to my Sportage. I keyed the fob and before I got in, I saw her stiffen before she opened her door.

"What's wrong?"

"Company."

I closed my door and turned around. Flippy McRoadkill and Skoal-boy, or Jackson and Davis as Chief liked to call them, were standing at the entrance to the parking lot between the bookstore and the police station. They had balls, I'd give them that. Brains, not so much.

"Hello, ladies. What can I do for you today?" I was already pissed. If they wanted to start shit, I was going to beat them to it.

Their faces darkened, and Jackson actually took a step toward us when a cough from behind him stopped him in his tracks. I hadn't even noticed Chief. His timing was as impeccable as always. *Damn it.*

"Jackson?"

"Hey, Bill."

"Whatcha doin'?"

"Just sayin' hi to the ladies."

"Well, didn't I warn you to stay very far away from them?"

"You did."

"And you didn't listen."

"There's no law against talking."

"I didn't warn you to stay away from them because of the law, Jackson. I did it to keep you from getting hurt. Those two ladies right there aren't the bar trash you're used to. Trust me when I say they will fuck you up. They've already done it once."

The whole time Chief had been talking, Jackson never turned around. I could see the anger playing across his face. His friend, Davis, on the other hand looked like he was about to blow mud in his probably less than pristine white undergarments.

I leaned over my car and put my head innocently on my arms, letting my eyelids flutter at Jackson.

"Dot," Chief called.

"Yes, Chief?"

"Knock it off."

"Yes, sir. Mister Chief, sir."

I could hear his sigh from across the parking lot. "Let's go, Jackson. They were just leaving, anyway."

His lips curled in a snarl and he turned around, grabbing Davis by the arm and dragging him around the corner. The tension immediately left Yuki's body and she relaxed, turning around and opening the car door, finally.

I walked around the car and handed her the keys. "Listen to the radio for a minute. Let me thank the chief."

"Uh huh."

"I'm just saying thank you."

"With your lips, probably," she muttered under her breath.

"Yes. I say thank you with my lips. I say most things with my lips. You kind of need them for speech."

145

"And other things." She got into the car, started the engine, and closed the door. I heard the thumping of K-pop through the sealed doors as I walked over to Chief.

"Thanks," I said to him with a smile.

"I'm just glad I saw them follow you into the parking lot."

"You were worried about me?" I grinned at him.

"No. I was worried about the paperwork I was going to have to fill out by the time you were done with them. Just saving myself from that hellish nightmare."

"Don't worry. I have serious doubts about my ability to claim anything as self-defense with the DA after my ass. I would have left them breathing."

"Through which orifice?"

"Turtles can breathe through their ass. Did you know that? I could have turned him into a turtle."

"Just stay out of trouble. If they show up again, don't do *anything* but call me. Please?"

"Fine." I gave him an innocent smile and kissed him. "Seriously. Glad you were there. Going to the mall covered in blood never goes well."

He rolled his eyes. "You're going shopping?"

"Yeah. I almost incinerated a bitchy customer, so Jason kicked me out of my own store. Told me to go buy something to blow off steam."

He gave me the look that said he didn't know if I was joking or not. I chuckled to make him think I was kidding. "I give up. Have fun. Go shopping a few towns over, please."

"Heading to Syracuse."

"Oh?"

"Big mall. I figured I could do some serious damage there with my credit card."

"Just stay far away from trouble there. The police don't play."

146

"I don't want to play with the police there. The one here is much more fun." I ran my fingertip over the front of his jacket and gave him a sly smile.

"You just want me to put you in handcuffs again..."

"Yes, please."

∞ ∞ ∞

"I can't believe all that shit fit in your car." Yuki kept looking over her shoulder, waiting for the mountain of presents stuffed in my trunk and back seat to fall forward, burying her for all eternity. We had made four trips to the car, dropping off boxes and bags. Yuki might have had vampiric strength, but she only had two arms and tiny little hands.

"Me, neither. Thought we were going to have to buy another car there for a minute."

"Har har."

"You're right. I'm joking. There's no way I would have let you drive one."

"Meanie."

"Am not. I'ma good witch."

She smiled at me. "You are."

"Awww. Thanks, Yukester." I turned on my turn signal, further proving my good witchiness, as we coasted off the highway. The roads were getting icy and it looked like we would be getting some more snow before the night was over. We were definitely having a white Christmas unless there was a freak heatwave for the next three days.

"We going home to unload?"

"Yep."

"Anything planned for tonight?"

"Actually, no. We'll see what everybody is up to and order Chinese or something."

"Goody," she said sarcastically.

"Shit. Sorry."

"No worries. It's only four, can we run to the blood bank after we drop everything off?"

A nervous ball of fear welled up in my stomach. It had only been a day, but Lord Abernathy had yet to make an appearance. It would be my luck that he would show up while we were there to make a withdrawal. I sighed. If he was there, he was there. I wasn't going to hide from him, I just wasn't looking forward to dealing with him. "Sure."

"It's still daylight..." She must have picked up on my nervousness.

"Oh. That's right!" I smiled and turned onto our street.

The house I bought next to mine was completely empty. The neighbors had *finally* moved out. I didn't take possession of the house until the end of the month, but I didn't mind. It was better to have no neighbors than the stuck-up bitch who called me a slut while drooling over my Dar. *Growl. Snarl.*

"It's weird nobody being here. I even miss Jaeren," Yuki said softly.

"Don't tell him, but I do, too. The joys of being an elven king."

"King of Crayola, maybe."

"He's kind of cute when he's not being a princess."

I put the car in park and popped the trunk. "Wait here," Yuki told me. "I'll bring everything in."

"That will take you twelve trips. I can carry stuff, too."

"Talk to me when you can lift a car." She got out of the Sportage and closed the door softly. I sighed and turned the radio on, scanning the channels until the subtle sounds of Christmas music filled the rapidly cooling interior. Pulling my jacket a little tighter, I closed my eyes and leaned back into my seat, humming along with the music.

The music drifted off into the distance without my noticing. Muffled notes were clear enough for me to hum along with, but the beat and tempo were lost as it slowed, almost as if it were being played underwater. It was the same with Yuki's voice. I could barely make out my name as she screamed it. "Jingle Bells, Dot where the fuck are you," wasn't how the song went…

I opened my eyes and was looking up at Yuki who was staring in through my open door, something akin to panic firmly etched upon her face. Red tears were forming in the corner of her eyes.

Master? Her voice broke through my muddled thoughts. The Christmas music had faded into nothing, but music still caressed my ears. Music I had heard before. The gentle melody caressed my entire body, touching places it shouldn't as it tried to seduce me into staying.

"Staying?" I sat up and snapped out of it, some of Yuki's panic settling in *my* chest when I heard my muffled voice. *Yuki?*

Oh, thank fuck. Where are you?

Sitting right in front of you, I answered. Realization dawned on me. I had parked as close to the house as I could, the roof casting a shadow over the driveway as the sun set behind it. Without even trying, I had slipped into the shadow realm. Or it had dragged me there. I could feel the shadows swirling around me as they sang. It hadn't been the music caressing me lovingly.

Uh…pretty sure you're not.

I reached up and poked the tip of her nose. *Boop.*

She screamed and fell backward, jean covered ass bouncing on the cold concrete. "Don't fucking do that!"

I laughed and ran the same finger through the air, tearing a hole back into reality. Unsure how to just shift from one realm to another, I had to get out of my car to literally come back to earth. "Sorry. Couldn't resist."

"Why were you in the shadow realm?"

"I must have slipped through the veil when I dozed off listening to Christmas music."

"Yeah. Christmas music makes me want to shift to a parallel world, too. Especially Jingle Bells."

I reached down and offered her a hand, pulling her up off the cold, somewhat frozen concrete. "Well, that was fun."

"At least you didn't land on your ass."

"No, just another world." I looked through the back window. She had completely unloaded everything, so I couldn't have been gone that long. Thankfully. I might not have been able to resist their song if things had been a little different. "Come on. Let's go get you some food."

CHAPTER 12

I put the car into park and looked up at the sky through the windshield. It had gotten a little darker, but the sky still had a cotton candy pink tone. We had *maybe* an hour before it was time for vampire wakey, wakey, blood and stakey. Hopefully Lord Abernathy travelled slowly.

"Too bad they don't have a drive-thru."

"That would be convenient," Yuki said, nodding thoughtfully. "Probably be a little difficult to explain to the normies, though."

"Normies?" I laughed at her description of normal humans.

"You've never heard that before?"

"No."

"You need to watch more anime."

"You keep telling me this, but I'm a little old for cartoons," I answered and pulled the tinted door open by the freezing metal handle. The sterile smell of a medical facility wafted to my nose, the stench of sanitizer burning my nostrils.

Yuki gasped. "Calling anime a cartoon is like calling a romantic comedy a giggle porn."

"And that is what it shall be referred to from now on. Thank you." I chuckled as we made our way to the counter. A bored looking woman in a gray business suit was watching our exchange with disdain and an upturned nose. She looked like a librarian.

"Hi. Withdrawal for Christopher Lee."

"Sign right here, please." She set a clipboard with hastily scrawled names slathered across its otherwise pristine page.

The whole scene was rather plain and boring. I was half-expecting to be led to a secret lounge with shirtless bartenders who catered to the undead. In books, vampires didn't own blood banks, they owned bars that served blood. It was *very* unsexy.

I should open a vampire bar. Give the local fang-bangers something to do other than brood.

"Who's Christopher Lee?"

Yuki snickered as she finished signing her name and slid the clipboard back to the receptionist. "My account name."

"The actor?"

"Yes."

"I fail to see what Saruman has to do with…"

"Seriously?"

"Orcs?"

"No. Dracula. Christopher Lee played Dracula in *ten* different movies."

"Oh."

"Noob."

I blushed as the receptionist shook her head and headed toward the back room. "She's fun."

"Yeah. Most Servants are."

"Servants?"

"Humans who devote their lives to serving vampires."

"Thought they were called Renfields."

"In the movies, maybe. Not in real life."

"Excuuuse me." I rolled my eyes.

The *servant* came back carrying a small insulated bag and set it on the counter in front of Yuki. "Will there be anything else?"

"Nope. That was it." Yuki pulled out a small wallet from her back pocket. It looked older than she was. I knew what I was getting her for Yule. I reached out and stopped her, pulling out my card from my wallet and handing it to the receptionist.

She seemed to hesitate to take my card but plucked it from my fingers and stuck it chip first into the machine below the counter. She waited a moment, punched a few buttons, and handed the card and my receipt back to me. I stuffed it all back in my purse without looking. I'd check the going rate for hemoglobin when I got back home.

Yuki grabbed the bag and pulled the strap over her shoulder, heading for the door. I followed without so much as a goodbye for the chatty teller.

"I'm surprised you didn't complain about the price," Yuki finally said as we got into the car.

"I didn't look. Should I have?"

Yuki blushed. "Well, I'm not clan or family anymore. Dear Old Dad is charging me full price for food now."

I fished the receipt out of my purse and whistled at the total. "How many bags is that?"

"Seven. A week's worth."

"Seventeen hundred bucks for seven bags of blood?"

"Two-fifty a bag. Sucks to be a vampire." She practically pouted. Her debit card was tied to an account I had set up for her when her father had cut her off. I'd been giving her sort of an allowance that didn't come *close* to seventeen-hundred dollars a week.

"How have you been eating?"

"Making it stretch. Quarter bag a day for the past month. Finally saved enough to buy this much. Didn't you see me shake my head when you wanted to pay?"

I sighed and leaned back in my seat. "Why didn't you tell me?"

"Because you would have tried to fix it or pay for it. It's not your problem, it's mine."

"How much did you *used* to get charged for blood?"

She shifted uncomfortably in her seat. "Fifty."

I frowned. That still wasn't cheap. Thinking of the kids in the diner, I wondered how they paid for their supply. Maybe they were pulling a Yuki and making it last. Or getting back to their roots when they could get away with it and were feeding discreetly from the local population. I hadn't heard anything, and I'm sure Chief would have mentioned people getting bitten by vampires if anybody had reported it. There was *nothing* lordly about Abernathy. He was a crook. "Do any other vampires in town have to pay full price?"

"Not if they swear fealty or loyalty to the clan. Then they get the family discount."

I was *extra* pissed off because I had set the whole thing up for him to take over the local blood bank. "Something else to talk to your father about when he shows up."

Yuki sort of scoffed. "Thirty minutes ago, you were worried you were going to run into him. Now you *want* to yell at him?"

"If he takes advantage of the people who are supposed to be under his protection? Fuck yes. That pisses me off. Almost as much as you not telling me you were skimping on meals because you didn't have enough money." I reached over to her and sighed when she winced, expecting a blow I would never think of delivering. Instead, I caressed her cheek. "Silly vamp. You're mine. If you *ever* skimp on another meal, I'll tell Jaeren you think he's sexy and want to spend more time with him."

She gave me a shy smile, a nod, and rubbed her face against the fingers I had used to rub her cheek. "Thank you, Master."

"For what?"

"Being you."

A bit of wetness slipped between my fingers and her skin. She was crying. "Well, don't make me have this talk with you again. You need something, you tell me. Got it, kiddo?"

"Yes, Mother." She let out a short bark of laughter and seemed to melt with relief against my hand. Remembering, I pulled it away. "Is that okay? Sorry. I didn't mean to touch you if you don't want to be."

She blinked in surprise. "You did it, and I didn't notice until I felt how comforting it was. I don't like to be touched, but I don't mind if it's you." She blushed. Hard.

"You're not..." I gave her the look.

"No! I'm not attracted to you. I mean, you're beautiful, but that's not my thing."

Sighing a little in relief, I nodded. "I love you, kiddo. But, I'm glad you don't..."

"Nope. I love you, too. But anything more than a caress, maybe a snuggle, and I'll bite your ankles off." She chomped for emphasis.

Laughing, I reached out and pushed the start button, letting the engine warm up for a second before I put it into reverse. We were about a block away when she started eyeing the bag sitting on her lap. "Eat if you're hungry. Nobody will notice and my windows are tinted."

"You don't mind?"

"Watching you? No." The memories of Ellis' hot blood hitting my tongue almost made me groan.

She nodded and pulled the Velcro apart, snagging a bag and ripping off the corner with her teeth. She put the open end in her mouth and suckled on it like a melted freezer pop. "Mmm," she started to say as the blood instantly flushed her cheeks.

"Make sure you eat the whole damn thing. No more skimping, Skimpy."

155

"Yes, Master."

We were almost in my driveway when we realized something was *very* wrong. It started out as stomach pains. I'd almost assumed it was from overeating after going so long without, until she started panting. Then she turned pale and started sweating. "You okay?"

"I think? Not feeling so hot."

By the time we turned onto our street, she was green and clutching her stomach, bent over and wheezing with her head between her knees. "Yuki?"

She held up her hand. When we *finally* pulled into the driveway, she opened her door frantically, and fell out onto the driveway. By the time I shut off the car and had my door open, I heard her retching the contents of her stomach. Practically running around the car, I skidded to a stop while she was throwing up black blood onto the pristine white snow beside the car.

"What the hell? Was the blood bad?"

She couldn't answer. Not for a few minutes while she expelled it all. All I could do was kneel beside her and try to comfort her. I grabbed a handful of snow and used it to cool my fingers before pressing them against her forehead with one hand, and her neck with the other.

"Does that help?"

She nodded between heaves.

We stayed there until the retching stopped and she fell sideways. Half of her was in the blood splattered snow, and the other half was on the driveway.

Worried, I got my arms under her and hoisted her as I stood. She felt like she weighed almost nothing as I ran for the house. My keys were in the car, but I didn't hesitate to kick the front door open, shattering the lock and splintering the wood around it. Blinking in surprise, I turned and slid inside, careful not to bang her head against the frame of the door.

Taking her to my room, I set her unconscious form on the bed while I stripped her and me before picking her up and taking her into the shower. Her body temperature usually hovered around room levels. She felt almost frozen. I wanted to get her under the hot water to warm her up and get the blood off her.

She didn't stir as I held her effortlessly with one arm and used my other to sluice the blood from her pale white skin. It only took a moment and then I just held her in my arms under the spray, letting it warm her.

How long we stood there, I didn't have a clue. It was the sound of footsteps that broke me out of the fearful trance I had fallen into. Slowly, the shower door opened, and Jimmy stood there with a baseball bat in one of his hands. "Is she okay? What the fuck happened?"

He dropped the bat and grabbed a couple of towels out of the linen closet. One he set on the counter, the other he opened and held out for me to put Yuki into. It was awkward, especially with the slippery shower floor, but I managed to get her into his arms without spilling her, or me, to the floor.

Jimmy wrapped the towel around her and lifted her up, straining a lot more than I had when she passed out, and took her into the bedroom and got her under the covers. He touched the back of his hand to her forehead and frowned. "Is she supposed to be hot or cold?"

"Usually about the same temperature of wherever she is. Why?"

"She's freezing. How long were you in the shower?"

"Twenty minutes at least."

He frowned a little harder. "Maybe she needs blood?"

I stood there, wrapped in the towel at a loss. I had no idea what was wrong with her or how to fix it. "I think that's what started this whole thing."

"What?"

157

"Blood. We stopped at the blood bank." I sat down next to Yuki and looked up at Jimmy. "She hasn't been eating because Lord Douchernathy jacked up the price of her blood supply. She downed a whole bag in the car and got *really* sick just as we were getting home. She puked in the yard and passed out. I brought her in and got her in the shower, trying to warm her up."

He leaned over, close to her head, and whispered her name. When she didn't respond, he said her name rather loudly and gently shook her shoulder. Frowning again, he lifted one of her eyelids and tilted her head toward the light. "Her pupils aren't dilating, but I don't know anything about vampire physiology."

"Me neither."

"Dot?"

"Yeah?"

"You don't think the blood was…poisoned?"

I started to shake my head but stopped. It was a possibility I hadn't thought of. I'd just assumed that maybe it was bad. There was only one way to test it. Taste test. "Grab the bag out of the car for me? The empty one on the floor, too."

He narrowed his eyes and nodded. I sat there watching my familiar until he came back into the room. "What the hell did you do to your door?"

"Panicked and kicked it open."

"You should have Bill hire you as the police battering ram."

"No jokes, please." I sighed, severely worried.

"Sorry. You know it's my coping mechanism. You should have seen how hard I was straining not to crack any while you were in the shower."

"Proud of you. Hand me the empty." It was the bag that got her sick. I'd start there.

"What are you going to do?" He handed it to me and opened the cooler bag.

Without taking the time to think about what I was about to do. I put the corner of the bag in my mouth and sucked some of the remnants into my mouth, swishing it around.

"Dot!" Jimmy tried to pry the bag from my mouth.

"It doesn't taste like poison."

He stared at me incredulously. "Uh. If Yuki drank the whole fucking bag, I'm sure she would have noticed. Not all poisons have flavor."

"Oh." I felt pretty stupid. When he used logic like that, I could have saved myself some uncomfortable tastes lingering in my mouth.

One thing I *did* learn was that human blood didn't do *anything* for me. Vampires, yes. Dark elves, yes. Humans, no. It was like drinking a can of pop that had been left open for a week. It was flat and gross, kind of syrupy. It tasted dead.

"I can call my buddy at the hospital. He runs tests on the blood of car accident victims. Maybe he can test it for poison?"

"You just happen to know someone who tests blood? Why am I totally shocked by this coincidence?"

"Dot. This is Cedar Falls. Everybody knows *someone* who does something."

"Makes sense. Please."

He took the empty bag of blood and the cooler, heading for the kitchen. I listened as he called his friend and made up some shit excuse about testing the blood one of his friends had gotten as an infusion, blah blah blah. He also shoved everything in the fridge to keep it from spoiling.

I caressed Yuki's cheek while she was unconscious. I could still feel the connection between us, and it flared with my touch. She stirred a little, whimpered, but didn't wake. She was fading. I could feel it.

Yuki?

There was no response. No matter how many times I mentally called out to her. Nervously, I started to bite my nail as I watched her for any sort of movement.

She is dying...

The goddess' voice echoed in my head.

"I know," I whispered to the air around me, surprised that the Lady had stepped in for a visit. She'd been very silent as of late.

Heal her.

"How?"

You always ask the questions you already know the answer to, Sister.

I'd gone from daughter, to niece, to sister. Blushing, I felt anything but. She was a god, I was...Dot. I was just keeping my father's powers warm for him while screwing everything and everyone around me with them. Because I couldn't control them. I couldn't control *me*. "The blood wasn't poisoned."

No. She is not what she once was. She is what you are making her. She could already walk in the light and you hadn't even donned the mantle of your father. You are changing her.

I'm killing her.

No. She needs fuel for the fire that burns within her...

Not blood?

I felt her mental shrug. *Does blood sustain you?*

It has.

But not the blood of the children of man...

And then it clicked. Just as it always did when the Lady spoke to me. She worked everything out in my head until she drowned me in understanding. I drank blood. But the blood of elves and vampires...

Without thinking about what I was doing, I brought my wrist to my mouth and tore it open with the fangs that I knew would be there when I needed them. Heat poured down my arm as my lifeblood wet my skin. Quickly, I

160

brought the wound to her slightly parted lips and pressed it against them.

Nothing happened for more than few moments until I felt her tongue gently slide over the gash in my flesh. I whimpered when her lips pulled apart, creating suction as she pulled the blood from my wound and drank.

Pleasure washed over me as Yuki moaned against my skin. I let her drink and drink and drink until her eyes opened and she let go of my arm with hands I hadn't felt.

"Master?"

"Welcome back."

Looking around the room, she finally realized where she was. "What happened?"

I shook my head, got up, and walked around the bed, sliding under the covers next to her. "You passed out in the driveway," I answered and put my head back against the pillow, offering her the crook of my arm. She rolled over and put her head on my shoulder, sighing deeply. "Do you feel better?"

"I feel. That's an improvement. I remember barfing and then blackness." She cocked her head, listening to Jimmy on the phone. "I was poisoned?" She sat up, noticing the towel. "Why am I wet?"

"You were freezing and covered in blood. I washed you off when Jimmy showed up."

"Why is there a bat on your floor?"

"He thought we were attacked, I assume."

"I was poisoned?"

Shaking my head, I didn't know how to break the news to her. "No. I don't think so." I sat up and brought my knees up to my chest, a little difficult in the towel, but I managed. Putting my arms over my knees, I rested my head as I turned to look at her. "Know how I wanted nothing more in the world than to eat those vampire kids?"

"Yes?"

I sighed and decided to rip the Band-aid off. "I wouldn't suggest drinking human blood again. Ever."

The front door was battered a second time as Dar shot through the house, sliding to a stop on the hardwood floor in front of my bed. "You're okay?"

We both looked up at him. Yuki nodded.

"Thank the Lady. What happened? I felt your pain and your surrender. I felt your spark fading!"

"Calm down, Darling. She's fine." I stared at him in confusion. Why was Yuki changing, but not Dar? They were both my familiars. He had been so worried that the binding we had shared would have changed me, but it was more likely that the complete opposite was going to happen. "Hey."

"Yes, Master?"

"How are you?"

"I am fine?" He gave me a quizzical look. "Should I not be?" He started patting his chest worriedly.

"Nothing's going on with you, right?"

"Such as?"

"Extra-long horns? Extra demony feelings? Hair in funny places? Is your voice getting deeper?"

"I do not understand?"

I shook my head. "Nothing. Just, if anything weird happens to you, let me know right away, okay?"

"Yes, Master."

"He said if he runs the test, he'll probably get fired. We're friends, but not that good of friends." Jimmy sighed and stuffed the phone in his back pocket before noticing a very awake Yuki for the first time. "Well, I'll be a vampire's uncle. She's okay?"

"Yeah. The blood wasn't poisoned," I answered confidently.

"Rotten?"

"You? Sometimes, but I love you anyway."

162

"No jokes, please," he answered drolly, throwing my words back at me.

I grinned at him.

"So, what was it?"

"Our little badass here can't eat people no more."

"Huh?" All three of them answered in unison.

CHAPTER 13

"Why are you pouting?" Jimmy reached over and turned the heat up a tad, warming the inside of his truck a little bit more. He must have noticed me shivering.

"I'm not pouting. Just didn't want to leave Yuki."

"She was perfectly fine and more than happy to go to bed with a big smile on her face. I think she likes Dar's blood more than yours."

After she had woken after her episode, I'd offered her more blood. She seemed tempted and hesitant at the same time. "I don't want to take too much from you at once," she'd answered before Dar helpfully volunteered a blue wrist. As soon as she bit his wrist, they both started feeling the pleasure. I had to leave the room to get the jelly monster to shut the hell up, and I hated feeling jealous. Especially when Dar was just looking out for the both of us. He should have been rewarded, not seeing me snarling in fury.

"I know. I'm just worried about her."

Dar's comforting hand touched my shoulder. He and Shea, who had shown up slightly after Dar, and then Jimmy decided that the four of us should go get steak to replenish the blood we had donated. Not that I trusted him, but the thought of a medium raw steak really sounded good. "It is not like we are ever apart from her. She will be fine and can contact us instantaneously if that changes."

165

"I know," I said with a sigh, giving up and deciding to enjoy the dinner and the company.

The parking lot was mostly empty as we pulled in. "Everybody must be getting ready for Christmas," Jimmy said with a smile.

"Three days," I said with a sigh. I still needed to decorate the house. Luckily, my mother had taught me her spells long ago. Maybe I would do it after dinner and surprise everyone. I loved Yule, but I'd been so busy with one thing after another, I'd hardly had a chance to enjoy the season.

"Technically, Christmas Eve is when the humans *really* start their holiday. That's two days away."

"I find the different religions of your world interesting," Dar said softly from the back seat.

"Wish the people of this world thought that way. Mostly they just like to argue. Or start wars."

"I find that fascinating as well. Horrible, but fascinating."

"Truth."

Jimmy shut off the truck and we all piled out, heading toward the front door of Bunyan's like a ravenous pack of hyenas. Except Shea. He calmly trailed behind us, a curious smile under the black hoodie I'd given him.

I slowed and draped my arm around his waist while we walked. "You seem quiet tonight. Quieter. Everything okay?"

"Yes, Lady." The nervous quiver in his voice told me that it wasn't, but I wasn't going to poke and prod him to tell me. I'd poke him and prod him for other reasons, but never that.

"Well. If you want to talk, I'm your witch."

He leaned against me and tilted his head against my shoulder. While we were walking. If I tried that, I'd have tripped over my own feet and gotten a mouthful of pavement for my efforts. Steak sounded way better.

166

"Hi! Welcome to Bunyan's. Just the four of you?" Tiffany, the hostess, practically drooled when she saw the guys. I found my happy Zen place and ignored the hungry look she gave them.

She sat us at a largish booth in the back. It took only a few minutes of menu browsing before Chelsea showed up. "Oh! Hi. Welcome back," she said with a fang filled smile. Every tooth was visible and sharp. How she didn't sever her own tongue every time she talked was a complete mystery to me. The fact that I couldn't see her glamour, even if I tried, bothered me. Her face, while still beautiful even with a gaping maw, was not conducive to eating.

"Hi, Chelsea. How are you?" I managed to say it with a smile.

"Good! Welcome back. Can I get you a round of drinks?"

Shea and I ordered wine. Dar and Jimmy opted for their usual beers. We perused the menu while she got our drinks. I looked up at Dar and he was giving me a grin. Nothing excited him like meat. We were a lot alike, he and I.

"Shall we?"

"What?"

He pointed to the back of the menu to The Babe. The sixty-four-ounce ox steak we had each polished off during our last visit. "Can we?"

"We can." My ravenous beast had died down somewhat, thankfully. But the thought of that much meat made me happy.

"You're going to eat all that?" Jimmy was staring at the back of his menu to see what we were eyeballing.

"Yep. Been there, done that. Literally got the T-shirt."

"That's four pounds of steak…"

"Yep."

"That's a lot of meat."

"Yep. I can handle it."

167

He chuckled. "I'm sure you can…"

I pinched his side, but grinned at him, knowing he was joking and not being an ass. "You gonna watch?"

"With rapt fascination."

"And a healthy erection."

"Bet your ass."

"Nope. That is, and shall remain, off limits for the foreseeable future." I was still paranoid after getting arrested with the butt plug incident. A fact that wasn't lost on James.

He chuckled into his menu. I swatted his leg. "You do not care for anal play?" Shea asked without any sense of embarrassment.

"Apparently, I do. Too much."

"I do not understand?" He looked around the table for an explanation. Jimmy was turning beet red, trying not to burst out laughing.

"When I was arrested, I had a toy that was controlled remotely in my butt. Jason didn't know I was in the back of a cop car and cranked it up." I figured it was easier to tell him the truth rather than try to make up some excuse.

"Oh. I understand."

"Yep." I flushed and set down my menu just as Chelsea brought our round of drinks. Jimmy was between her and I. She reached in front of him and set two glasses of wine down in front of me, and one in front of Shea across from me before giving the boys their beers.

"You need a few minutes?"

"I think we're ready," I answered, looking at Shea for confirmation. I didn't know if he liked steak, so I hoped he found something appetizing on the menu. His nod was all the answer I needed. "Yep. We're ready."

She looked at me and I grinned at Dar.

"Two Babe's, medium rare with baked potatoes."

"Make that three. I'll try it, too," Jimmy added. Chelsea nodded and scribbled our orders down before looking at Shea.

"I'll have the smothered chicken, please."

"You got it. I'll have it out to you soon." She grabbed the menus and headed toward the kitchen.

Sipping my wine, I sat back in the booth and leaned against Jimmy, who seized the opportunity to kiss the top of my head. "You look beautiful."

"You're just trying to butter me up."

"I wouldn't use butter. Maybe whip cream or drizzled chocolate."

An image of me, covered in confections, and the three of them surrounding me and making me their dessert fluttered across my brain and sent tiny shivers of pleasure to all the right places. "Oooh. We might have to try that. Later."

"In the privacy of your bedroom?"

"Uh…yeah?"

"What fun would that be?" Jimmy laughed evilly.

Knowing full well that he had seemed a little too happy when the three of us agreed to go to dinner with him, I sighed.

"You don't want to play?" He didn't sound disappointed, just making sure I was in the mood after everything that had happened. He might be a perv, but he was a considerate one.

He earned a grin. "After the day I had, I want to say no, but you always make me feel so good, so how could I?"

The evil grin made its way back onto his face. Lowering his lips to my ear, he gave it a little lick. "You're over-dressed," he whispered.

Looking down at my outfit, a shiver of fear swept through me. I'd taken my jacket off and hung it up when we walked into the restaurant. That left me in leggings and an oversized sweater. "Uh… I'm literally wearing two pieces of clothing. How can I possibly be overdressed?" I whispered my response, not wanting the others to hear. Glancing over, I should have known it was futile. Dar was smiling into his beer and Shea was looking from Jimmy to me, not understanding, either.

"You should definitely take off your pants. That sweater is as long as a dress."

Not bothering to whisper, I stared at him. "You want me to sit here, in a restaurant, completely naked from the waist down?" He had lost his mind. I'd made it a moral imperative to never get arrested again. His plan posed a serious risk to my imperativeness.

He kissed my ear again. "Your sweater is long enough, and you wear dresses without panties when we go out…"

"That's a dress. This is a sweater."

"Are you afraid?" He gave me a little smile.

"Yes!"

"Good. That will make it better."

"Make what better?"

"What we're going to do to you."

And there it was. He said, "We," not, "I." Dar began to sniff the air and got a glazed look in his eye as my excitement seeped into my leggings. Between the promise of being played with by all three of them and the fear of getting caught, I didn't stand a cookie's chance in Josie's lunchbox. Glancing around the restaurant, the nearest people were three booths away, and they were more focused on each other than anyone else around them. "I can't," I found myself saying, but *wanting* to. Wanting to more than anything.

"Shea, would you help her get out of her pants?"

"It would be my pleasure," he said and slipped under the table like a stick of melted butter. *Damn elves and their bendy parts.* If I had tried to what he did effortlessly, I would have ended up in traction. Which might have been fun, too.

170

I was staring at Jimmy when I felt Shea's hands slide up my thighs, under my sweater, and begin tugging on the waist of my leggings. He got them down to my ass with no problem, and I momentarily debated not listening to Jimmy, but my ass lifted off the seat on its own volition. My pants didn't stand a chance. They were down around my ankles in a fraction of a moment. The cool leather felt soothing against my bare ass cheeks.

Shea lifted my feet out of my pants, and then suddenly Dar was lifting them above the table and smiling at them. "Stop!" I hissed the word across the table, wanting him to hide them beside him or something. Instead, he grinned and brought the crotch of them to his face, inhaling deeply. My thighs parted and I felt Shea's lips kiss me gently across my folds as I mewled and buried my face into Jimmy's shoulder.

"I think she might be a little embarrassed," Jimmy said with a small chuckle to Dar.

"I think you might be right, James. But she does smell exquisite." He finally put my leggings down on the bench beside him.

"She tastes that way, too." Shea's muffled voice reached our ears from under the table before he planted one last kiss and slipped his tongue between my lips. I gasped and involuntarily thrust my hips toward him. He didn't take the bait and I felt him pull away from me. I watched in rapt fascination as his head appeared back above the table as he slithered back into his seat.

"Happy now?" I stuck my tongue out at Jimmy who shook his head.

Reaching under one of my legs, he lifted it and put it over his, fully exposing me beside him as his fingers slid under the table and ran lovingly and teasingly through the hair above my practically gushing sex. "Now, I am."

"Jimmy," I whispered his name, practically begging him to touch me lower.

171

"Can I get you a couple more beers? Wine?" Chelsea's question made me squeak and try to close my legs, but Jimmy held me still, not stopping what he was doing.

"I'll have another," Jimmy said. "Dar? Shea?" I hadn't even touched my wine so I reached out and downed one of the two glasses while Jimmy teased me. I couldn't even look up at our waitress.

"Please," Dar answered.

Watching Shea, he nodded but didn't tear his eyes from mine. "Yes, please."

"What about you, sweetie? Need another one?"

She was talking to me while my boyfriend was exposing me to her and playing with my nether regions. I was going to come and he wasn't even touching my pussy, just letting his fingers drift through my tuft of hair.

As much as I didn't want to look up, I did. Her eyes were staring at the hand in my crotch and she was biting her lip gently between her pointed teeth.

"Yes. I'll have another, please."

Her eyes shifted to mine and she nodded. "I'll make s-s-sure the h-h-hostess doesn't seat anyone near you. Have fun," she whispered and turned around to get us some more drinks.

Dar snickered and Shea grinned at me. His grin was more sinister looking than Jimmy's and I felt myself get a little wetter. Unable to stand it, I gasped and buried my face into Jimmy's shoulder again.

"Should we give her a little release, or should we keep teasing her?" Jimmy put it to a vote, letting his fingers slide down and over my lips, collecting some moisture and rubbing it all over me. My hips started bucking and I started sliding against the leather. As quickly as he started, he stopped, trailing slick fingers through my hair again and just teasing me.

"I do not think it matters. One way or another, she is going to come," Dar said appreciatively.

"I think you're right," Jimmy answered him with a small laugh. "Isn't that right, baby girl?"

I just nodded against him, my breath coming in ragged gasps.

"You want me to plunge my fingers inside you? Do you want me to rub your clit? Or do you want Shea to make you come with his mouth? How about a pen, do you have a pen I could borrow?" His grin grew twice as big.

Ignoring him, I looked over at Shea and nodded, my choice at least made by me, not giving Jimmy time to think of something better or worse. Like straddling his cock in the middle of the restaurant. I sincerely doubted my ability to say no at that point.

Shea smiled at me and slid back under the table. With my leg over Jimmy's he had plenty of room to work his magic on my sensitive clit with his lips and tongue. My breathing morphed into near hyperventilation as he swirled his tongue in dazzling circles over my flesh. Jimmy's lips locked against mine and his tongue darted into my mouth in an effort to muffle my moans. When two of Shea's long fingers plunged inside me while his tongue danced across me, I came. I came hard. The restaurant darkened, and I didn't know if it was the Shadows surging into reality as pleasure fired every nerve in my body, or if my vision just faded from the intensity of my orgasm.

When I could finally see and sit up, Shea was back in his seat and Chelsea was setting food in front of us. "I hope you enjoy your chicken as much as your before dinner dessert," she told Shea with a grin as she set his food in front of him. "And I hope you enjoy your steak almost as much as your lover's lips," she told me with a wink and left us to our meal.

I knew one thing. The color of my cheeks probably matched the color of my medium-raw steak.

173

∞ ∞ ∞

Jimmy locked the door behind him. He was holding a can of whip cream in his hand as he grinned at me and walked toward the bed. As soon as Shea, Dar, and I had gotten into the room, they removed the sweater that had been the only thing I was allowed to wear for the remainder of our meal and the ride home and lay me in the center of the bed, spread open with my hands by my sides. Then they undressed each other as they planted little kisses all over each other right next to me. They were beyond beautiful together and by the time they finished, a wet spot had already formed on my comforter beneath me. Every time I had reached down to touch my aching pussy, one of them reached out and stopped me by grabbing my wrist.

Jimmy set the can of cream on the dresser and shrugged off his shirt and jeans. He picked the can back up and strode confidently toward the bed just as Shea popped Dar's cock into his mouth and started sucking. I didn't know where to look or who to watch. They were all equally gorgeous.

Jimmy knelt on the floor by the bed and tilted the can, letting enough out to cover each of my nipples before trailing a line of cream down my chest, over my stomach, and not stopping until just above my clit. The cold wetness caused my back to arch against the bed as the heat of my body melted the cream. Dar latched on to one nipple and Jimmy the other as Shea pulled Dar's cock from his mouth and crawled up the bed between my legs. He started licking the cream from my stomach.

Groaning, I melted into their mouths. "Fuck me."

"Who?" Jimmy asked curiously.

"I don't care. I need a cock in me now."

Jimmy chuckled and volunteered as tribute. He stood behind Shea and gently stroked his hip. Shea understood

174

the message and turned, lying alongside me and settling down with his cock by my head. I didn't need to be asked twice as I turned my head and pulled him into my mouth at the exact time that Jimmy parted my pussy with his cock. I hissed against Shea's flesh as Jimmy slid his entire length inside me with one long, hard thrust. I put my feet flat against the mattress beneath me and spread my knees as he pulled back and thrust into me once again.

"Fuck, fuck, fuck," I managed to mumble with my mouth full.

Dar stood and walked around the bed. With Shea's cock in my mouth, his ass was on the edge of the bed. Dar lifted Shea's leg and lightly let his fingers trail over the cock I was sucking and the balls beneath it.

"May I?" Dar asked something of Jimmy who stopped thrusting inside me. I whimpered.

"Help yourself," Jimmy answered.

Dar's fingers massaged the flesh of my lips around Jimmy's cock, collecting my wetness against his fingers. Then they reappeared below Shea's balls and began lightly stroking Shea's ass while I sucked. My eyes widened as Jimmy started pounding inside me again, and the tip of Dar's cock touched the spot he had lubed up with my wetness. Slowly he inserted himself into Shea, mere inches from my face. Not going to lie, that was pretty fucking hot. Between Jimmy's cock and that, I had my first orgasm since we got home. I had three at the restaurant by the time we finished dinner. Jimmy even traded seats with Dar, so that each one of them had a chance to make me come.

Dar must have been watching Jimmy. Hell, they were probably high fiving each other above Shea and me. His strokes into Shea matched Jimmy's into me and without warning, Shea gasped and unloaded into my mouth as Dar and I brought him to the point of coming.

I gently stroked the soft skin of his hip as he emptied himself into my mouth while I tried very hard not to let any of it spill from my mouth. Relentlessly, he shot over and over against my tongue.

Jimmy grunted and his thrusts became erratic as he came inside my pussy. I was already wet, but he added to it as he lowered his lips to mine and found my lips with his. "I love you," he whispered as he pulled away and stood up.

"I love you, too."

Dar pulled himself from Shea's ass and walked into the bathroom. He shut the door and I heard the sink running for a moment while I caught my breath. When the door opened, he grinned at me and moved to the spot Jimmy had vacated before plunging himself into my pussy as Jimmy brought his cock to my lips.

Still not satiated, I reached out and pulled him to my mouth, tasting his come as well as mine as I slowly started bobbing my head against him.

"Fuck, that feels good."

Shea got up from beside me and put a leg over me, straddling my stomach and working his legs backward toward my head. With my free hand, I began rubbing his ass as I wondered what he was up to. When his tongue found my clit, I gasped.

Dar's cock pulled from my pussy and found Shea's mouth before plunging back into me while Shea's tongue played with my clit. They kept repeating the motion while I sucked Jimmy. It was the most erotic thing ever, and I couldn't have felt more loved as the four of us pleasured each other in unison.

Dar announced that he was going to come, and Shea suckled my clit as his fingers encircled Dar's cock just outside my entrance, squeezing him while he emptied his balls inside me. I was just about to come, when Dar pulled away, giving Shea the opportunity to clean all of our combined juices from me. His fingers slid around my clit, tugging and teasing while he did it and I didn't stand a chance against the onslaught of pleasure. I groaned against

Jimmy's cock as I came, and he came again. Instead of swallowing it, I pulled away and let him come against my lips as I stroked him, feeling his hot wetness splash against my skin and dribble down over my neck. Dar began to kiss my face and neck, removing all traces of Jimmy's pleasure as I sighed in contentment.

"That was fucking hot," I said to no one.

The three happy grunts around me sounded like an agreement.

CHAPTER 14

I was dreaming someone was driving a ten-penny nail through the center of my forehead. Needless to say, I woke up screaming and sat straight up in bed. Candace squeaked and dropped to the floor.

"Candace?" I sounded groggy and looked at the alarm clock next to my bed. It was six o'clock in the morning, and I groaned. I had actually fallen asleep for three hours and if it weren't for Candace tapping me on the forehead and inducing nightmares, I might have slept for several more hours. "What is it?"

She got up off the floor, pulling herself up by my mattress and staring at me intently. Leaning closer, she whispered, "Something is wrong. I feel people outside…"

That was enough for me to fling the covers off myself and practically run to the front door. Luckily, I had been a little chilly after my shower last night and pulled on a heavy sleeping shirt. I was mad enough to have run out the front door naked.

I undid the deadbolt and turned the knob. My kick last night had snapped the latch from the knob and splintered the wood around it. Luckily, I had been able to magick the whole damn thing back together. Flinging the door open, I turned the porch and floodlights on, illuminating the yard in a brilliant white glare.

There was nobody there.

That was enough to set my nerves on edge. I trusted Candace's feelings more than my own eyes. Readying a stun spell, I stepped outside in my bare feet, ignoring the cold seeping up my legs from the frozen concrete beneath my feet.

"Who's there?" I said it with authority, leaving no doubt that I knew *someone* was there.

The sound of something hollow and metal striking the driveway, and the shadow of someone running from the side of the house and around the fence of the neighbor's property, caught my eye.

"*Ná bogadh*!" My car must have blocked the spell, because they kept running. I charged after them and almost slipped on the step. And stopped when I caught sight of their feet as they landed in the bed of the big blue pickup truck as the driver gunned the engine, surging down the road and whipping around the corner in a squeal of knobby tires.

It was my two buddies. There wasn't a doubt in my mind. Sighing, I walked over to my car and stopped, snarling in anger. Beside my front tire was a can of spray paint. It had made the noise I'd heard when Davis dropped it. That wasn't what had pissed me off. It was the gouges in my paint. They had used either a screwdriver or a knife to carve upside-down pentagrams into both doors and slashed both tires on the same side. The other side, the one facing the house, was fine.

"Amateurs," I grumbled and turned toward the house, determined to fix the damage later. After Chief saw what his town troublemakers did.

"Candace, bring me my phone," I called toward the door.

The bastards spray painted my garage door, too. Horribly. It was almost illegible and not even spelled correctly. *Thow shale not suffer a which to live.*

180

I didn't know whether to call Chief or the grammar police.

Candace came out the door in her slippers and coat, careful not to drop my phone as she picked her way across the icy drive. "Was someone here?"

I pointed at the door in the pre-dawn light.

"Was it kids?"

"No. Just adults with a third-grade education. They got my car, too," I answered as I took the phone from her and called Chief. He answered on the third ring.

"What's wrong?"

"Good morning to you, too."

"Sorry. But if you're calling me this early, it means something's wrong…"

"Yeah. You dressed?"

"At the diner."

"Good. Come over to my house and if you see your friends in the big blue pickup…bring them with you."

"Shit."

"Yeah."

The line clicked dead. "Coffee?"

I blinked at Candace, staring at me with a peculiar look on her face. "No, sweetie. You get back in bed. You have to go to work soon."

She turned and headed toward the house while I waited for the cavalry. Before he showed up, Candace came back outside carrying a tray with three mugs of coffee steaming heavily in the frosty air. She handed one to me, set the tray on the hood of my car, and took one for herself.

"Thanks, sweetie. Why you no listen?"

"Because it is cold, and you need coffee. But you would never ask."

I leaned over and kissed the top of her head. "You're right. Thank you."

"You are welcome." She gave me one of her patented, sunlight infused grins, and I felt a little warmer inside.

Flashing blue lights illuminated the end of the street, but there were no sirens wailing. I'm sure my remaining neighbors would appreciate the kind gesture.

Chief pulled into the driveway behind my Sportage. His face went from worried to exasperated in a fraction of a second. I saw the change through his windshield. Killing the engine, he opened his door and got out of the Jeep.

"Morning, Sunshine," I said with a little smile.

"Lemme guess..."

"Okay, but the first two don't count."

He slammed the door and walked over to me. "You're okay?"

"Yeah. Everybody but my garage door and car are fine." I pointed at the etched damaged and wounded rubber.

"They didn't go after you at all? That would turn this into an assault charge."

"Nope. Davis ran as soon as I hit the lights and came outside. I got off a stun spell but missed."

"You missed?"

"Pre-coffee aim and he was using my car as a shield."

"You saw him?"

"His shoes as he leapt into the bed of the pickup."

"Well, there's cameras on the corner on Main. I'm sure I can find the footage of him shitting his britches in the back of the truck. That should be enough to pin the both of them at the scene."

"If the DA prosecutes, you mean." I rolled my eyes.

"If he doesn't, I'll file a complaint. I'm getting pretty tired of this bullshit and it needs to stop before someone gets hurt, namely Jackson and Davis."

Candace took the opportunity to hand Chief a cup of coffee. He nodded his thanks and took a sip. "That's good. Thanks, Candace."

"You are welcome. If you need anything else, let me know. It is too cold out here."

"Thank you, sweetie," I called after her, getting a little wave over her shoulder in response.

"Well, let me take some pictures for evidence. Maybe I'll be able to get some prints off the spray paint, but with as cold as it is...he was most likely wearing gloves."

"I don't think he's that smart." I leaned against the hood of the car and cast a small warmth spell around me, watching Chief get to work, scooping up the can of paint into a large bag before sealing it up. There was lots of bending over on his part, and smiles and eyebrow raisings on mine. He was a pleasure to watch and sexy in his uniform.

"How did you know they were out here?"

"I didn't. Candace felt them and came and woke me up."

"Your wards didn't go off?"

I blushed in embarrassment. "They were human and didn't intend me harm. I'll fix it to include intent to harm my property as soon as you're done."

He rolled his eyes and shook his head.

"Shut up. You didn't even use shields before I rolled into town."

"True." He sighed. "I'm just worried. Between the DA, the Doc, and these two clowns, things could go south pretty damn quick."

"At least it's warm in the south."

"You know what I mean."

"Yeah. And I've got a little more for you to worry about. I was given a heads up by a nice gentleman at the diner that they are holding anti-witch meetings somewhere in town."

Chief nodded. "I'd heard the same thing but haven't seen or heard anything concrete."

"Everyone fears the unknown. We'll get through this. Somehow."

"I just hope it's without someone getting hurt."

"Jackson and Davis?"

"I was thinking more of our witches. If someone ends up getting burned at the stake…"

"I won't let that happen."

"I know." He nodded and took the last of his pictures.

"Sorry to interrupt your strawberry pancakes."

"Don't be. I wasn't eating. Marge called me in a panic, so it was business, not breakfast."

I stood up, moving a little closer. "What happened? She okay?"

"Yeah. She said she saw someone in the walk-in cooler, but they disappeared."

"Ran past her?"

"Walked through a wall…"

My heart stopped. "Marge…saw a ghost?"

"I doubt it. Marge is getting up there in years for a human. She probably imagined the whole thing. Besides, you can't see them unless there's a mirror, right? You taught me that much."

"Apparently shadows work just as well…"

He stopped moving. "Yeah. Uh…that whole walk-in cooler is one giant shadow filled box…"

"Let me get dressed. I'll head over there and check things out for her. You go do something about Frick and Frack. You don't even have to arrest them, but at least warn them I'm done being nice."

"You just threatened them in front of the chief of police…"

"Gonna arrest me?"

"Hell no."

"You're learning."

∞ ∞ ∞

184

As soon as I pulled open the door, I could see something was wrong. Marge was behind the counter, but her eyes were darting all over the diner. Not that I could blame her. After my encounter, I'd been pretty fucking spooked, too.

Finally, she noticed me. I pointed at my booth and sat down. Nobody was close enough to overhear any conversation we might have, so I made her come to me instead of the other way around. "Hey, Dot."

Even her voice sounded scared. "Hey, yourself. Heard you had a visitor this morning. Sit."

Her face turned deathly white, but she set the mug and pot down on the table and took the seat across from me. Not trusting her shaking hands, I poured my own coffee and took a sip. "Dot, it was horrible. I've seen death before, but this… That was no living man."

"Ghost?"

She seemed hesitant to nod, she even looked around the diner first, but then she leaned forward and did. "Do you think I'm crazy?"

"Was the ghost burned?"

She sat back in shock. "How did you know? This wasn't one of your pranks?"

"Nope. There were three of them in the bookstore the other morning. Scared the fuck out of me."

"You?"

It was my turn to nod. "Then one of them attacked Jason."

"They can? Is he okay?" She went from shaken to stirred.

"He's fine. I banished them from the bookstore and threw up a protective barrier. Want me to do the same for the diner?"

I offered, but my biggest fear was that Marge's ghost was one of the ones I kicked out of First Moon Books. It was my fault the ghosts were manifesting, according to my

185

mother and grandmother, but if it was one of the ones I sent packing... Then I was *definitely* to blame. I didn't know whether to hope it was a fourth ghost, or one of the three I did kick out. Either way, I needed to figure out how to lay them to rest permanently.

"Finish your coffee first. I assume Chief told you about the problem?"

"Yeah. I had some witch hating vandals at the house this morning. Keyed my car, slashed my tires, and spray painted my house."

She gasped and then got angry. Really angry. "Was it those two boys in the pickup?"

I nodded, still sipping my coffee. "Yeah. Chief's gonna scare 'em straight. Hopefully they leave me alone after that."

She looked at me thoughtfully for a moment. "You...uh. You don't want to scare them away? Might work a little better than the long arm of the law. I'm just sayin'."

I laughed and shook my head. "Throwing around my power to scare people never ends well. It just makes me a bully."

"But they're bullying you!"

"True. But... Shit, Marge. There's no way to say this without sounding like a braggart, so I'm just going to go ahead and say it. People like that...they're kind of like ticks. They can't hurt me."

"Ever hear of Lyme Disease?"

"Well, yes. But that only happens when you rip their heads off. I'm not to that point yet."

Marge laughed, ghosts momentarily forgotten. Until I pointed toward the kitchen. Her face darkened as she nodded and got up. I set my mostly empty coffee cup down on the worn linoleum and stood after her, following her toward the swinging door.

"Hey, Dot."

"Hi, Herb."

"Everything okay?"

"She's here about the *problem*."

Her rolled his eyes. "Marge, I'm telling ya, you just need to take some time off!"

"She saw them in her store, too, *Herb*." She made his name an insult.

"Really?" He looked at me for confirmation.

"Unfortunately."

Herb grabbed a gigantic ladle from the wire rack next to his griddle and brandished it like a billy club. "Miguel. You have the conn."

"Aye aye, Cap'n," he answered with a thick accent.

Herb marched us back to the walk in cooler and flipped the switch on the outside of the wall before opening the door and leading the way in. The space wasn't overly huge, but the three of us fit in with plenty of room to spare.

"See? Nothing," he said and lowered the ladle.

"The two of you stand outside. When I say so, turn off the light."

They looked at me like I had chickens sprouting from my head. "It will be pitch black in here," he answered.

"No. You're going to leave the door open."

"Oh." He wiggled past Marge and I and popped the door open. Marge practically ran out of the frigid space.

"Go ahead," I told him.

He reached over, never tearing his eyes from me, and flipped the switch. The lightbulb, encased in glass with a wire cage around it, flickered as it died. Shadows cast from the lights outside darkened.

The frigid temperatures of the cooler dropped as darkness swirled and the ghost became visible against the far wall. Sightless eyes, long burned from its charred skull, stared blindly toward me. It, there was no way to tell its gender, started hobbling toward me as arms raised, reaching for me.

187

"Dot," Marge hissed. "Get the fuck out of there!"

I held up my finger beside me, wanting a minute to think. According to my mother, the ghosts wanted to be laid to rest. To rest they needed to be purified. "Hey, Herb. Got any salt?" It was worth a shot.

"One sec."

A moment later, a paper jug of iodized sodium-chloride rolled over the floor and hit my foot. Without taking my eyes from the slowly moving specter, I reached down and grabbed it. Flipping it open, I poured a large amount in my hand and tossed it at the ghost.

Unsurprisingly, it passed right through it and landed on the somewhat clean concrete floor. "Hey, Herb."

"Yeah?"

"Got a broom?"

"Was that supposed to do something?"

"It does on TV." I dropped the salt and called my power, hands and arms illuminating in black flame. That was a new one on me. They usually just glowed.

"Woah," the two of them said behind me.

I strode forward, tired of waiting, and swung my fist at the ghost. With the amount of power I poured into it, I expected it to burst into a million pieces, a spray of ectoplasm, or even just turn to smoke. It didn't. Instead, it flew back from my solid right uppercut and hit the back wall with a loud *thud*.

I hadn't dispelled it. I'd given it form. "Black flames bad," I muttered and looked at my hands.

"Dot?" Herb and Marge *both* sounded like they were going to have to run home and change their undergarments.

"Well, the good news is, it's not a ghost anymore."

The bad news was, Cedar Falls had its first zombie.

It struggled to its feet, clawing the stainless-steel wall behind it, still completely blind. Sniffing the air, it wheeled around toward me and snarled.

"Dooottt?" Herb's terrified voice broke my heart.

"Shut the door!"

"Get out of there," Marge begged.

"Just shut it!"

At least Herb trusted me. Or was sacrificing me to save everybody else. I hoped for the former but was okay with the latter. The zombie was my fault, anyway. Whatever his reasoning, I winced as the door slammed shut behind me.

"Hey, little fella. You hungry?"

The zombie stopped moving and tilted its head. It snarled once and reached out slowly, feeling the air in front of it for me.

Reaching for the shelf next to me, I grabbed the closest thing, an apple from an open cardboard box, and tossed it to it. Forgetting momentarily that it couldn't see, the apple bounced off its forehead and broke against the concrete floor in front of it.

Zombies, apparently, are not fans of flying fruits. It snarled in outrage and ran at me, full bore.

Without thinking, I called power to my hands again and pushed it to the side as I moved out of the way. The black flames sizzled its skin as it howled in agony, falling to the floor and writhing. Its pain only lasted for a moment before it spun on the ground and scrambled across the smooth concrete, hands and feet slapping wetly as it raced like a deranged spider. Before it hit the wall, it leaped and drove its two hands through the back wall of the cooler, prying the metal apart with its hands as it tried to escape.

Herb's gonna be pissed. "Stop!"

It stopped moving, arms still in the wall as its feet settled to the ground. I stared at it, waiting for it to attack or anything. For all intents and purposes, it looked like a horrific art sculpture someone had thrown at the wall a little too hard.

"Why aren't you moving?"

It made a series of rasping gargling sounds. I was sure if its tongue hadn't been burned from its head, I might have

189

been able to understand it. It sounded like speech and it felt like it was trying to answer me. It was obeying me.

"Hop on one foot."

One leg lifted and the creature bent down and thrust upward, the hands stuck in the wall tearing wetly against the jagged metal of the cooler. Black, foul-smelling liquid started running down the wall. I gagged and a little bit of coffee found its way into the back of my throat, not helping the situation any.

"Stop!"

It did.

"Oh, that's fucking gross."

It turned and looked at me over its shoulder and tilted its head.

"Sorry. Not your fault."

The situation had taken a completely different turn. Instead of a ghost to banish, or a ravenous zombie, I had an obedient pet. It would be a cold day in hell before I walked it on a leash or took it to PetSmart for obedience training, but at least it listened. I needed to get it out of the diner and figure out what to do with it after that.

"Herb?"

"Dot?" His reply was muffled through four inches of metal and insulation, but I could hear him.

"It's okay. You got something I can wrap this thing up in?"

The door opened. Marge took one look at the zombie hanging out of the wall and fainted. Herb managed to get his leg under her, softening the landing, but she rolled and hit her head against the door.

"Shit." I started to move toward her, but the zombie started squatting in the cooler, intent on obeying my every command. "No! Not you. Stand. Don't move. Don't shit. Nothing!"

I breathed a little lighter when it straightened back up. I *really* didn't want to know what zombie crap smelled like.

190

The thought made me want to hurl, and I gagged again as I turned toward Marge.

Herb had already scooped her off the floor and was holding her against the door, lightly tapping her cheeks and calling her name.

"She okay?"

"Yeah. She doesn't do too well with dead things. Dot, what the hell is going on?"

"Apparently, I turned your ghost into a zombie. How I gave it a body, I haven't got a friggin' clue, but I did. But, it's a good zombie and obeys me. So, I'm going to get it out of your kitchen and then figure out what to do with it."

"Yeah. I'm pretty sure that's a health code violation."

"I'm sure that's several thousand violations. Do you have anything I can wrap it in?"

"Garbage bags and tape?"

"Yeah. Cuz that won't look like a body."

Marge woke up and saw the zombie again, slinking down the door, completely out cold. Herb put his hands on her hips and looked down at her. "Well, she's just going to keep doing that until we get *that* out of here." He pointed at my new squishy friend.

I had a flash of brilliance. *Yuki, I need you at the diner. Bring me pants, a sweatshirt, and a jacket.* I looked at the undead thing. *Bring a hat and scarf, too.*

What?

I'll explain when you get here.

Yes, Master.

CHAPTER 15

Opening the back door, I peered around at the empty smallish parking lot behind the diner. Herb's car was there, a dumpster, and nothing else. I just hope it stayed that way while we got Squishy to the car.

Squishy had earned his name while Yuki and I attempted to get him dressed. Yuki's fingers had gone through his flesh, not once, but twice while putting an old pair of my leggings, that no amount of washing would ever get clean enough to wear again, on his legs. Subsequently, that was also the time we found out it was a he. The other reason for the name Squishy.

When *it* fell off, Yuki lost the contents of her stomach, splashing blood into the sink of Herb's dishwashing station. If the Cedar Falls Health Department showed up at any time in the next several hours, it would be a million years before he reopened after the number of fines and violations he would have accrued.

When I glanced up at him apologetically, he looked about three seconds away from adding to the mess Yuki had already made.

I just wanted the day to be over.

Yuki cleaned while I magicked the cooler back together, repairing the Squishy-sized hole in the back wall. Herb whistled in admiration as the wound slowly closed in the metal.

"Sorry, Herb."

"Looking at the bright side. There's no ghost in my cooler."

"You are a wise man, Herb." I stepped outside, took one last look around the parking lot and nodded at Yuki in the driver's seat of my car. Herb had given us about thirty garbage bags to line my trunk with. I hoped it was enough. Yuki hit the button and popped the trunk. "Squishy, get in the trunk," I whispered to the winter garbed zombie just inside the door.

It moved faster than I would have thought. Movies and television did little to accurately portray their speed and it practically dove into the open space, sliding across the plastic and lying still. Without checking, Yuki hit the trunk button. Unfortunately, Squishy's foot was hanging over the bumper and the door reopened.

"Squishy, pull your legs in," I said as I walked past and got into the passenger's seat. "Now close it." I nodded at Yuki.

It whined as it pulled shut with a satisfying click. We'd done it. We got the zombie in my car. "Now what are we going to do with it? Please tell me you're not going to keep it."

"I need to figure out how to put it to rest. I don't want him staining my carpet."

"Ew."

"Big time."

"So, where am I going?"

"To Grandmother's house we go."

"Where?"

"Over the river and through the woods."

"I hate you."

"No, you don't. You wub me. Take Main toward the hospital. Make a left on Second."

"Okay." She put it in drive and gunned it, spinning the car sideways before rocketing out of the tiny lot.

194

"Uh… Maybe I should drive."

"Relax, Boss. I got dis bitch."

As soon as we hit the street, a horn blared behind us. Followed by the distinct sounds of police sirens. I turned my head ever so slowly and simply stared at Yuki as she gulped and pulled over to the side of the road. The car behind us honked and I saw the couple inside laughing as they passed.

"Got this bitch, huh?"

"Kinda sorta, yeah. Your accelerator is kind of mushy."

"So's your head, Yuki."

"Well, don't blame me. You're the dumbass who let me drive."

I sighed and rolled down my window. Chief had gotten out of his car and was walking toward us with his hands on his hips and a smile on his lips. "Mornin', Ladies."

"Heya, Chief."

"Yuki. I thought I told you no more driving in city limits. Do I need to expand that to a state-wide ban?"

"Sorry, Chief. Kind of a zombie apocalypse emergency situation goin' on right now."

"Zombie apocalypse?" He laughed and looked through the back window, screeched, and drew his firearm.

I sighed and put my face in my hand.

"That thing is afuckinglive?"

"Chief this is Squishy," I said while rubbing my temples. "Squishy, say hi to Chief."

The zombie lifted his head and groaned, "Glaaaaaaah."

"Dot?"

"Yes, Chief?"

"What the actual fuck? I mean come on. *Work* with me here. Dingbat comes flying out of the parking lot, almost sideswipes the Chesterfields, and you've got a damn zombie in the back of the car?"

"Would you rather I left it in Herb's cooler?"

"You found it. In Herb's cooler?"

195

"Kinda. It used to be a ghost until I hit it with my flaming fists of corporeal being, and then it turned real and kind of zombieish."

"Go. Go wherever you're going. I don't want to know. But *you* drive."

And with that, he turned around, got back in his Jeep, and sped around us.

"Wow. That was easier than flashing him your tits."

"Shut up, Yuki. And switch seats."

"*Hai.*"

It might have taken *me* a few minutes longer to get to my grandmother's house, but we made it in once piece and didn't get pulled over. Or run anybody off the road, fall off a bridge, or run over any old ladies with walkers.

As soon as I pulled into her driveway, she *and* my mother stepped out on the front porch and stared at my car.

"Were they expecting you?"

"No."

"Did you forget Mother's Day or something?"

"No."

"Why are they staring at you?"

"I'm more worried about why they are together. Refrain from using the word 'apocalypse' ever again, please."

"*Hai.*"

Taking one last deep breath, I coughed from the putrid smell overwhelming me, and got out of the car. "That's nasty. I can *taste* it."

Yuki got out right after, chuckling. "Shoulda named him Stinky."

"Squishy's cuter."

"There is nothing cute about that thing."

"Maybe we should call him Bob."

"Bob?"

"Yeah. Like Ka*bob*."

"That's just gross."

"Dorothea?" My mother made my name a question.

"Oh. Hey, Mom. How are you?"

"Child," Nana interrupted. "What is in your car?"

I turned to Yuki. "They can sense Squishy. It wasn't me." I gave her a wink and turned back to my mother and Nana. "Have a bit of a situation…"

"I can see that much. Bring it inside."

"Uh… Is your back gate unlocked?"

"Yes?"

"I'll bring him around."

"Him?"

"Yeah. His name is Squishy."

"I assume his name is why you do not want him in my house?"

"Yeah. I probably should have named him Juicy."

"The back gate is unlocked." With that, she and my mother went inside.

It took a few minutes to get Squishy out of the trunk and around the house. Mother and Nana were standing in the exact positions they'd been on the front porch on the back patio. They were even wearing the same expressions.

"Nana, Mother…say hi to Squishy."

"What have you done, Child?" Nana stepped forward and held out her hand. If I looked closely, I could see silvery tendrils of power flowing from her fingertips and settling over Squishy's flesh.

"Punched a ghost so hard I knocked it into Zombieland."

"It is as we feared, Mother." My mother was staring intently at hers.

"What is?"

She shook her head at me while Nana continued probing my zombie. "You gave its spirit flesh, how?"

"Black fire."

She stopped probing and narrowed her eyes. "Show me."

197

I held up my hand and called my power. Once again, the black fire enveloped my hand, flames flickering about six inches above my fingertips.

"Amazing," Nana said and reached out with her hand. As soon as the flames licked her fingers, she yanked her hand back. I stared in shock as they started to decay in front of my eyes, but with a cough and a bit of concentration, they healed. "I would suggest not touching any of your lovers with this power."

"Yeah." I nodded, wide-eyed.

"Hand job of doom," Yuki said with a giggle. I shot her a reproachful look, but my mother and Nana cackled in agreement.

"Have you touched your zombie with it?"

"Once, when I didn't know he was mine to command. He didn't like it."

"What happened."

"He made a *graaaaah* noise and ran away."

"Try it again."

"Huh?"

"Touch him with the fire, but picture it healing him instead of hurting him."

"Uh. It's fire. Pretty sure you can't heal someone by burning them."

"Indulge me. Ninety-nine percent of magic is intent. You know this."

"Fine. But if he turns into a marshmallow in your yard, it's not my fault." I turned toward Squishy and held out my hand. "Sorry, bud. This might hurt a little bit." I pictured the flames licking across his skin, undoing what time and fire had done to his corporeal form. When the flames actually touched his flesh, it spread across him like flashfire, leaving whole flesh in its wake.

Yuki whistled. No one would *ever* think he was alive, but at least he was whole. He blinked shriveled eyes and stared at the sun above us. His flesh was pasty and gray, he still smelled funny, but he looked a hell of a lot fresher.

"Next time, picture the corpse in this state instead of just punching the ghost."

"Next time? You think I *want* to make more zombies? I want this one to go to its final rest. Not wake more up."

"We do not always get what we want. This is more of your power and you have it for a reason. Keep that in mind." She looked at my mother, my uncharacteristically *quiet* mother, and narrowed her eyes.

"What?" Curiosity got the better of me.

"Nothing," Nana muttered and looked at me instead. They were keeping more shit from me, but I let it go. I'd find out on my own or they'd spill the beans when they had to. Asking them would just get me more runaround. "You made it. Lay it to rest."

"How?"

"With the tool of your necromancy. The black flames. Use them to send him to his rest."

"So… Picture him buried in the ground, unanimated?"

"If that is your ideal of passing on? Yes. It might be as simple as picturing him as not being. It is your power. It will answer to you."

"Yeah. Because shit always works the way it's supposed to when I try new shit." I sighed and stared at the zombie in front of me. "Squishy, you're a good boy, but it's time for night nights. You want to go to sleep?"

"Gaaah."

"I'll take that as a yes." With a sigh, I closed my eyes. Picturing Squishy seeping into the earth and going to his final rest. It was the only thing I could imagine as I opened my eyes.

The fire flared from my hands and engulfed him. He didn't shriek or writhe in agony. He simply slowly lowered into the ground while standing upright. The four of us stood around him in a circle as he slowly disappeared. Just before his chin touched the dirt, I swear I saw him smile.

"You did it, Child," Nana said proudly.

"Yipee. I melted the zombie."

Yuki prodded the ground with her foot after his head disappeared. "That was the coolest fucking thing I've ever seen."

I rolled my eyes and shook my head. "You need to get out more."

∞ ∞ ∞

After the Squishy Incident, as it would later be known as, my mother and Nana had clammed up. Even as to the reason why they had been together. I'd even offered to buy them lunch, but they made some excuse about a pre-existing engagement.

"They're going to a strip club," Yuki said once we were in the car.

"I don't want to know."

"Why?"

"Because it's my mother and grandmother."

"It's not like they look like old ladies. Hell, they look almost as young as you."

"Gee, thanks."

"Don't get me wrong. You're more beautiful, but... I don't know. It's more in their air. They're almost regal while you're..."

"A helpless cause?"

"No! You're more down to earth and alive. They look like they would kill you, clean you, and fucking eat you if they could get away with it. You're more fun."

Yuki wasn't big in the compliment department, so I took her words to heart and got a little sniffly.

"So, where we going now?"

"Home to take a shower, and then I figured we could swing by the bookstore and check on things. Grab some lunch after."

"Diner?" She asked drolly.

"Sure."

Pulling into my driveway, I smiled at my pristine garage door. After Chief had done the whole police rigamarole, I magicked *it* and my car back into their former, pre-vandalization condition.

"Still can't believe those bastards fucked up your house."

"And my car."

She nodded. "What are you going to do if they do it again?"

"They won't get a chance. If either of them so much as set a toe on my property, they're going to get their schnitzel sizzled."

"Can we set up some security cameras so we can watch the show?"

"Sadist."

"Hey. It's not my fault if people are stupid. Might as well get some entertainment from Darwin's Theory."

Shutting off the car, I got out and headed for the front door. Yuki trailed behind me until we were inside. She headed for one shower while I headed for the other. Dealing with Squishy had left us both feeling a little less than clean.

She was out and dressed before I even finished drying my hair. "I should cut all mine off. Think spiky red will go over well?"

"Hey, they liked you completely bald. Go for it."

I shuddered at the memory. Not something I would ever want to repeat again. "No. I'll just deal with it."

"Want me to brush it for you?"

"I'm keeping you forever," I told her and handed her my hairbrush. Sitting down on the end of the bed, wrapped

201

in a towel, I almost fell over as she jumped on my mattress and landed on her knees behind me.

"You better."

"You're good with that?"

She stopped brushing for a moment. "Yes. Dot... I like it here. Thank you."

"You're welcome, kiddo." I smiled at her in the mirror on top of my dresser.

Ten minutes later we were in the car and listening to Christmas music on the way to the bookstore. "Lunch first?"

I took my eyes from the road and looked at her. "You're hungry?"

"Puked up my breakfast."

"You forgot, didn't you."

"Forgot what?"

"That you can't drink regular blood anymore. Marge's stash is useless.

Her eyes narrowed and she frowned. "Fuck."

We were going to have to think of a solution. She couldn't feed off Dar and me every night. I toyed with the idea of starting a supernatural blood bank, but the whole train of thought completely ruined the mood and reminded me her father was most likely going to be in town sometime that night.

"Let's just check on everyone. Make sure everything is okay and we'll get some lunch. They're probably hungry, too."

She nodded without looking at me.

"Look at the bright side."

"What?"

"I don't know. I'm drawing a blank, too. If you think of anything, let me know."

CHAPTER 16

"That will be seventeen dollars and eighty-nine cents."

I watched as the woman reached out with a shaky hand and slowly held out her debit card for me to take. She was human, but probably the same age as my Nana. She *looked* close to a thousand years old, and she was adorable. "Thank you, honey."

I smiled at her. "You just put your card in that machine in front of you, ma'am."

She looked down and nodded, tried three times and finally got it in the slot. Almost immediately, SALE DECLINED popped up on the register screen in front of me. "You're all set," I lied and shoved her book into one of the paper bags Jason had ordered with First Moon Books emblazoned across it in green lettering. "Enjoy your book!"

I hit cancel sale on the register and pushed the bag across the counter. Her gnarled hand wrapped around the handle as she happily took her book and headed for the door.

"You're gonna go broke if you keep being that nice. That was the third one today and you've only been here an hour." Jason cocked an eyebrow at me.

"Meh. It's only money," I answered and stepped back, letting him back at the register.

"Thanks for the lunch and the break."

"My pleasure. Any luck in hiring people?"

"Dwight works tonight. Shea is off today. Dar is stocking as fast as he can. I had seventeen applications yesterday. I have four of them coming in for an interview this afternoon."

"Sweet."

"Do you want to do the interviews?"

"I'd rather get kicked by a mule."

"I figured you'd say that." He chuckled and rang the next person up.

"Seriously. If you can tolerate them, hire them. If they don't work out, so be it. Just get some damn help."

"You got it."

A loud *bzzzt* noise echoed through the building before a thunderous *pop* killed every single light in the store. At least there was enough filtering through the front windows that the customers weren't in danger of tripping. "How come the registers are still working?"

"UPS."

"Postal service? I'm confused."

"Uninterruptable power supply. Big one in the back with surge protection."

"This is why I love you. You're all brilliant and stuff."

"I'll go check the breakers."

"No. Stay. I'll go. I know where the panel is." I headed toward the stock room. Dar fell into step behind me.

"That was very loud."

"Yeah. Didn't sound like a breaker popping." I pushed the swinging door open and automatically reached for the light switch.

"There is no power, Master."

"Yep. Force of habit," I said and held up my hand, letting loose with a little light spell. The glowing ball hovered a few inches above my palm.

Flipping open the gray metal door, I pushed every breaker to the on position, not trusting the little indicator windows built into them. Unfortunately, they were all on. It wasn't a breaker, just like I'd thought.

"You smell something burning?"

Sniffing the air, I nodded at him. We both turned and looked at the metal door leading to the back of the store. Walking over, I hit the release bar and stepped outside.

The main electrical panel was propped open, and the lock was cut, lying on the ground next to a smoldering piece of rebar. "Sonofa fuckbitch."

"Dot?" Dar stepped outside and looked down to what I was staring at. "Oh."

"Yeah. Go tell Jason to call the power company."

"What are you going to do?"

"See if I can fix it."

"I suggest waiting…"

"Just give me a minute."

"Yes, Master."

He turned and walked away while I pulled my cell out of my jacket pocket. Dialing Chief, I put the phone to my ear.

"If this has *anything* to do with zombies, I'm hanging up."

"You next door?"

"Yeah?"

"Go out the back and come to the rear of the store."

"Why? What's going on?"

I shut the phone off and stuffed it back into my pocket. "Maybe it *is* time to rip the head off the tick."

I heard the rear door of the station open from where I stood. A few seconds later and Chief was there, winded from running. "What happened?"

"*Somebody* pulled my main panel open and threw a piece of rebar at the contacts."

"Holy shit. Is everything okay?"

"Just take some damn pictures so I can try to fix it."

"Dot, that's not like accidentally touching a plug. That's the main line for the store. Two-hundred and twenty volts or some shit."

"And I throw lightning at Italian Restaurants. I have a store full of people and no time to call an electrician."

"Close the store! Take some time off while this gets fixed the right way."

"Just take the damn pictures."

He sighed and pulled out his phone. "You're uh…not going to take matters into your own hands, are you?"

"With the power? Yes. With your little fucknut yocals? No. If anything happened to them right now, I'd just be proving the DA's case."

"Thank the Lady," he said in relief. The phone made a few shutter noises as he snapped off a few pictures, then he bent down and took a couple of the smoldering rebar and cut lock.

"This is their last free pass, Chief. If they do anything else, the DA won't have enough evidence left to convict me."

"If they do anything else, I'll help you find them."

I nodded and stepped closer to the box, putting my hands on the outside of it. Sending a tendril of power into it, I gasped as the line feeding in scorched me a little. It wasn't pleasant, but didn't hurt me physically. It *did* make my teeth wiggle a little, however.

"*A bheith mar a bhí tú,*" I whispered to the large metal box between my hands. The metal warmed beneath my hands as my magic seeped inside. The contacts themselves were isolated from the box, getting the magic to them was a little more difficult, but with a push of power, I changed the shape of my spell into a globe that encompassed everything.

"Woah," Chief said softly behind me.

The metal stopped smoldering, paint thinned and changed back to its original color. The plastic shielding on the thick copper wires repaired itself while the shorted bits of metal thickened and shined in the sunlight behind me.

"Is that it?" I blinked as I released the magic.

"You might have to throw the main. I'm sure that popped when the feed was shorted." He moved over a little and looked at the meter. "Yeah. It's not spinning."

"Where is the main?"

"Probably on the other side of this wall. You want to fix the lock?" He pointed at the cut lock lying on the ground.

I almost said no, for as much good as it did. My luck, some kid would walk by and lick the terminals like a Tide Pod. Sighing, I bent down and grabbed it, repeating my spell and re-locking the damn thing through the hasp. "There."

"Come on," he said and reached for the door. The handle-less exterior, exit only door.

"Shit."

"Now we have to go through the front like some sort of barbarians," he said and chuckled to himself.

"Yeah, yeah." I headed around the building into the parking lot between the station and the store, and then around to the front of the store. By the time we got inside, most of the customers had left, but there were a few stalwarts waiting with their books. "I thought the registers were still running?"

"UPS only gives it enough power to shut them down safely."

"Oh. See about getting a backup generator installed. Power should be back on in a second," I called, heading for the storeroom.

"Did you get it fixed?" Dar asked as we entered the storeroom.

"Yes. Were you in here?"

"I just returned and was about to open the door."

"Yes. It's fixed." I walked over to the wall and saw the main panel. There was a huge, rubber switch on the front of it. "It says it's on," I said to Chief.

"Yeah, but the disconnect inside probably tripped. Shut it off and turn it back on."

"That's the solution for everything." I grabbed the switch in both hands and pulled it down. Waiting a second, I pushed it back up into the on position and there was a *clack* as power flooded through the store again. A few of the customers cheered inside the store.

"All right. I'm going to go find Jackson and Davis. Have fun," Chief said and kissed the top of my head before leaving.

"Do you wish me to look for them, too?" Dar lifted a questioning eyebrow.

"Not yet."

"Very well."

∞ ∞ ∞

"At least we're closed tomorrow," I said with a resounding sigh, locking the door with the key. Tomorrow was Christmas Eve, and while some large chain stores might force their employees to work, I was not a bastard. Even if the people who worked for me were just as pagan as I was.

"Let's just hope the store is still standing when we reopen on Monday." Jason didn't sound too happy. When I'd told him what happened, he almost ran out the door to go looking for Jackson and Davis, himself.

"It'll be fine," I said and pulled the key from the lock and patted him on the shoulder.

"Is it bad that I'm kind of hoping for a small structural fire? Not too much damage. Just something that will take a week to fix?" Josie was pouting. But she was tired, she always pouted when she was tired. It was her thing.

Elbowing her in the ribs was Candace's. "Guard your words, love."

"Dot knows I'm kidding, Candy."

"But the gods do not."

"Dot knows I'm kidding, Candy."

Candace rolled her eyes. "Would you rather not have any customers? You wish to buy our own house. It is difficult without money…"

Josie hurriedly shushed her with a kiss, but I could feel her eyes darting toward me. *She wants to move out but doesn't want me to know… Bwahahahaha. Dreams do come true, little sister.*

My car screeched to a stop on the street in front of the store at the exact moment my phone started ringing. I'd let Yuki pull the car out of the lot and onto the street, but I motioned her to get in the passenger seat while I answered Chief's call.

"Hey, sexy."

"Are you alone?" He sounded almost angry.

"Yuki and Dar are with me," I answered, winking at Dar in the back seat via the rearview mirror.

"Park. I need you to come to the station."

Every hair on my body stood on end. "Am I being arrested again?"

"No. Just a couple of questions this time."

A low throbbing buzz started at the base of my skull. "What about?"

"Just come next door."

"Why?"

"Dot. Please."

"On my way." I got out of the car and shouted at Josie. She, Candace, and Jason were just about to round the corner to the parking lot.

"Can you take Dar and Yuki home?"

She looked at Candace who nodded. Technically, it was her car. At least until they were married. "Yeah. Everything okay?"

"Yeah," I shouted, but shook my head ever so slightly.

Getting back in the car, I pulled it into the parking lot and shut off the engine. "You sure you don't want me to stay with you?"

I shook my head at Yuki. "Hopefully this won't take long. I *really* didn't do anything this time."

"This time." She winked and got out of the car. Dar, on the other hand, hesitated a little longer.

"Go. I'll be fine."

"As you wish."

I got out of the car and walked around the corner. Chief was standing in the door. Unsure if he was waiting for me, or just didn't trust me, I narrowed my eyes. He opened the door and motioned me in.

He didn't say a word until we walked through the entire station and he motioned toward the chair in front of his desk. "Where is it?"

"Where is what?"

"That damn zombie of yours."

"Squishy? That's what this is about?"

"Yes, Dot." He shook his head incredulously.

"I laid it to rest in my grandmother's yard."

"You buried it. In Nana's yard?"

"I didn't bury it. I laid it to rest. Kind of like dispelling the magic that kept it going and it sort of melted into the dirt. No digging."

"And you're sure it's dead?"

"Yes? Out of curiosity, why?" He tossed his phone across the desk. There was a picture on the screen and I stared at it, trying to understand what I was seeing. "Is that?"

"Yep. Jackson and Davis."

"What the fuck happened to them?"

"I was hoping you could tell me?"

"Wait. You think *I* had something to do with his?"

He sighed. Probably to choose his next words very carefully. Or that's what I would have done if I were him. "No. I'm *asking* you if you had anything to do with this. There's nobody in town with more motive than you. Add that to the fact that somebody literally ate the flesh from their bodies, factor in the zombie in your possession..."

I sighed, too. Kind of seeing his point. "No. If it were me, I would have just told you. Squishy didn't leave my sight, and he's gone now."

"How many zombies did you make?"

"Just the one." *That I know of.*

He reached over and grabbed his phone. "We have another problem."

"I didn't do that, either."

"Their bodies had been dead for at least six hours."

I blinked at him in confusion. "Then how did they vandalize the bookstore?"

"That's my point. It wasn't them. It couldn't have been them."

"What the fuck?"

"Somebody else doesn't like you very much, either."

My phone started ringing in my pocket. I pulled it out and didn't recognize the number, so I hit end and set it on Chief's desk. It started ringing again, so I set it on vibrate and declined the second call. As soon as I set it down it started rumbling and sliding across the desk. Chief's started, too.

"Hang on, it's the mayor." He answered the call and stood up, facing the wall. "Hello, Mayor."

Master? Dar's voice sounded hesitant in my head.

Dar? Everything okay?

I was just about to ask you that, too. Why are there several news vans outside your house?

News vans?

211

"Wait, what?" Chief pulled the phone away from his ear, stared at it for a moment, and put it back before turning around and typing something on his laptop keyboard.

Yes. News vans. What should we do?

Go home. They can't block you. Just tell them I'm not with you.

Chief stood up. "We'll just say it was a prank," he said into the phone, turning the laptop and moving it to where I could see the screen.

He had Youtube open and a video was playing. I was standing behind the back of the bookstore hands on my electrical box, pouring magic into it. There was a subtle glow over everything. That was about as well as magical energy showed up on a camera lens. Unfortunately, the camera was of good enough quality that you could clearly see the wires, plastic, and metal all kneading themselves back together and repairing themselves.

I'd just been outed.

As a witch.

On the internet…

"Fuck me."

"Now isn't a good time." I didn't know if Chief was talking to me or the mayor. "Hang on. Here she is."

He handed the phone to me. "Sherry?"

"Hey, Dot."

"They set me up."

"I kind of figured. Otherwise why would they have a camera set up, pointed at your electrical box."

"There's news vans in front of my house. This isn't a case of someone catching some stranger in public using magic. They deliberately outed me and gave my name and address to the press."

There was a moment of silence on the other line.

"Sherry?"

"Dot, who would gain the most for outing you as a witch?"

My brain short circuited as I thought about it. The list was long and full of nothing. "I haven't got a clue."

"Think about it."

Then two little initials finally clawed their way to the forefront of my cerebrum and pissed off my medulla oblongata on the way. "The DA."

"Yep. And he gets to hold his very own little witch trial right here in Cedar Falls…"

CHAPTER 17

For the fifteenth time, I listened to the heater kick in and blast the house with warm air as I stared up at the ceiling while sleep eluded me. "Why can't I sleep?"

Nobody answered me. They weren't having any problems. Even my vampire familiar was asleep in her bed, snoring away.

I probably could have blamed it on my nerves. Getting home with all the news vans had been like landing an F-18 on a fully loaded aircraft carrier deck. I banked the turn into my driveway going at least thirty miles an hour, nearly sideswiped Candace's car, and skidded to a stop just before ramming the back wall of the garage. Yuki and Dar had cleared the runway and she palmed the door close as soon as I stopped. They both were staring at me like I'd lost my damn mind and rightfully so. I might have lost my marbles, but I didn't have to deal with the fucking press.

Avoiding them at all costs had been Sherry's last bit of advice before I hung up the phone with her. That, and don't do anything stupid. I could almost hear her winking over the phone.

Flinging the comforter off me, I turned and winced at the clock as I dragged my sorry ass out of bed. Five in the morning. I *used* to go to bed that late. Getting up that early was an affront to my sensibilities.

Pulling on my seldom used robe, I walked out through the living room and pulled out a mug from the cabinet above the coffee maker. With all the practice I'd been getting, I was almost as proficient as Candace and smiled as I hit brew.

When I closed the cabinet, I screeched. Dar was standing there, and I hadn't even heard him walk up. "Holy shit. Warn a master."

"Sorry. I did not mean to frighten you."

"What are you doing up?"

"That was my question for you. I *was* asleep on the couch until you started making coffee."

"Want a cup?"

He nodded and I pulled another mug out. "Is everything okay?"

I sighed and pulled out the now full cup and handed it to him, putting the other on to brew for me. "I guess. Just a shit ton going wrong and I just have that feeling that shit's getting out of hand."

"Deal with the problems as they come. Do not let them compound."

"From your lips to the Lady's ears."

"No. From mine to yours. My kind has never worshipped the Lady."

I nodded, not wanting to get into a religious conversation. Too close to home. His people worshipped my father. The corner of my lip curled in a little bit of anger while I watched my coffee brew. *Why couldn't I have a normal father? Even a human one who was disappointed he had a girl but still felt the urge to teach her how to play catch in the yard?*

I still wouldn't have been disappointed. I ignored his response. It was just like him. Ignore the important stuff and respond to the stupid shit.

Because that is when you need me the most.
Shut up.

216

If that is your wish. Just like that, I felt him leave and I hadn't even noticed his presence to begin with. I may have inadvertently found the true definition of frustration.

"Are you okay?"

Dar's voice brought me back to reality. And that reality had a steaming mug of coffee in it. Pulling the mug from the machine, I inhaled deeply before sipping carefully. "Yep."

"Would you care to sit or are you planning on staring intently at your favorite kitchen appliance until the rest of the house wakes up?"

"Sitting is good."

He turned around and headed for the couch, looking over his shoulder to make sure I was following him. I did. But only because he had a nice ass. I liked drinking coffee at the table, but if he wanted to be comfy, I was good with that. He asked for so little, it was nice doing small things for him when he let me.

He sat down on the end and offered me his side. I wasn't about to turn *that* down and plopped down next to him, careful not to spill either of our coffees. Thankfully, I wore my robe. I had all the grace of a moose going downhill in rollerblades. He shook the coffee off his hand and wiped it on his sweatpants.

"Sorry."

"I was born on the plains of Gehenna. Coffee poses no threat."

I wasn't taking any chances. Gently, I grabbed his wrist and pulled his hand to my lips. I licked the remainder of the coffee from his skin before planting several kisses over the wound. It was better to be safe than sorry.

"Thank you, Master."

I took a sip of my coffee and let my head rest against his shoulder, staring out at the snow covered back yard through the sliding glass door. Taking a deep breath, I closed my eyes and relaxed into the moment, relishing in

217

the quiet and the closeness with Dar. His vaguely cinnamon scent made me smile.

"You are sure you are okay?" Concern tinged his voice.

"Dar. I'm fine. You can relax."

"I was relaxed. Then you made coffee."

"Sorry I woke you up."

"Do not be. I am not." He smiled at me out of the corner of his mouth, flashing a bit of demonic fang.

He was insanely hot as an elf. I had trouble keeping my hands off him whenever I was near him. As a demon, he was a sex god and I decided to give into the impulse to touch him. I put my hand on his thigh and began lightly palming circles over the softness of his sweatpants.

"Do you, as the humans say, need a hug?"

Grinning at him, I took his coffee mug and set both of them on the coffee table. "Yes. Yes, I do."

He opened his arms and I slid into them, leaning over his hips and pressing my face to his chest as he pulled me tight. Ever so gently, I felt his lips trail through my hair as he kissed the top of my head.

"Thanks, Darling."

"You are welcome."

Staying there for a long moment, I made to slip back into my seat next to him, but he refused to let me go. "You like holding me?"

"There is nothing in this world or mine that I would rather do."

He made me a little sniffly and I rubbed my face against him. Finally, he let me go and rolled me on my back in his lap. Sighing happily, I looked up at him and gave him a smile.

"Feel better?'

"I didn't think it was possible, but I do. Your hugs might be infused with demon magic."

"As is the rest of me."

Chuckling, I rolled a little and kissed his T-shirt covered chest. "I'll agree with that statement."

"You are beautiful," he said simply, trailing a finger along the skin of my cheek.

"You're not allowed to say that."

"I am not?" He gave me an apologetic stare.

"Nope. Not at the same time I am thinking it about you."

"You think I am beautiful?" He blinked in surprise.

"Duh. I have eyeballs."

"But I have horns and…"

I silenced him with my finger over his lips. "You might look different, but that doesn't mean you're not absolutely gorgeous."

If you've never had someone smile at you while you were shushing their lips with your finger, I highly recommend the sensation. "The same for you with your flaming hair, the light dusting of freckles over your cheeks, and your overly large beautiful green eyes." I pulled my finger away when he started talking. I should have left it there. It might have softened the blush on my cheeks with the light dusting of freckles I tried so hard to ignore.

"Sweet talker."

His chest rumbled as he laughed softly, almost a growl that sent a shiver over my arms. "Hey, Dar?"

"Yes, Master?"

"Would you kiss me?"

"It would be my pleasure." He leaned down and lightly grazed my lips with his.

"Harder."

"Yes, Master." His pressed against mine and as my mouth parted, his tongue slid against mine. I moaned into that kiss as his hand slid under my robe and settled on my bare stomach, his fingertips tracing patterns just above my belly button.

I was still kissing the air when he pulled away. "Was that satisfactory?" One corner of his mouth curled in a smile. He was teasing me and I loved it.

"Not even close."

"Yes, Master."

I was starting to get the impression he enjoyed calling me master. Especially at times like that. Which worked out well, because every time the word left his lips, it made me a little wetter. They were going to have to start calling me *Squishy*.

While he kissed me, his hands slid up my sides and somehow, he wrangled me into straddling him on the couch without ever breaking that kiss. More demon magic.

My hands found the bottom of his shirt and lifted it up over his head and off his arms. We had to break the kiss for that one. His clothes supply was limited, at least until he opened his Yule presents. I'd been a very busy master. Almost as busy as the closest Amazon distribution center responsible for my order fulfillment.

As soon as he was shirtless, my hands slid over his chest until I felt his nipples slide across my palms. "Your skin is on fire," I said softly and meant it as his flesh warmed my hands.

"Not just my skin. All of me. You make me burn with need."

"Quit talking and kiss me some more." I leaned into him, never taking my hands from his chest, kneading the flesh beneath them.

I felt him, through his sweatpants, as he throbbed against me. My bathrobe had draped around us and I was naked underneath. Grinding myself against him, I became lost in that perfect kiss.

"I am not the only one on fire," he managed to gasp as he pulled away.

"No shit." I arched my back, lost in the sensation of our limited contact.

His fingers found me, pushing his cock out of the way and slipping along my very wet lips and teasing my clit. I stopped grinding and lifted myself off him a little, giving him all the access he wanted.

"May I taste you?"

"That is something you *never* need to ask."

He smiled and leaned over on his back, rolling and pulling me onto his chest. I was straddling him, knees on the sofa beside him, open and wet. His smile widened as he stared at me, not all of me, just the part in front of his hungry face. "Beautiful," he said simply, pulling me closer until I could feel his hot breath against my wetness.

"Dar..."

It was all I managed to get out before his lips kissed me softly, his tongue darting inside me, as he groaned into me. The vibration of his mouth drove every last thought from my lust-fueled brain.

"Fuuuck," I whispered, trying not to wake everyone up.

"You taste like heaven."

"How would you know? You're from the opposite direction."

"Because if I said you taste like Hell, you would have gotten angry." He chuckled and resumed licking me.

"It's Gehenna," I threw his words back at him and closed my eyes. He was going to make me come and we'd just started. My hips started making lazy circles, grinding me against his him, and pushing my sex against his undulating tongue and mouth.

It was hopeless. Not standing a chance against him, I came. Grabbing his horns in my hands I held on for the ride, hips bucking against him as I let out a long hiss of incoherent noise.

When I was finished, I pulled back and smiled down at him. "Holy fuck."

"You seemed to enjoy that almost as much as I did."

"Yeah. I'm betting I enjoyed it a *little* more."

"Perhaps." He winked.

I slid back, working my knees alongside of him and reaching behind me. As my fingers found the waistband of his sweatpants, I pushed them down and exposed his cock as I kept working my way over his abs until I felt him nudge me from behind. More demon magic. The tip of his cock perfectly aligned with my *very* wet entrance.

"Master?"

"Yes, Dar?"

His hands slid over my shoulders as he pushed me down onto him as he leaned up and kissed me. "I love you," he whispered after he had impaled me.

Sitting up, feeling him throbbing inside me, I looked down at him and smiled. "I love you, too."

Enjoying everything about the moment, I started swirling my hips over him, gasping as every ridge of his cock shifted inside me, pushing my walls in every direction and sending pure jolts of pleasure through every nerve in my body.

"Fuck, you feel good," I said and closed my eyes, concentrating on the feel of him inside me.

"As do you."

Lazily, I let my fingers slide down over my stomach, through my hair, until they found my clit. I let them gather a bit of wetness before rubbing against it in time with the movement of my hips.

"I like this," he said softly.

"Me fucking you in the living room?"

He shook his head. "While all of our play has been glorious, this might be my favorite."

"Why?"

"Because it is just you and I. That makes it very special."

I gave him a sad look, almost apologetic. "It is," I agreed.

"I hate to ask…"

"But you'd like to do this more?"

"Would you mind? I do not wish to monopolize your time, but this, *this* is more than I ever hoped for."

I leaned over and kissed him, not breaking my rhythm. "Most definitely."

His smile was reward enough. "Thank you, Master."

"Don't. It is me who should be thanking you. You put up with me, love me, and never demand anything of me."

"It is my pleasure."

"Nope. Pretty sure it's mine." I grinned and picked up the pace.

He groaned in response, his breathing changing as I started lifting myself off him and dropping back down. Then his eyes started glowing. I probably should have been scared, but something inside me responded. My feet slid forward, one pressing against the cushion beneath us and the other dropping to the floor beside us. My head leaned in farther and I stared into his eyes as I truly began to fuck him, using my legs to slide up and down his throbbing cock until just the head of him strained against my parting lips.

"Are you going to come," I snarled at him. His eyes widened as he stared back, eyes not daring to leave mine. "Good," I said and grinned wickedly, my talons sliding over the flesh of his chest. Reaching out once more, my hands curled over his horns as I used them to steady myself as I drove myself down against him, grinding my hips before lifting myself back up. Over and over, I repeated the motion as his breathing reached its peak.

"Come," I commanded him and finally his eyes closed as his hips bucked against me. It was enough to push me over the edge and I dropped down atop him, my lips finding his neck as my teeth pierced his flesh. Not enough to tear, but for me to taste the wetness of his blood as my pussy spasmed around his throbbing cock.

We stayed there, just like that as our breathing slowed. Finally, I kissed the slowly closing wound on his neck and sat up and smiled. He was happy, but then stared at my face as his eyes widened. "Master?"

"What?"

There was an internal conflict playing across his face as he debated telling me something that I wasn't going to like.

"What?"

"You're…"

"What? What, Dar?"

He gulped and looked into my eyes. "Your eyes are glowing, and your fangs have returned."

Sighing, I nodded. "It's the vampire powers in me. I've been going a little vampy lately when I get excited."

He shook his head. "You are not a vampire."

"I know. I just get a little long in the tooth and hungry for blood. It's more like a side effect than actually turning into a vampire. It's not like I can bench press a bus or anything."

He grabbed my hand and held up my talons in front of my face. The same talons I had used to rake his flesh and hadn't noticed at the time. "Vampires do not have *talons*."

"What? Wait…" I felt the fangs sticking out over my lip. They were much thicker and not quite as long as the ones I'd been sporting lately. Pulling myself off Dar and ignoring the mess that followed, I hugged my robe around me as I ran to the guest bathroom and flipped on the switch. My eyes *were* glowing with an ethereal red light inside. I wasn't vampiric, I was demonic. It had happened to me before, when Dar performed the mating ritual. Us mating must have triggered it again. Sighing, I shut off the light and turned to see Yuki staring at me in the doorway.

"Nice look."

"Don't get me started."

She looked very disheveled, but she was ten times cuter with her hair all mussed and the blush on her cheeks. "Can I go back to sleep now?"

"Yep. All done. Sorry about that."

"No, you're not." She flashed me a brief smile as she stared at my eyes and then just above. "I guess it could be worse, you could be horny."

Inadvertently, I ran my fingers over the side of my head. No bumps, no horns, nothing. For *that*, I sighed in relief. "Yeah. That would be a little tough to explain."

"Not really. Everybody knows you're a horny old broad." She winked and went back into her room, shutting the door behind her.

CHAPTER 18

Marge gave me a curious glance as she filled my mug with coffee. She greeted me normally and pointed to my usual booth, but as soon as she got within three feet of me, she got jumpy.

"You okay?"

Sighing, she sat down across from me and stared at me intently. "Is that thing gone forever?"

"Squishy?"

She nodded.

"Yep. Laid him to rest. He's not a zombie anymore."

"Oh, thank heavens." The tension drained out of her and she visibly relaxed.

"That's what you were worried about?"

"Yeah. Blame Herb. He took me to a horror movie about zombies when we were a lot younger. Haven't been able to stomach the damn things since. Wasn't expecting to run into one in real life."

"Yeah. Sorry about that."

"No worries, hun. At least the diner is ghost *and* zombie free, thanks to you."

And probably infested in the first place because of me. I was definitely a hazard to the normal townsfolk. "My pleasure," I lied through my teeth.

"You guys doing anything fun tonight? It's Christmas Eve!"

"Think we're going to order Chinese and watch movies. Nothing exciting. What time should we be here tomorrow?"

"We get the turkeys in the ovens around eight in the morning. Herb comes in earlier than that to mix up all the stuffing, but we won't need any help until about nine or ten. Whichever is easier for you."

"We'll see you at eight," I told her with a little wink. Getting twenty something turkeys into the ovens couldn't be an easy task.

She smiled and nodded. "Hungry? Or did you just want coffee?"

I glanced at my watch. It was closer to noon than morning. "Cheeseburger."

"You got it, sweetie."

She slapped her hand against the top of the table as she stood and headed for the kitchen. I smiled and relished my hard-won cup of coffee. As soon as the sun rose, the news vans that had been parked at the end of the street took up position in front of the house again in a silent vigil as they waited for me to leave. I'd cheated and called Shea, asking him to shadow walk me to the bookstore. He'd readily agreed but had already made plans to take Dar Yule shopping. As soon as they dropped me off at the closed bookstore, they departed, leaving me to my own devices.

The diner was always a good place to start.

The door chime rang merrily behind me, and my smile got a little bigger. I smelled him before I felt his presence. "Hey, Chief," I said without looking.

"Miss Blackwell. I didn't expect to see you out and about this morning. How did you sneak past the paparazzi?" He chuckled as he sat down.

"Little shadow walker snuck me out."

Chief looked around and pointed at the seat he was sitting in, questioningly.

"No. He and Dar went shopping."

"Ahh. They seem to get along great."

"Yep." I laughed softly.

"What?"

"They're…uh. They're together when I'm not around."

"Together, together?"

"Yep."

"Huh. They actually make a cute couple."

"Want me to ask if there's room for a third?"

Chief grinned at me. "You'd enjoy that too much."

"I'm more afraid of you enjoying it too much."

"Yeah. So not happening." He winked. At least he didn't mind me teasing him. "So, what are you up to today?"

"Nothing. Figured I'd wander around town since every news van in the county is parked in front of my house."

"That's kind of brilliant."

"I thought so."

Our conversation was interrupted by Marge, who dropped off two Cokes and two cheeseburgers. "Enjoy!"

"I swear she keeps a cheeseburger behind the counter for when you walk in." I shook my head in suspicion.

"No. She knows what time I eat lunch when I'm working."

"That makes sense. In a Marge sort of way, but what if you don't want a cheeseburger one day."

"Why would I not want a cheeseburger?"

"Doesn't it get boring, eating the same damn thing every day?"

He took a bite of burger and gave me a wicked grin. "Nope. There are most definitely things I wouldn't mind eating every single day for the rest of my life."

A bit of heat crept up to my cheeks. "That better not have been your idea of a proposal."

"Nope. Just stating a fact."

I grinned at him before taking a bite of my food. We sat in companionable silence chewing our food until his phone rang. Hastily setting down the last few bites of his burger, he wiped his hands on his napkin and pulled the phone out of his uniform shirt pocket.

"What's up, Marcus?"

I watched the color drain from his cheeks. "What?" A cold feeling of fear washed over me as I stared at him, waiting for him to say something that would give me a clue.

"On my way," he finally said and hung up.

"What's going on?"

"Come on," he said and stood up, tossing a twenty down on the table. "We might need you."

"What is it?" I took another bite of burger and washed it down with a sip of coke.

"The DA called the station."

"Oh." I slowed down to a walk. Disinterested in helping further.

"Dot, there's a zombie in his house."

"Serves him right."

Chief sighed. "Please. Maybe he'll be grateful and drop the charges."

"He would have to be a decent human being for that to happen." He gave me puppy dog eyes. My kryptonite. "Fine," I said angrily and headed out the door he was holding open for me.

We walked around the police station and got into his Jeep that had been parked out back. He started the engine, put it into gear, and hit the sirens and lights.

"You wanna slow down, Yuki?"

He did a double take. "Uh…police business. I'm allowed to drive this fast."

"Uh huh."

"I'm an excellent driver."

"Uh huh."

"I haven't been in an accident in…two years."

"Uh huh."

He shut up after that. Probably because everything he said went in one ear and out the other as I grabbed the oh-shit bar above my head and chanted a litany of prayers to the goddess.

We slid, not skidded, to a stop in front of a *very* large house by Shea's apartment complex. The same subdivision where Doctor Shapiro lived. It had to have been the *posh* part of town. The only two people I knew that lived there were a doctor and lawyer.

"He lives here?"

"Yeah." Chief left the engine running but opened his door.

"What a snob."

"You didn't know he lived here?" His question had a particular lilt to it that I didn't like.

"No? How would I?"

"I don't know. Magic?" He got out and headed toward the back of the Jeep and popped the trunk. I followed after him to find out what the hell he was getting at.

"What? Why would I use magic to find out where he lived? The only people I know in the area are Shea, who lives in the apartments, and Doctor Shapiro. Why would I care where the DA lives?"

He sighed, pulled out a shotgun, and closed the trunk. "I didn't think you did. I'm just being a cop."

"And by cop, you mean asshole?"

"How am I being an asshole?"

"You just accused me of sending a zombie after the Dickless Attorney."

"District."

"Whatever. You really think I would do something like that?"

He cocked an eyebrow at me.

"Fair enough, but no. I didn't. It would have been kind of brilliant and I'm sorry I didn't think of it first, but I'm innocent."

He nodded. "I believe you. Just making sure."

"Fair enough." I pouted and crossed my arms.

"Just gotta admit, first Jackson and Davis. Now the DA. Kind of a *huge* coincidence."

Even I had to admit that it was. "Weird." Fear twisted my stomach in an icy fist. *What if? What if they were protecting me?*

"Yep. Weird." He headed toward the house. I trailed behind, not unwrapping my arms from around myself. I had a bad feeling and that wasn't a coincidence, either. "Marcus. Where you at?" Chief yelled through the house from the entryway.

"Back here," came the distant reply. "Master bedroom."

Chief started walking in the direction of the voice and I followed behind him. Staring at the shotgun slung over his shoulder, I wondered at the effectiveness of the weapon. I might have to pick one up.

Marcus was standing in the bedroom and pointing his gun at the zombie slowly clawing its way through the wood paneling lining the interior of the walk-in closet. It wasn't having much luck against the stainless-steel plate behind it.

"Where's Materos?"

Marcus turned to look at Chief. "He's in his safe room," he answered and rolled his eyes.

"Money well spent if you ask me. Why is the zombie still alive?"

"Chief. I've shot the damn thing twelve times. It didn't even get pissed off at me."

I snickered. They both turned and gave me a dirty look. "Mind if I give it a shot?"

Chief made a be my guest motion with his hands. I tapped his chest as I walked past him and stopped just inside the closet. "Uh, Squishy Too?"

The zombie stopped clawing and turned slowly, regarding me with its overly dehydrated eyeballs. I kind of wanted to give him a bottle of Visine. "Could you stop attacking that man and come with me?"

"Glaaah."

Squishy Too was a little more intact than Squishy. Not as burned, but still very much dead and decomposed. "Come on. Follow me."

I headed out of the bedroom, turning to make sure it was following, and it was. He was trudging behind me and dragging one foot behind him.

"How'd she do that?" Marcus sounded confused.

"She has a way with men."

I rolled my eyes at his joke and headed for the back patio. I could lay Squishy Too to rest, but probably not through hardwood floors. I sighed at the grandeur of Materos' house. Most, if not all, of his DA paycheck had to have been going towards his mortgage. The only thing I was *truly* jealous of was the mirrored, wood trimmed bar built into the wall. I whistled as I passed it and stopped for a moment to let Squishy Too catch up.

"You want a drink?"

"Glaaah."

"Okay. Might be your last chance though."

"Glaaaah."

"You're a good and sober man, Squishy Too."

I gave one last wistful glance at the bar. I caught the zombie's reflection in the mirrors behind all the bottles of top shelf booze and my heart stopped beating. The zombie was quite visible, but so was the spirit animating it. The one hovered, superimposed, over the fleshy body. Lately, I'd been able to see spirits under two conditions. One, in mirrors. Two, in shadows. When I saw them in the shadows, their features weren't very visible. In the mirror, however, I could see every last detail. The ghost standing next to me was one of the three I'd kicked out of the bookstore. I would have bet a very large sum of money that Squishy was one of them, too. Unfortunately, it had been in

233

the very dark walk-in cooler that I'd seen him. There was no way I would have recognized him.

Fuck. Shit fuck. There's one more out there somewhere.

When I'd inadvertently given Squishy a corporeal form, I must have done the same for the other two without knowing it. Gulping, I said, "Come on. Let's get you to bed."

It took me a moment to unlock the sliding glass door and head out into the back yard. The snow was pretty thick, tall trees shading the yard and keeping it from catching any real direct sunlight. I cleared a patch with my foot. "Stand there," I told Squishy Too.

Saying a little prayer for him would have been kind of like talking to myself, so I forwent. "Be at peace and go to your final rest," I told him, calling the black fire to my hands. Without ceremony, I willed it to engulf the zombie and watched in fascination as he melted into the ground, just like his predecessor.

"Maaan. Shit is *never* boring when you're around."

I let out a soft bark of laughter and bowed to Marcus. He and Chief were standing behind me, having caught the whole show. "Thanks."

"You! You did this! You're trying to kill me! Chief Bates, I want this…*woman* arrested for attempted murder!" District Attorney Materos was standing in the doorway, red with rage. Veins were popping out on his forehead and sweat was freeze drying on the rest of his face. He looked like he was one ghoul away from popping a casket.

"You do, huh?"

"It is your *job*."

"No. My job is to uphold the law. Not to do what the DA tells me to. You see, Miss Blackwell has a rock-solid alibi. She was with me the whole time. So, she *couldn't* be responsible for whatever the hell that thing was trying to get into your little saferoom. Have a nice day." He motioned us toward the back gate, not wanting to get close to the raving lunatic or go through his house. I didn't blame him, neither did I.

"You know what? Fuck you, too. You better start looking for another job, you friggin' *witch* lover!"

He looked over his shoulder. "Yep. I do love her."

"You think my little video on Youtube was the end of this? I'm just getting started!"

Not going to lie. The blood in my veins froze. It was one thing to *suspect* him of setting me up and another to hear him admit it. Chief's hand shot over and he firmly entwined his fingers in mine, silently telling me to let it go. A firm believer in karma, I sighed and decided to be the better human. I wouldn't hurt him, I'd let the universe sort it out. He looked like he'd been about to have a heart attack, anyway. Marcus opened the gate and let us pass, putting himself between us and him. I gave him a sad smile as I walked past him. "Thanks."

"I love you, too," he said with a chuckle and a wink. That brightened my mood a little.

As soon as he pulled the gate shut, the screaming started. At first, I thought it was Materos just venting his frustrations, but it was a little hard to pretend the gurgling, gut-wrenching wail of being killed for anything else.

The gate automatically locked from the inside. "On three," Chief said levelly, and we shouldered it open and fell into the snow. In unison, the three of us gasped when we saw Squishy the Third covering DA Materos' body with his, gnawing on his open throat. At least he had stopped screaming.

"Does this mean those other charges are dropped?" I had to ask.

CHAPTER 19

I blinked at the setting sun just going down over the back side of Materos' wood fence. After laying Squishy the Third to rest, we figured out he had clawed his way under the fence on the opposite side of the back yard, out of sight. I kind of sort of felt a little sort of bad about the whole oversight, but not that heartbroken. The guy was a dick. Did he deserve to die? No. Would I spend countless nights, wandering the halls of my humble abode unable to find a moments rest because of the wracking guilt slowly eating away at me from inside? Hell no. Did I feel like an idiot for not looking around right away for the third zombie? Maybe. A little.

"It's not your fault," Chief said for the umpteenth time, sliding his hand over my shoulder as he walked past me as he did his Chiefly duties. There were no zombie bodies to pin the murder on and none of us, including Marcus, were going to mention the Z-word. Not if we didn't want to end up in a padded cell. The cause of death had been officially listed as an animal attack. One look at Materos' body and Herb opened his mouth to say something, looked at the three of us, and nodded.

"Looks like a small bear attack," he said and finished examining the body before carting it off.

Even the mayor had stopped by to pay her respects. Or to make sure he was dead. I wasn't really sure. She gave me a wink as she left, so I was pretty sure it was the latter. Materos wasn't very well liked. By anybody. His wife had left over a year ago with the kids. The neighbors didn't even know his name. Even the assistant DA, who just happened to stop by, didn't seem too bothered by the sudden loss of his direct supervisor. He was probably already banking on a pay raise. The only one who showed even a *modicum* of sadness was Dr. Materos. His equally dick headed brother. He seemed to know our story was bullshit and kept staring at me the entire time he was in the back yard. Finally, he left, and I could feel the foreshadowing flowing from him. This wasn't over, but at least *he* wasn't the district attorney. The most he could do was refuse to take my insurance if I ever ended up in the emergency room, but I had a feeling he was going to *try* to make my life difficult.

For me, it was a Christmas miracle. Materos' death had even gotten the reporters off my ass. They were now swarming the front of *his* house intent on interviewing everyone and everything in the surrounding area. Marcus had grabbed an extra jacket, hat, and sunglasses out of his patrol car. I looked like Deputy Doohickey in the getup, but at least they didn't recognize me.

We were still standing around in the back yard when the sun finally went down.

"You want me to grab the work lights, Chief?" Marcus hollered across the lawn, to get his attention.

Chief looked around the yard. "No. Let's wrap it up. We're done here."

Thank fuck. I'm hungry. Memories of my half-eaten burger made my stomach twist in a knot.

"You ready to go?" He pointed to the open gate.

"I've been ready for a couple of hours now."

"I know. Sorry this took so long."

"Think they'll find the bear?" I laughed softly.

"Probably not. If it wasn't hibernating like it should be, it must have been sick." He winked. I hadn't even thought about that. That's why he was the Chief and I was the exorcist.

"We make a pretty good team. You handle the paperwork and details. I can take out the zombies."

"Shhh. There's still a ton of ears around."

"Sorry," I whispered.

"Come on. Let's get you home," he said and pushed the shattered gate out of the way for me. He was such a gentleman. We almost made it the entire way to his Jeep when the searing pain behind my eyes started. I wobbled on the street and Chief caught me before I fell. "You okay?"

I shook my head. It was all I could do. "No. Give me a minute."

Witches didn't get migraines. This was something completely different and new, and I didn't like it. Something was tearing apart my brain and I didn't have a clue what it was.

Master? Dar's voice sounded pained.

You feel that?

Yes. What is it?

I don't know. Yuki? I sent her name down the link we shared and felt it flitter away into nothingness. *Yuki?*

Is she with you?

No. At the house.

I am with Shea. We will go there now.

I felt him sever the link. They would get there before Chief and me. "Home."

"What's wrong."

"Yuki is gone."

"What? Gone, gone?"

"I don't fucking know. Get me home, please." I opened his door and slid into the passenger seat.

239

He got in and started the car, slamming it into gear and gunning the engine, sirens on full blast. Everybody got out of the way as he skidded around the corner, taking us to Main.

I was fighting the pain in my head. The link to Yuki was raw and throbbing. That had to be the cause. My heart cracked and refused to beat. I sat motionless in his seat, hoping for the best and fearing the worst.

"She'll be okay."

"I'm not so sure. Go faster, please."

He stepped on the accelerator, pinning it against the floorboards and not slowing for anything. Not even the train tracks. We landed on the other side, and I didn't even bat an eyelash, let alone scream. I wanted him to go faster.

Master?

Is she there?

No. The house is...destroyed.

Fuck the house, find my Yuki.

Yes, Master.

The two of them were standing outside when Chief jumped the curb and landed in the snow-covered grass. I was out of the vehicle before he even put it in park.

"Where is she?"

"Taken," Shea said sadly.

"Who?"

It was Dar who answered. He held out his hand and wrapped it around my shoulder. "From the damage to your house, I would have to guess vampires. I shifted to make certain. Their smell is all over everything."

"No..." Panic seized me. Her father had come to town.

"Dot?"

"What?"

Dar looked afraid. "Candace's car is here..." He pointed at it sitting in the driveway. I hadn't even noticed.

"They're not inside." I didn't ask, I told. He had taken insurance. Lord Abernathy wanted something, what I didn't

240

know. Me, Yuki, answers…the possibilities were endless, but he was determined to get what he wanted.

Chief jogged over and stopped when he saw the looks on our faces. "What's wrong?"

"Everything." I should have known. Things were going *too* well. That's when disaster always chose to rear its ugly little fucking head.

"Where are we going?"

I turned to him and pressed my face against his warm chest. "You're going to go. I…uh. I need you to sit this one out, Chief. For me."

"Like hell I will. I'm tired of sitting on the sidelines while you run off and face the nasty shit by yourself. I helped with the damn demons, didn't I? No offense, Dar."

"None taken."

"Chief. This isn't demons. It's an entire clan of vampires and their lord. They have Yuki, Josie, and Candace. This isn't a full-scale invasion, gather the witches and man the fucking cannons. This is a stealth mission. We're going to sneak in, get them and get out. And possibly nuke the fucking place when we run away."

"You're going to shadow walk in." He glanced over at Shea, who nodded, and then Chief lowered his head until it was level with mine, staring me in the eyes. "This is the plan. No fighting, no taking on this vampire lord by yourself. You're just rescuing your family."

"Yes."

"Do you promise me?"

"Yes. This is the plan."

"Okay. I believe you. And I'll do as you ask. But, so help me Lady, Dot. If this turns into a goddess damned war and you don't call for backup, I'm going to lock you in my cell for a fucking week."

"On what charge?"

"Stupidity without a license. Go, before I change my mind. And I'm gathering the coven. And your damned mother. So, if shit goes south, you call me, give me a mental shout, send up a flare, or blow up a fucking building and we will find you and help. Do you understand?"

"Yes. And that is a good plan, too."

"I didn't say your plan was a good one. But with the two of them with you, you might be able to pull it off."

"It's not just me. I have the shadows, too."

He shuddered and nodded before he leaned in and kissed the shit out of me. "Be careful."

"I will."

"Come back."

"I will."

"I love you."

"I love you more," I said with a little grin.

"I fucking doubt that," he answered with a huff and stormed off to his Jeep.

"Is this really the plan?"

"Do you really think it will be that easy?" I answered Dar's question with my own.

"No. I do not. Are you going to call for back up?"

"Nope."

"I did not think so."

"You guys don't have to go with me…" I gave them an earnest look, meaning the words that came out of my mouth.

"Somebody needs to keep you alive," Shea answered without hesitation, reaching out and grabbing my hand.

I looked at Dar. "You could stay here and keep the hearth fires warm…"

"And miss a glorious battle with my mate?"

I grinned at the two of them. "You mean mates."

Dar looked at Shea and gave him a shy smile and nodded earnestly. "Let us do this, as they say."

"Where are we going?"

"The only place we can. To the clan house."

"Yes, Lady," Shea said and squeezed my hand, pulling us into the shadow realm.

∞ ∞ ∞

Shea stepped out of the shadows from the copse of trees on the empty lot next door. The moon was bright overhead, and I sent a silent prayer to her to guide us and keep all of us safe. And then I said another that Yuki was still alive.

"There are no lights on," Dar said, stating the obvious.

"Vampires don't need them."

"Do we ring the bell?"

Shea slipped his dagger from his belt and peered in through the window closest to us. "No shadows," he said softly.

"Dar?"

"Yes, Master?"

"Think you can make a door?"

"Yes, Master." He shifted into his giant hellhound form and backed up to the edge of the woods. I grabbed Shea and pulled him away from the window as Dar charged full force at it. His head broke through the glass, but his body tore through the wall underneath it like a hairy wrecking ball. We followed in right behind him, ignoring the debris still falling from above.

"Thank you, Dar," I said and headed for the bedroom door.

He growled in response, not bothering with mind speech.

I didn't bother turning on the lights, I could see the vampire sitting calmly at the dining room table, sipping a cup of what I assumed was blood.

"Amir."

"Lady," he answered, tilting his head in acknowledgement.

"You don't seem surprised to see me," I said as Dar shifted to fit through the doorway.

"I volunteered to wait here for you. It made sense that you would come here first."

"Why did he take Yuki?"

He sighed and took another sip. "I warned him. Do you know how much courage it took to warn the fucking lord of our clan that he shouldn't mess with you?" He slammed the cup down on the table. "No. The lure of walking in the sun and marrying off his daughter to the Clan of the Steel Dawn was just too much for him."

"What? Wait. Slow down. He's going to marry Yuki off?"

"That is his plan, yes. After he learns from her how she walks in the sunlight. He's almost obsessed about that. I would even wager that he cares more about that than the threat you pose to him. He killed them you know."

"Who?"

"The younglings who said you felt like a vampire lord. He took it as a challenge to his power. He accused them of being traitors and that they wanted to join you to walk in the sun."

I was in shock. None of this sounded like Lord Abernathy. Not the one I knew. Not the one I helped take over the local blood bank.

"Why did you volunteer to wait?"

He pushed the cup away from him. "You know the reason."

"Why, Amir?" I put my hands down on the table and leaned forward.

"Because my loyalty lies with you, not him. Even if my sister does not feel the same way. *You* were the one who saved us. Not him. You gave us shelter, freed us from our

244

bonds. I am sorry I was so obsessed about joining a clan that I ignored my friend. I am sorry."

He was telling the truth. I could taste it in the air.

"Where is he?"

"Meeting with the lord of the clan from California. He means to give him his daughter tonight."

My blood boiled. Arranged marriages were barbaric. Forcing your asexual daughter to marry someone...was evil. There was no way I was going to let it happen. Not as long as I still breathed. "Where?"

"Graveyard. He told me to tell you to come alone or your witches would die at the fangs of his vampires."

"Not if I snap them off first." I turned around and paused for a moment. "Thank you, Amir."

"Dot..."

"What?"

"Do not do this. I have to, in good conscience, tell you not to. He is a monster. You might be extremely powerful, but you do not know the full power of a vampire lord."

"I don't have a choice, Amir. Yuki is my friend. Just as you are. I protect my friends, no matter what."

"I know."

"Will you come with us?"

"I wish I could. If I were to go with you, the moment he set eyes on me, I would become a detriment. He is lord. I am clan. He could control me with a mere thought."

I nodded.

"I do promise to stay far away. I will not fight you now, or ever, my Lady."

"If the night goes as planned, you'll be free again."

"Then I doubly wish you luck."

We walked out of the house through the hole we made.

CHAPTER 20

Lord Abernathy couldn't have picked a worse spot to make the exchange. They were in the center of the graveyard, Yuki bound at his feet as they stood in front of three tall vampires in black suits. They stood in front of a white limousine. Unfortunately for all of them, the moon high above us had cast a thousand shadows in the shape of tombstones all around them.

Shea wasn't my familiar. He was close, but no cigar. I had no way to communicate with him mentally. Fearing I would have been overheard, even if I whispered, by the kiss of vampires, I pointed at Shea, then Dar, and then toward the opposite side of the graveyard.

You want him to shadow walk me to the other side? Box them in?

Yes.

Shea rolled his eyes, grabbed my hand and Dar's, and pulled us into the shadow we'd been standing in. "We can talk freely here."

"Oh. Duh. Sorry."

"It is all right. You may be able to walk in the shadows, but you lack the experience."

"Ouch."

"Just stating the truth." He blushed.

"It is. True, I mean. But experience is a fine teacher. You take Dar to the other side. Drop him behind the largest of the tombstones. You come out behind them and wait. I'm trusting you to be stealthy. If they hear, see, or smell either of you, the game is over."

"Yes, Lady. May I ask what it is you will be doing?"

"I was supposed to come alone. And that's exactly what I'm going to do. Walk straight up that road and keep their attention on me."

"You are going to make a spectacle of yourself?"

"Big time."

"I have faith in your abilities," Dar chimed in with a little smile.

I kissed them both and stepped out of the shadow on my own. Not relying on Shea.

"Fidget?" I whispered, not caring if they heard me. I had come alone, just like Lord Abernathy wanted.

Fidget squawked as he slid out from the sleeve of my jacket.

"Just you and me bud. Keep me safe, okay?"

Chirp.

The dusty and dirty road was too frozen to kick up much as I strode down the middle of it, heading directly at the unsurprised looking vampires and a fearful looking Yuki. Candace and Josie were nowhere to be seen. I just hoped they were safe.

"Phillipe," I called out Abernathy's fist name, dispensing with the titles and respectful sounding surname. He had stolen from me. That made us equals. Or, at least that's what I tried to tell myself to bolster my confidence.

"So good of you to join us, Lady Blackwell."

He made my name sound condescending. First point to him. "You stole my familiar, Phillipe. You knew I would come take her back from you."

"She is no longer yours. I know you felt me sever the link between you. I thought that would have been enough incentive to keep you away. I had *hoped* you would ignore it, but I didn't think you would have that much courage in you. I should have expected more from your mother's child."

"Courage?" I kept walking, forcing my legs to close the distance between us. "I don't need courage. There isn't anything I wouldn't do for my friends. How did you break the familiar bonds? You told me you couldn't."

"Friends? This useless creature?" He kicked the bound Yuki in the side. "She has been nothing but trouble to me since the day she was born. It is only my love for her mother that has kept her alive. I thought by sending her out here to you, my troubles would have been silenced. I see I was mistaken. As to your bonds, it took months to find a sorcerer up to the task. Again, she has cost me a fortune."

"But you have no trouble using her."

"No. She is my creation. I do not."

The closer I got to him, the more his voice dropped in volume. He was almost speaking in normal tones. I'd gotten close enough for him to stop yelling. "We don't have to do this. Give her back to me and I'll go away."

"You're going to go away even if you keep walking."

"Yuki, you okay?"

She looked up at me, red rimmed eyes clearly visible even in the moonlight stared at me in utter hopelessness. I didn't need mind speech to know what she was saying. She was begging me to run away with a look.

Hang in there, kiddo. I got this, I told her, just on the off chance she could still hear me. Not really believing she could, I had no trouble lying to her face. The odds of them getting out of the graveyard alive were pretty good. I'd make sure of that much. The odds of me following after them…those weren't so great. Yuki would live, her father had severed the bond between us. Dar… Wherever he was in the world, if I died, he would most likely follow. He knew that and still followed me into battle.

"Last chance, Phillipe. Give me back my Yuki."

"Mine!" His voice echoed through the entire graveyard, tiny reverberations of the word bouncing from every slab of marble in the field.

"Like hell she is!" I snarled and picked up the pace.

As soon as my feet started running, Abernathy smiled and raised his hand. Two vampires standing in a copse of trees behind him stepped out, their hands on the shoulders of Josie and Candace.

"You will stop." His voice was barely a whisper and my feet skidded to a halt. "Now. You will turn around and walk away or they will die. Keep walking and all three of you will perish."

Now. My mental voice signaled the attack. Dar slid out sideways in his hellhound form from behind the largest mausoleum in the graveyard. He bayed at the moon above. The tone was enough to make me want to cover my ears in agitation. The sound was not meant for mortal, or immortal, ears. It wouldn't hurt either me or them, but that wasn't its purpose. Dar bayed to draw attention to him.

Abernathy wasn't fooled and didn't take his eyes from me, so he missed Shea slipping from the shadows and slicing through the necks of the vampires holding Josie and Candace with his silver blade. It wouldn't be enough to kill them, but the silver would keep them from healing right away and the blade had severed their throats, not giving them a chance to call out. Silently, they dropped to the ground in shock, clutching the wounds in their necks. As soon as they were incapacitated, he pulled Josie and Candace back into the shadows to safety.

Just as Dar stopped howling.

"You missed your chance to attack. You didn't think I would be stupid enough to take my eyes from you while your little pet barked at the moon?"

"I was counting on it." I pointed behind him.

He glanced over his shoulder and I saw the look of disappointment pass over his features. "You can't even *make* good help these days." He reached down and picked Yuki up by the neck, holding her out in front of him.

"What are you doing? The day walker is ours. You gave us your word."

He looked at the three vampires in front of him. "And have her you shall. After she serves her purpose to me." He turned her, pressing her back against his chest as his sharp fingers grabbed the front of her throat. "This is your last chance, Blackwell. Leave or she dies, you die, your dog dies. I'll find your mother and kill her, too." He grinned at me evilly.

Yuki looked down at the hand at her throat. She hadn't been around any vampires in a while. Not since the change had come upon her. Not since she found she fed from them instead of humans. The proximity of his hand to her throat drove away her fear and was replaced by hunger. She looked back up at me incredulously.

That's it, baby. Show Daddy you're not that scared little girl anymore.

Her legs might have been bound, but she lifted them up and drove them underneath her as hard as she could, catching Abernathy square in the shins as she launched herself from his grip. She didn't land very far, just a few feet away before she rolled across the frozen dirt.

"You sniveling little shit!" He strode forward, intent on hitting her in the face when my fire spell hit him in the chest. There weren't many things that could hurt a vampire. Fire was one of them.

Or, so I thought.

His rage became focused on me as his face contorted in rage, suit blacked from my blast, but otherwise unhurt. "Kill them all!" His voice was exponentially louder than the first time he yelled.

The graveyard was situated in the middle of the surrounding woods, creating a serene place for people to bury their loved ones. From those trees, scores of vampires poured into the moonlit fields.

He had an army.

I had a Shea and Dar.

It wasn't going to be nearly enough.

Even the vampires standing in front of the limo were laughing at me. Shea stepped from the shadows of their car and launched himself at Yuki. He had almost connected with her, intent on getting her to the shadow of the headstone closest to them, when Abernathy's hand shot out and snatched him from the air.

"Well, if it isn't the little librarian," he said and grinned. Until Shea's dagger slashed against his wrist, nearly severing his hand from his arm. Shea dropped to the ground and Abernathy pinned him there with his Italian leather shoes while he stared at his wrist, watching it heal.

It's now or never.

My feet launched me toward him. It was a suicide move, but all I needed was to get him away from Shea and Yuki. They could get to safety, Dar could get away, and maybe by the grace of the goddess, I could slip away to safety, too. It was our only chance, and we only had a few seconds before Abernathy's vampire army killed every one of us.

At least my sister is safe.

Without even tearing his eyes from his arm, Abernathy reached out and caught me by *my* throat. He held me there for the last remaining moment it took for the wound to close before he turned his head toward me. His eyes narrowed as he smiled and tilted his head in mock sympathy.

"Foolish witch."

"Foolish vampire," I answered and called the black flames to my hands and grabbed his arm.

Inspiration can come from the strangest of places. Being choked to death is one of them. My thoughts flashed to the zombies melting into the ground. Zombies were undead, just like vampires.

Abernathy's eyes widened as pain shot up his arm and his veins bulged, alight in black fire. He let go and went to smash my forearms, intent on breaking my bones. Fidget slid from my sleeve and took the brunt of the attack, but the fire stopped burning and didn't send him to the hell he belonged in.

"Whore!" He kicked me, faster than Fidget could protect me from, launching me at a tree twenty feet behind me. I hit the trunk and wasn't sure if it was it or me that cracked in a sickening crunch. Either way, I slid down to the frozen ground, unable to move as pain wracked every nerve in my body.

I stared at him, chuckling noiselessly since my lungs had lost the ability to force air over my vocal cords. Shea had grabbed Yuki and dragged her kicking into the shadows. I had won. Partially. If only my sweet Dar wouldn't have to pay for my arrogance.

In the distance, I saw him. The vampires had closed in and were clawing him mercilessly. Some had even wrapped their arms around him and were bleeding him with their fangs. He was a hundred times stronger than any of them, but not all of them. They were crushing him with their sheer numbers.

At least he wouldn't be alone when he died.

You are a god, daughter.

I blinked in surprise. My father never intervened when it mattered. To hear his voice now was a shock. It was always my goddess who came to me in my time of need.

Isn't it about time you started acting like one?

I don't know how.

It isn't a matter of knowing. It's a matter of feeling. Look around you, what do you see?

Vampires and death.

Yes.

Isn't there some sort of manual you could give me and quit with the games?

His mental sigh was like music to my ears. *You have so much of your mother in you.*

Sure. Insult me before I die.

Your mother is one of the strongest women and witches you have ever laid your eyes upon, and you know it.

I know.

Good. Daughter, I love you, but sometimes you are too dense for your own good. You should think long and hard about that. As you lie there. In a graveyard. Full of bodies. Goddess of the underworld.

Well, shit. When you put it like that...

I love you, he said again as his voice faded from my mind.

I didn't watch Abernathy as he was closing the distance between us, a self-satisfied smirk on his face. I looked at the crop of headstones around me and let my senses fling from me like a finely cast net. Purple lines settled over the entire graveyard and I could sense every bone of every body in every grave around me. Some had been there for over a century. Some barely a year. I knew each and every one of them.

I lifted my barely healed arms up above the ground, smiled at Abernathy as I called the black fire, and slapped the ground beside me.

For a few moments nothing happened. Abernathy glanced around him nervously. As the moments passed, his smile returned. "Was that a bluff or did your power fail you?"

"No. It worked."

He narrowed his eyes and tilted his head. "What did?"

"It takes a few moments to claw through six feet of dirt," I answered with a smile as bodies burst from the ground all around him.

254

"How? That is not possible." He started shuffling backward.

"That's what I thought." I chuckled and stood slowly, my body still healing. I took a deep breath, my lungs healed and ribs reknitted. My back still hurt like a bitch, though. "Kill them all," I shouted, my voice echoing over the graveyard like rolling thunder.

More bodies burst from the ground. My zombie army had finally appeared.

Dar. Get away.

Trying.

Zombies dragged vampires from his thrashing form until he was free enough to bound away, standing at the edge of the clearing.

The vampires were strong, but not zombie strong. The three by the limo were quickly overwhelmed and I turned my head as they were slowly ripped apart. Their screams weren't something I would forget for a very long time.

"What are you?" For the first time since I had met him so many years ago, I heard fear in Abernathy's voice. It was that fear that triggered the hunger inside me. I had been grievously wounded. My body expended vampiric energy to heal that. It needed blood to replenish that and Abernathy sounded *so,* so tasty.

I licked my lips as I walked toward him. He started to back away faster. Without so much as a word of command, two of my zombies grabbed him and held him still as I stepped up to him and sniffed his chest.

"You smell delicious."

"You're a witch! You can't eat a vampire!"

"Oh, but that's not all I am," I answered as my fangs slid lower than my lip and my eyes began to glow with blue fire. I could see them reflected in his. He started screaming even before my fangs slipped into the flesh of his neck.

EPILOGUE

Mindlessly, I wrapped the extra-wide tinfoil sheet over the disposable aluminum pan with half a sliced turkey nestled safely inside. "Forty-eight," I told Herb.

"That's the last one," he said and pumped his fist. He pulled the pan from my hands and slid it onto the rolling rack beside him. "Put it in the van, Miguel. You guys get on the road."

Miguel looked at his watch and nodded. "We should have everything delivered by four. A lot of people are going to be eating good tonight, Mr. Herb."

I watched him as he wheeled the cart toward the back door of the diner and finally snapped out of it. "I need to go get showered."

"Yeah. You do smell like a turkey." Herb poked me in the stomach and pulled me into a hug. "Thank you, sweetie. You made this old man's Christmas a little brighter this year." He turned and looked at everyone in the kitchen. Chief, Jimmy, Dennis, and Jason. Shea, Dar, and Yuki. Candace and Josie. Even my mother and Nana had offered to help. "Thank you all."

I couldn't help it. The tears started pouring from my eyes as I wrapped my arms around him and held on tight. As soon as the fight in the graveyard had been over and Lord Abernathy fell dead at my feet, I collapsed, wailing for the father who had finally helped me after a hundred years of floundering on my own. He didn't utter another fucking word and I hated him. Herb was more of a father to me than the god who had abandoned me.

"You okay, sweetie?" He pulled back until he could stare into my eyes.

"Just a rough few days."

He playfully slapped me in the back of the head. "Then you should have gotten some rest."

"And miss all this fun?" I did my best to give him a smile.

"It was, kinda. Huh?"

I nodded. "Best Christmas ever."

"Wait 'til next year," Marge chimed in. "We'll do this shit tanked on eggnog."

"I can't wait," my mother answered and rolled her eyes.

"I haven't had eggnog since..." Nana paused to think about it. "Just after the black plague, I believe." She shrugged and walked away.

"She's joking right?" Marge looked like she was about to faint again.

"Hardly, Marjoram," Mother said, slurring a little as she swirled her glass of wine. "Except, I believe she is referring to the black plague that wiped out the creatures in the Mesozoic Era." Mother cackled.

"It's just Marge, Mother."

"That's what I said. Merge."

I chuckled and tossed the carving board and knife into the huge sink beside the prep table.

"What time is dinner, Daughter?"

"Six. I told Nana to make sure the both of you aren't late."

"Very well. We shall see you at your overly-humble abode."

"See you tonight, Mother."

She nodded and followed after Nana. Surprisingly enough, Nana had insisted that Mother check out of

Farrell's motel. I laughed when she used the excuse of the hotel needing the space for the holidays, but let it go. Maybe absence really did make the heart grow fonder. Maybe they both were just getting senile in their old age and needed each other to remind the other to take their meds. It didn't matter, as long as they could both stay under the same roof without killing each other. Just a few months ago, it was hard enough to get them to live in the same town without blowing it up. Baby steps were for amateurs.

"See you tonight, Herb. Marge."

"Bye, Dot."

I turned and grabbed Yuki by the ear, pulling her away from the pie case. Every time she walked past it, she stopped and stared lovingly at the contents. "No. Let me stare for just a minute longer!"

Vampires can't eat pie.

I know. But it looks soo damn good!

I smiled at the happy tone of her mind speech. As soon as her father died, she had latched herself on to one of my still closing wounds and drank her fill of my blood. I had planned on offering her the opportunity to *not* be my familiar anymore, but she squashed my well-intentioned plan with a nasty glare and a happy smile as she rolled my blood around on her tongue and told me I tasted yummers. Crazy kid. I loved her.

It was kind of funny, but as I sat there healing, I wondered how I was going to explain how badly everything had happened when the cavalry I *didn't* call, showed up. They were being led by my shining knight in brown polyester riding his steed with flashing blue and red lights. Everybody had showed up, battle ready. Even my mother and Nana. When they saw it was over, they all took turns hugging me and crying. Especially my boys. Each one of them held me close and whispered how much they loved me into my ears. My body might have healed itself, but they healed my heart.

"Let's go home, Yuki."

"'Kay." She grabbed my hand and pulled me toward the exit. I stopped her for a moment, not wanting to collide with the ghost hanging by the exit. Another victim of a nameless fire. I bowed with respect and he fluttered away. Since the battle, my sixth sense, the one that let me see ghosts and the underworld of graves beneath our feet, had been amped up exponentially. Before, I could only see them in mirrors or shadows. Now I saw them everywhere. It made life a little more interesting.

Without even asking, Yuki got into the driver's seat. I rolled my eyes and let her have her way, climbing into the seat next to her and staring out the window as she *slowly* drove us home

∞ ∞ ∞

"For such a simple guy, you're awfully hard to shop for," I told Chief and set his present down in front of him, narrowly missing his empty plate of food.

As a surprise, I'd had an entire seafood meal catered from one of the fanciest restaurants in Amersville. I'd had to pay them triple to agree to deliver on Christmas day, but it was money well spent. I sure as shit didn't feel like cooking and after the day the whole clan had, nobody felt like fucking turkey. Jimmy maybe. The perv. The looks on everyone's face as the very merry catering servers brought in chafing dish after chafing dish of lobster, shrimp, and crab made me happier than I'd been in a very long time.

"What did you get me?"

"Open it and find out."

He tore through the paper like a little kid and ripped the cardboard box into shreds to get at the gift inside. Hand shaking, he pulled out a framed picture of the two of us I'd sneakily had Yuki take. I had the image blown up and framed. He pressed his lips together and gulped, trying not to cry. The big softie.

He had pictures of his late wife all over his house, but his office...he kept a picture of me there. I knew I had a very special place in his heart, and I figured he could use a picture of the both of us. It would make him happy. "Thank you, Dot."

"Not too sentimental?"

He sniffed and shook his head, not daring to look at me. I could see the tear finally roll its way down his cheek and I kissed it away before anybody saw it. They never would have let him live it down. "Love you," I whispered as I went to grab my next gift.

Jimmy smiled as I brought it to him. "Happy Yule, Jimmy."

"It would be happier if you had let us get you presents."

I held up my hand and held out his gift in the other. "I have all of you. That is all I could ever want."

"Still say it's not fair."

"Besides. You got me that Mr. Nutsack. Your gift giving days are over. Just give me kisses from now on." I rolled my eyes and patted him on the head. Luckily, I had talked Dar into keeping it at Shea's house. Their first pet together. They named it Golum, but I refused to call it anything other than Mr. Nutsack.

Jimmy carefully tore the wrapping paper from the small gold colored box. He pulled open the lid, grinned, and closed it. I could practically hear the wheels turning in his head.

"Well? What is it?" Curiosity was tearing Yuki apart.

Jimmy slid the box across the table to her. I wanted to stop her from opening it, but I just shook my head and waited for the laughter.

"You got him a five-hundred-dollar gift card to the adult toy store in Amersville?"

"Could you think of a better present for him?"

"Nope. You done good, Boss."

"This one is for Jason…" I put the box in front of him.

He tore it open, lifted the lid off the box, and blushed.

"What is with you guys. You have to tell us what you get. Or show us. It's the rules," Yuki said exasperatedly.

"It's a remote controlled buttplug…" Jason glanced up at me. "I thought you swore you'd never use one again."

"Oh, sweetie. That's not for me. That's for you." I held up the remote.

Marge started cackling. My mother started wiggling her eyebrows. Jason quickly closed the box.

"Dar, if you look in Yuki's room there's a huge scratching post for the nutsack. Sorry, it was too big to wrap and put under the tree." He shot up, kissed me, and ran into Yuki's room to check it out.

"Dennis," I set his box in front of him.

He kind of gave me a shocked look, not really expecting anything, but smiling as he pulled out the entire box set of Star Wars DVD's. I'll admit, I had to turn to Jimmy for advice. Dennis wasn't the most vocal of boyfriends, and I didn't know what to get him. He turned and looked at Jimmy and laughed.

"What?"

"Jimmy's a dickhead. He knows I hate Star Wars. I'm a Trekkie."

I slapped the laughing Jimmy in the back of the head. "I'm sorry, Dennis."

"Don't be. I don't think there's a present in the world that would have made me smile that much. Plus, it's from you."

"Shea. You're up next." I grabbed his present and set it down in front of him. He pulled his dagger, scaring Marge and Herb until he deftly slid it between the folds of the wrapping paper and pulled the entire thing off in one solid sheet. Which he folded neatly and set aside. I chuckled a little.

He reached in and pulled out the titanium pocket flashlight from the box and gave me a quizzical look.

"That is a tactical flashlight with ten thousand lumens."

A smile spread across his face as he hugged it to his chest.

"I don't get it," Yuki said, staring at me.

"It is so I can always escape."

"Yeah. Still don't get it."

"If there's no shadows around, he can make his own," I said with a grin, not expecting him to get up from his chair and run to me, burying his face in my chest.

"What did you get me?" Josie grinned at me from the end of the table. I'd been planning on saving her for last, but if she wanted to be impatient, I'd learn her.

"Oh, something *very* special."

Her face fell. "Dot. I told you not to get me anything special. I'd be happy with booze. You already do too much for us." She hugged Candace a little closer.

"Yes. But it's my job to take care of…my best friend." I'd purposely hesitated, just to watch my mother squirm.

Petty, thy name is Dot. Bwahahaha.

I walked over to the tree and pulled a tiny box from the branches and walked over to them. "This is actually for both of you. It's a Yule and pre-wedding gift rolled into one. I hope you like it."

I set the box down between them. Josie pushed the box toward Candace who eyed it suspiciously. Finally, curiosity got the better of her and she lifted off the lid of the gilded box.

There was a layer of glittered cotton covering the gift, which she reached out, pinched it between her fingers and lifted out. There sat a single silver key on a ring.

"A key?" Candace looked up at me.

"Yes."

"You got us a key for Yule?" Josie was confused.

"Well, the key is to open your present."

"Please tell me you didn't get us a new car," Josie said sadly, shaking her head. "That's way too much."

"Of course not! That's not a car key." I winked.

"Josie?"

"Yes, Candy?"

Candace gulped, staring at the key. "I believe that is a house key." She sniffled.

Josie peered at it and then up at the smile on my face. I nodded.

"No fucking way."

"Yep."

"You bought us. A fucking house?"

"Sort of."

"Where?" Candace looked a little worried.

I pointed at the north wall. "Right next door."

"You bought us the fucking house next door?" Josie's voice had almost slipped into the ultrasonic frequency.

I nodded once again

They looked at each other, then at me. Then they started screaming, pushed their chairs backward with their asses, and ran over to me and tackled me.

"Best Yule ever?"

"Yes!" The both screamed together and then started kissing me all over my face. I couldn't stop laughing until the doorbell rang. An ominous fear settled over me as I sat up. "I'll get it," I said worriedly.

"Let's just hope it's not another ex-boyfriend," Jimmy said jokingly. Yuki smacked him in the head.

I walked over to the door and slowly reached out for the knob, twisting it and pulling it open slowly. Jaeren was standing there with a grin on his face. "Merry Yule! I come bearing gifts for my Lady!"

"Oh, thank fuck."

"Pardon?"

"Was just expecting something horrible. That's how these holiday things and get togethers usually end for me."

"Fear not. May I come in?"

"Of course. You could have just come in. You're always welcome here." I stepped out of the way and let him walk in.

"I took the liberty of sneaking your gift into your back yard. I hope you do not mind," he said and headed for the sliding glass door.

"How'd you get it in there?"

"Magic." Apparently, he wasn't kidding.

"It took me quite a while to figure out the perfect gift for you. Especially after your gift of color sticks. I thought it would take a miracle to equal such thoughtfulness. Luckily, inspiration struck. Meet your gift." He slid the door open and whistled.

A single spiraled horn, glittering in the sunlight, brought a collective gasp from everyone in the room. Then the pure white snout, piercing blue eyes, and gorgeous mane peeked in through the door and gazed at me adoringly.

"Jaeren…"

"Yes?"

"Is that…"

"A unicorn? Yes, it is!"

Jaeren. The King of Elfhame Autumn Glade had gifted me a living, breathing unicorn. Because I bought him a box of fucking crayons.

"Holy shit!" Yuki giggled. "That's awesome!"

I grinned at Jaeren. "Thank you!"

At least it's not a hairless cat…

Shut up, Yuki

"Introduce yourself!" Jaeren pushed me toward the door.

I sighed in relief. Jaeren's gift was far from the ominous disaster I'd been expecting when the doorbell rang. Maybe, if I spent my life expecting bad things to happen after good things did, they wouldn't. That had to be it. I'd just unlocked the secret of the universe.

Greetings, Lady.

"Unicorn?"

My name is Delanir.

"That's kind of pretty."

Thank you. Lord Delron bids you hello. He knows how to get you to Tartarus. I am to take you to him, immediately.

"Oh, come the fuck on!"

Bonus Scene
Another's Darling

Enjoy this bonus scene from Dar's point of view!
Takes place approx Chapter 7

His hand felt so different in mine than my master's, not better, not worse, just different. His skin was softer for one, and it felt stronger, more dangerous. There was no doubt he could use that hand to bring me pleasure or slit my throat. He was an assassin. I knew what that meant far more than Dot did. When she looked at Shea, her vision was clouded by his feelings for her. She had lived his life, seen it through his eyes. She knew how he felt about her and how his one and only desire left in the world was to protect her.

Now, my vision was getting as cloudy as hers when I looked at him. He was as beautiful as any woman I'd ever lay with, even among my own kind. The kind of beauty where your heart skips a beat when they smile at you. The predator in me saw it as a trap. The demon in me saw it as something to be cautious of. The rest of me saw it as the chance at happiness.

Do not misjudge my words. My heart belongs to my master, it always has and always will, but she is not meant for the likes of me, him, or any of us. She is meant for all of us. She did not belong to us, *we* belonged to her.

The assassin gently, yet eagerly, tugging my hand through the realm of shadow was the same. We both shared that love for her, and yet something had sparked between us. I had felt it in our lovemaking with her, this bond between us as well.

Had she not been very outspoken and encouraged it, I would not have accepted his invitation for wine and a movie. I believe she knew of the feelings I was having for the diminutive half-elf. Knew and approved. She would never admit it, but I could see the guilt in her eyes for not being available to each and every one of her lovers every night. I cannot speak for the rest of them, but I wish there were some way to reassure her. Even one night spent out of a thousand would be amazing. She burned like the fires of k'vothar and soothed like the nectar of al'isithel.

We stepped from the shadows into his living room and Shea flashed me a shy smile. "We are here."

"We are."

"What kind of wine would you like?"

I chuckled, my experience with wine ranked up there with making small talk with dark elves. He blushed as he pulled his cloak from his feminine frame. "I shall defer to your expertise, Shea."

"I have just the thing then." The grin he gave me should have worried me. "Sit, see if you can find something for us to watch."

Blinking in surprise, I stared after him as he headed for the kitchen of his small apartment. When Dot wasn't around, he wasn't as nervous, seeming more animated. His nervousness around her kept him from expressing himself so much. If he had, her heart would have melted long ago. It doubled his beauty and I had to fight my desire to run my hands over him with every smile.

Making my way to his couch, I sat on the edge and picked up his television remote. There was a thin layer of dust over it and I chuckled. It might have been the first time someone touched it since he had his cable installed. "Have you ever seen GHOST BUSTERS?"

"I have not. My experience with movies is rather…limited."

I didn't need to look over the back of the couch to see his embarrassment, I could hear it in his voice. "I've had a crash course the past few months," I admitted. "There is little else for me to do but sit on the couch and watch the human entertainment."

"Feel free to come over if you're ever bored." And just like that the embarrassment turned into eager hope.

"You are lonely, too?"

He walked around the edge of the couch, carrying two glasses of clear wine. Not yellow, there was almost no pigment to it whatsoever. "Sometimes. But it has been that way most of my life. Up until I moved to Ashville all those years ago. Things have gotten better, and since I've moved here, they have improved even more." He handed one to me as he gave me one of his little smiles. Curling his feet under him, he sat on the couch beside me.

The movie started and I took a sip of my wine, it burned for a moment but then practically evaporated on my tongue without the need to swallow. It was a peculiar effect, and not one I minded. "What is this?"

"It is known as sublimation wine. The heat from your tongue turns it directly into gas, leaving no need to swallow."

I couldn't resist cracking a little joke. "But what if I like to swallow?'

He chuckled, a musical of notes that were almost as light as the wine. "Do you now?"

"Sometimes. Depends on what it is." I gave him a little wink. There was no need to beat around the bush. Not yet, but hopefully soon. I wanted him in a bad way and if he kept dropping hints, I was going to pounce on him like a Seruvian D'nethal.

"Are you cold? I keep the temperature in my apartment a little lower than I should."

"A little, but I am not uncomfortable."

"I could move closer…"

"You could, but I can't see you generating enough heat to warm a pippip."

"Pippip?"

"It's a small plains marsupial. Quite adorable and very tasty."

"Something you wouldn't mind swallowing?"

"As I said, quite tasty."

He scooted closer and pressed himself to my side, sighing a little as he stretched out his feet in the spot he had just vacated. "*You*, on the other hand, are very warm. I could get used to this."

"My warmth is yours. Offered freely."

"I shall take you up on that." He took a sip of wine and let it roll around his tongue. "I chose this wine for another reason."

"Oh. What is that?"

"Ask nicely and I'll show you."

"Show?"

He nodded, flashing another mischievous grin. My heart sang. This was the side he rarely showed to anyone else and it made it all the more special. However, rushing things was unnecessary, we had all night. The company and the movie were a good start to what I was sure would be a memorable evening.

"Have you told her yet?"

"That we have gotten closer?"

Shea shook his head. "No. Your secret."

I sighed, not wanting to kill the mood. My secret was something I *needed* to tell Dot. I just hadn't built up the courage as of yet. "No."

"She will find out eventually. If she does on her own, her reaction will not be favorable. You should just tell her. I am sure she will understand."

270

"That I am a prince of *B'rith*? That I have sensed others of my kind in this land searching for me? I cannot leave her. I cannot go back. To know that there is a danger of me being dragged away would only cause her pain. I do not wish to cause her pain."

"You are being foolish. What do you think she will think if you suddenly disappear?"

"That, I do not know. Let her deal with her own problems first. Mine can come to light once she has rescued her father."

"Do you think she will succeed?"

"With the help of her family, she just might."

Shea nodded and took another sip, making a little groaning noise as he appreciated the complex flavors. "Do not drink too much at once. It will not have a chance to sublimate." His warning came as I brought the rim of the glass to my lips with purpose.

"What would happen?"

"The alcohol content would be absorbed into your stomach as a liquid instead of a gas in your sinus cavity."

"And?"

"You would become very drunk."

I took a swallow and gave him a challenging stare.

"Oh. And it causes pain."

The liquid burned like fire as it went down. I gave a little cough and a puff of vapor flew from my mouth. "You could have led with that part."

"And missed seeing the fierce fire-breathing demon? I think not." He laughed and leaned his head on my shoulder.

"Wow. That is um…very warming."

"Me or the wine?"

"Both."

"Shall I show you the other reason I chose this wine?"

"Does it involve fire shooting from my lungs again?"

"No. But it might involve some shooting…"

I was intrigued. Let's be honest, who wouldn't be? "I would like that."

He set his wine down on the table in front of me and turned a little more toward me, giving me an expectant look that spoke volumes. I leaned over and before I could touch my lips to his, he devoured mine, his tongue slipping quickly into my mouth.

Shy Shea took a secondary role to excited Shea. He might be demure in his nature, but when it came to things sexual, he became less inhibited and more in control. I melted into the back of the couch as he crawled closer. While he kissed me, his hand deftly unbuttoned my shirt and slid over my chest, down my stomach and stopped at the top of my pants. He pulled away and looked down to unclasp my belt and unfasten my jeans one-handed.

He dove back into that kiss and fished me out with his delicate hand, tugging at the tip as he pulled me free from my pants and stroked me. I moaned into his mouth.

Pulling away, he whispered, "The pleasure has only just begun." I felt myself throb in his hand and a bit of moisture drip from my tip.

He pulled his hand to his mouth and licked the drop from his skin, "Are there any large tasty marsupials in Gehenna?"

"Many."

"What is your favorite?" He gave me a curious glance as he reached for his wine.

"D'valeth. Their flesh, while firm, is quite delicious."

"Then you shall be my D'valeth. And I will be your Pippip." He took a mouthful of his wine, set the glass back down, and lay down on the couch on his stomach, pulling my rigid hardness toward his mouth. He gingerly let me slip between his lips, careful not to spill a single drop of drink and swirled it around the head of my organ.

There was a flash of discomfort as my skin came in contact with the strong spirit, but then a numbing feeling swept over it to be replaced by a veritable hum from the liquid as the heat of my flesh hastened the evaporation process. I was in heaven between it and the gentle ministrations of my lover's tongue on the underside.

"Mmmm," Shea hummed happily as he began bobbing on me.

"That feels incredible."

He just nodded and I did not want to think how he learned of the little trick. I didn't want to know. We had found each other, and the past did not matter, but it still threatened to force me to turn into a ravenous jealous beast and render his past lovers into an unrecognizable slurry of paste. He had shared some stories of his past. They had not been gentle.

I ran my fingers through his beautiful hair as he made love to my member. He didn't suck it, he didn't give me a blowjob. He made love to my flesh, kissing it as one would kiss a long lost lover and he appeared to enjoy it as much as I was.

"You are going to make me explode, little pippip."

"That is the idea."

"Slowly. We are in no rush."

He nodded, my flesh still in his mouth as he bobbed merrily but slowed his pace. Suddenly, he pulled me from his mouth and stood up. I watched with rapt fascination as he stripped his clothes in front of me, confounded by his feminine beauty. If he had breasts and a little flare to his hips, there is not one person in this realm who would ever think him male. When he was naked, he moved in front of me, facing me, and straddled my legs. "Take off your pants."

I gabbed them from my hips and pushed them down, lifting my posterior from his leather couch and leaning forward to work them completely off. While I was there, I tenderly kissed the tip of his cock, and gently licked the underside before leaning back. I half-expected him to impale himself on me, but he didn't.

He straddled my legs and lowered himself, scooting forward until our organs touched, and then he closed the distance between us, taking both of us into his hand and standing straight up between us. Leaning back a little, he began pumping us as one, his small fist struggling to encompass both of us. I was leaking pre-cum almost furiously at that point and it welled between us, creating a slippery barrier between us as we were squeezed together expertly by my little lover.

"That feels almost as amazing as your wine and your mouth."

"We should have our Lady impale herself on both of us like this sometime."

That sent a shiver of pleasure down my back and he grinned wickedly when he noticed.

"Sorry," I said with more than a little embarrassment.

"Do not be. I liked the thought just as much as you."

"In fact," I said with a grin. "We should practice our techniques often to better please her, don't you agree?"

"I do." He leaned over us and found my mouth with his again, kissing me as he stroked us between our stomachs. We were both dripping with desire and creating a mess between us. "I think we are sufficiently lubricated. Wouldn't you agree?"

All I could do was nod as he lifted himself off me and reached behind him, spreading himself as he lowered his hole to my tip. "I want you to come inside me, Dar."

Again, all I could do was nod as his anus stretched over my over-swelled tip. Once it was past, he sighed in pleasure as he constricted around me and slowly lowered himself until he was again sitting on my legs. Reaching behind him, he grabbed our glasses of wine, mine I hadn't even noticed he had taken from me as we played. He handed mine to me and held his out in a toast. "To us," he said and smiled at me.

"To us," I reiterated and clinked my glass against his. As we sipped, he began to rock his hips in gentle circles, my cock plunging in and out of him with every rotation. His cock made the same motions against the flesh of my stomach, dancing across my skin.

"I love the way you feel inside me."

I nodded in assent and reached down, taking his hardness in my hand and slowly stroking him as we slowly made love in his living room. "You are so gorgeous, Shea. Gorgeous, sweet, and deadly."

"Deadly?"

"You are like that knife you carry. Wickedly sharp and beautiful. Well balanced and dangerous. You were also made to fit in my hand," I chuckled and stroked him a little faster, pleased at my own innuendo.

He blushed and looked away, but I let go of him and turned his face back toward me, shaking my head at him.

"No. Looking at your face and seeing your pleasure only heightens mine and makes my heart sing. Do not turn away from me, ever. Please."

He nodded and leaned over, kissing me again, and quickening the movement of his hips. I started to breath heavier into that kiss and reached back down to stroke him.

"Are you going to come?"

I nodded, pulling away from that kiss.

Taking my wine from me, he set them again on the table and grabbed my hips, pulling himself forward and pushing back, driving me in and out of his tightness.

"Not long," I managed to stammer as he rode me expertly.

"Do it. Fill me."

He began to buck his hips, his pleasure equal to mine as I felt him start to throb in my hand. Until he reached down and pulled my hand from him. He had to have been just as close as I was.

I felt the familiar tensing as my orgasm approached and just like that, I was staring at him wide eyed as heat flooded around my cock inside of him. He gasped and pressed his head to my shoulder, not stopping as I spurted time and time again inside him. I growled as I pumped into him, curling my hips beneath him.

Suddenly he stood, a look almost like panic on his face as he started pumping his cock in front of me. Quickly, I reached behind him and pulled him into my mouth, his hands gripping my horns as he unleashed himself in my mouth.

The first splash hit me in the back of the throat, and I swallowed as quickly as I could, making room for more. Much much more. He called out my name and held on as surge after surge of his seed escaped him. Reaching up, I encircled the base of him with my thumb and fore finger, stroking him as I sucked the last of the liquid from him.

Finally, he pulled away from me with his hips and laughed. "Gently. Woah. That was..."

"Amazing?"

"Too simple of a word to describe that."

"Perfect?"

"Yes. Perfect." He sat back down on my legs and we enjoyed a lengthy kiss before he grabbed a single glass of wine that we shared.

"Dar?"

"Yes, Shea."

"Would you stay the night?"

Panic seized my chest. We had Dot's blessing, but if she should wake in the morning and not find me there... I shook my head, driving the thoughts away. This isn't just what Shea and I wanted, it was what she wanted, too. I needed to let go of the fear. "I'd love to."

"Are you sure? I understand..."

"I'm sure."

The smile he gave me lit up the room and drove away the last of the chill. "Care to have a shower with me?"

"Care? I'd love to."

"Good. I'll wash your back."

"Is that all?"

"And front. And everything in between." He gave me a little wink, drank the rest of the glass, and set it on the table. He stood and reached out, taking my hand.

Again, I was mesmerized by the feel of it in mine, but feeling it belonged there.

Author's Note

Reviews are important for new authors and I greatly appreciate everyone who takes a moment to leave one, even a line or two! Thank you so much for reading my reverse harem series! I'm writing away and more books will be out soon!

Follow me on Amazon to be sent updates on my new releases!

Come join my Readers Group on Facebook for news, fun, games, teasers for upcoming books, and naughty shenanigans! 18+ recommended.

Coven of the First Moon

About the Author

A late comer to the writing game, Jacquelyn had always been a fan of romance novels and lately become addicted to the reverse harem category. I mean seriously, who wouldn't? Sitting alone one night she flipped open her laptop and said, "I'm going to give this a whirl." And thus, the Lovin' the Coven series was given life. She has designs on other series as well, but only time shall tell.

As for her, she is five-foot-something, with graying hair, wicked eyes, an eager smile, and an annoying laugh. She lives at home with her dog, a cat, and that is about all she is comfortable sharing.

Other Works

Lovin' the Coven Series
(Reverse Harem- 7 book series)

First Moon
Second Blood
Third Charm
Fourth Rite
Fifth Essence
Sixth Sense
Seventh Seal

The Fox and the Hounds
(Reverse Harem – trilogy)

A Tail of Woah
A Tail of Two Kitties
The Tell Tail Heart

Other

Girlfiend (standalone YA Paranormal Romance)
Succubus Soccer Mom (Reverse Harem Standalone)